GOOD MORNING, DINAH

EMILY HOLYOAK

INCLUDAS
Publishing est. 2015.

ISBN 978-1-949983-12-8 (Paperback Edition)

ISBN 978-1-949983-14-2 (Hardcover Edition)

ISBN 978-1-949983-13-5 (Ebook Edition)

Printed and bound in the United States of America

First Printing, 2022

10 9 8 7 6 5 4 3 2 1 | First Edition

Library of Congress Control Number: 2022947544

Cover Illustration by Sadie Hutchings

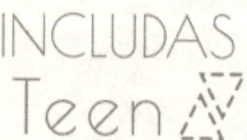

An imprint of INCLUDAS Publishing®
Salem, OR
includas.com
Bringing disability diversity and inclusiveness into the book world.®

For Sabrina,
My brave trailblazer.

CONTENT WARNING

Note to Reader

This book includes references to underage alcohol and drug use, minor physical abuse, emotional meltdowns, ableism, and animal injury.

CHAPTER 1

THE ITCHES START at my scalp and slither down my back. Every inch of my skin is on fire. My foot refuses to budge, as if it's full of lead.

"Take your time," Jenny's high-pitched voice calls through the door. "Use your tools." She's been my best friend for years and has helped me through so many ups and downs. She prepared me for high school and held my hand when my parents divorced. Even though she's my aide, we've grown close over the years.

I don't want to get in the shower. I stand on the mat in my comfy robe, trying to break the barrier that's between me and the ceramic death chamber. I rub individual pieces of yarn on the mat between my toes, and that helps stop the itches.

Our basement bathroom is remodeled, so there's a door between the actual bathtub and the countertop area.

"Remember what we talked about?" Jenny reminds me unnecessarily.

I know what we talked about. Nearly everyone showers

for hygiene reasons. I understand that not everyone is privileged to have running water and some bathe in rivers. Jenny needs to understand that the water pattering on my skin intensifies the itches.

I've done it before, plenty of times. Sometimes, I just don't wanna.

"Breathe..." she adds slowly and softly, trying her best to calm me down.

I breathe the chilly basement air in through my nostrils and out of my mouth, shut my eyes tight, and will my feet to step into the shower. I slide the glass door shut. An invisible force is holding them in place, supergluing them to the ground.

I grip the faucet and turn the handle to the right with instant regret. The high-pitched sound of the shower squeaking is too loud. My eardrums ring as the pressurized water pounds against the ceramic. I imagine the hard droplets piercing my skin like flaming arrows in a Tolkien book battlefield.

Nope. Not today. Retreating to my happy place in 3... 2... 1...

My brain swells, about to burst through my skull. Intense pain shoots through my shoulder blades as I bend over in agony. My tools of freedom emerge. Spectacular, glossy, feathered wings spread open in the bathroom. They crowd the small space. Bending my knees, I take off, breaking through the basement ceiling and then the main floor's ceiling, disrupting my mother's morning coffee.

The cool, brisk wind of liberation soars over my skin and through my wings. They beat the air and carry me off to a kingdom far away where I will rule in peace.

"Dinah?" Jenny's voice invades my seventeen-year-old senses.

Right. I'm still in the bathroom.

I want to tell Jenny that today isn't a good day for showering—what pounding water does to me—but the words don't come. I resort to my usual answer: I can't.

If only escape were that easy. I'll have to run.

I slowly open the door to see Jenny's arched eyebrow and high blonde ponytail greet me.

"No," I say. Time to find Higgins.

I'm fast. Jenny doesn't always catch me. I fling the bathroom door open and run down the hallway, careful not to let my robe fall off. I pass Mom in the kitchen, who whips her head around as I race past. I practically fly to my room and slam the door, locking it behind me.

There he is, just lazily lying on the bed, enjoying hogging the covers all to himself. I grab Higgins' fur and rub it between my fingertips. The soft bristles melt my heart and pump my veins full of calm-down juice. I bury my face into his golden fur, reveling in the swooshes of love it spreads over my skin.

I appreciate that Jenny gives me three minutes to calm down before she knocks on my door. "All right, Dinah. We'll try showering tomorrow. I'll draw you a bath because you escaped and locked your door, so I can tell your anxiety is through the roof."

I pull my face back from Higgins and look into his black eyes. He pants and smiles at me, his teeth showing while he wags his tail enthusiastically. All I have to do is touch his fur and look into his eyes, and I know he's mine and no one else's.

"Guess I have to, huh, Higg?" I ask him.

His shiny, golden tail pounds against the carpet. I sigh, accept defeat, and open the door to find that Jenny is already down the hall, no doubt on her way to the basement to draw my bath. I catch up and get inside the tub.

Baths are so much better. The water pressure gives me a hug instead of attacking my face at thirty miles an hour. But... I want to learn to take showers so that I can get ready quicker in the mornings. Mom agrees and says it'll prepare me for "life."

I grumpily wash myself as I hear Jenny going through the vanity drawers on the other side of the door. She pulls out a hair dryer and sets it out on the counter, as well as a brush; I can hear the clunk of both objects.

When I'm finished and robed, I emerge reluctantly into Jenny's presence.

"Because you decided to run away this morning, I call hair dryer," she says cheerily.

"You suck."

Jenny smiles in the mirror, making eye contact with my mirrored self. I'm a little above average height, my pickiness and hyperactivity help me stay around average weight, and my dark hair, eyebrows, and eyelashes don't require much makeup. I usually gloss my lips and maybe, if I'm feeling wild, throw on a pinch of peachy blush.

"Fine, but I have to pet Higg," I answer, testing the waters for striking a bargain.

Higgins helps me through my morning as I clutch the fur between his shoulders. I rub it between my thumb and fingers in a clockwise motion, trying to ignore Jenny drying and styling my hair. The hair dryer screeches a horrific tone, like a banshee. I grit my teeth to try making the experience pass faster. My hair isn't too frizzy when Jenny is done. It's naturally straight.

"Get dressed and get on up to breakfast." Jenny smiles. "Then we'll go over the proposed schedule for the day."

I choose a smooth and itch-free lavender bra. All my bras are the same, but at least they're different colors. Underwire bras feel like I'm suffocating in a corset. I choose a jersey-knit T-shirt—my favorite because of the silky touch. Leggings are always a must because jeans are too painful, and dresses don't work because I want my thighs to be hugged. I top it with the softest thing I can wear to school—a pink hoodie.

I have to wear cotton sweaters and hoodies. Khaki, denim, wool, and pretty much every other material under the sun feels like I'm wearing cactus needles.

I make my way to the kitchen, singing.

Someone's in the kitchen with Di-nah.
Someone's in the kitchen I know.
Someone's in the kitchen with Di-nah.
Strummin' that old banjo.

Every time I go into the kitchen, I have to sing that song. Maybe because my dad used to sing it when I was young. He loves my name. After all, he convinced Mom to give it to me.

I have to sing it every time because if I don't, something doesn't seem right. It can throw my entire day off. I have to or else my body gets the itches, and I implode from my pinky toe up to my neck. Every part of me kind of explodes.

When I was ten, my mom took me to a psychologist, where I had a few behavioral tests. She was concerned with how emotional I became when something wasn't going my way. It turned out I was on the spectrum. Not only do I have

OCD but also anxiety, auditory processing disorder, and sensory integration disorder.

This basically means that I need to have control over everything to make sure I'm comfortable, and I overthink everything. I process sounds at a higher rate than others, my taste buds are stronger, and I feel things so much deeper. I also love to read. A lot. I reached a twelfth-grade reading level in the sixth grade.

Jenny glances up at me from the table, where she's typing on her laptop. My mom is seated next to her, clutching her second or third cup of coffee. Higgins is on my heels, as usual, as I grab a mixed-berry yogurt and apple juice from the refrigerator.

My mom exhales slowly through her nostrils before she pleasantly greets me with, "Good morning, Dinah."

"Morning, Mom... *Someone's in the kitchen I know*," I sing, pretending to tolerate the day ahead.

As I pour my glass of apple juice, Jenny mutters something to my mom, and they do that grown-up mumble laugh.

"Okay, I ran away this morning," I admit.

Jenny's blonde ponytail flips around so fast that I swear she cracks her neck. She smiles at me like she always does. I'm positive it's required in her job description.

"We weren't talking about you, Dinah, but that's okay. Did you take your anxiety meds?" Mom says between sips. Her glasses slip down the bridge of her nose a bit, but she doesn't slide them up.

I try to focus on my yogurt, but I can't. Glasses. Glasses. Glasses. Glassesglassesglassessssss...

I step over to my mom, tap the bridge of her glasses and slide them up to her eyes.

"Sorry," I whisper as I step back to my yogurt on the counter.

My mom takes a noticeable deep breath, takes a large gulp of her cooling coffee, and sighs. "Thank you, dear."

Jenny has told me that keeping my hands to myself is polite. I try to do it, but sometimes the urge is too great to ignore.

Higgins puts his head on the counter and stares longingly at me for a taste of my yogurt. I let him finish the rest.

A muffled high screech sound comes from Nattie's room. My fifteen-year-old sister likes to scream into her pillow for dramatic effect when she can't find something, like her favorite tank top or tacky anime backpack. It'll be a minute before she comes down. I'll be long gone before that because I like to take my time walking to school. Besides, she's too cool to walk with me. She and her friends carpool together.

"Time to put Higgins' harness on," Mom reminds me, even though I would never forget something for Higgins. He wags his tail and sits up obediently, waiting for his duty to begin.

I drape and fasten his service dog harness around him. It has a giant enamel pin shaped like a rainbow that reads: "AUTISM DOG DO NOT SEPARATE FROM HANDLER." I give him a kiss on his fur and grab my backpack from the granite counter.

"Love you, Mom. Bye, Jenny," I call as I head out the door.

I grab my slip-on sneakers and start the fifteen-minute walk to see what awaits us at school. The September Wisconsin sun warms my cheeks. It's the third week of senior year, but the anxiety of what could possibly happen today makes it like any other first day of school for me.

I think today will probably be a good day. I'm clean, I'm comfortable. Higgins and I are in a pleasant mood. Higgins is just as smart as a human being; it's why he's allowed to walk me to school. Jenny and I may have had a rough morning, but the truth is, she's my rock. Just thinking of her and her smile reminds me I'm going to have a great attitude today.

School is bearable if I wear my noise-reducing headphones. I used to get lots of stares from the other students, but now they know they're something I have to wear to endure the day. The opening and closing of lockers, the buzzing of thousands of conversations, and even the class bell is enough to give me the itches. When I wear my headphones, I picture myself in far-off places, mostly the magical realms of fantasy books I've read. I'm walking Higgins along the greenery of Hobbiton, I'm dancing at the Count of Monte Cristo's lavish party, or Higgins and I are lying in a beautiful field in Narnia after the long winter has finally melted away.

I find myself more comfortable in imaginary worlds than reality.

Higgins and I spend half of my school day in the disability classroom at Hepburn High. Mom says it's for "social" purposes. I guess I am antisocial and awkward enough to make neurotypical students uncomfortable. It's okay with me because my feelings toward most of the other students are mutual. The exceptions are my friends in the disability classroom, especially Andrew. There's also Jimmy, Tate, Pedro, and Hannah. We've been through a lot together over the course of twelve years.

The classroom isn't anything special. There are desks and a few beanbag chairs scattered throughout, where I like to read if Higgins and I ever have free time. Some classrooms in my school have lots of windows, but this classroom is centrally located, so there's just one window in the door for fewer distractions. There are more cupboards than in other classrooms to hold therapeutic toys and equipment. A lot of disabled kids have therapy fused with their education.

Andrew Blumenthal has Down syndrome. His parents push him to do cross-country skiing in the Special Olympics, but he'd much rather be playing *Thelena's Wrath* with me. He lets me control the characters how I want. Mr. Peterson doesn't think my need to control is healthy. He would rather have us play something else during study hour.

"How about *Monopoly?*" Mr. Peterson asks as he grabs a box from the game cabinet.

"How about it, Andrew? Would you like to ruin our friendship today?" I ask him.

Andrew shakes his head so vigorously that his glasses almost come sliding off. "I want to play *Thelena's Wrath.*"

"You play *Thelena's Wrath* every day," Mr. Peterson says. If he's annoyed, I can't tell. "Yes, the role-playing and magic cards are fun, but we need something that Dinah won't control."

I throw Mr. Peterson a grumpy expression just as the classroom door opens. Ms. Underwood, the principal at Hepburn High, walks in with two boys—one younger than me and one probably my age. They both have light brown hair and striking blue eyes, so I surmise they are brothers. The younger one tries to escape the room, but his older brother has their arms interlocked so they enter together.

They struggle until they're at the big table where we're setting up *Thelena's Wrath*, the younger one takes a seat by me. Higgins' ears perk up beneath the table to make sure I'm protected.

Mr. Peterson stands up to greet them. "Good morning, gentlemen! Ms. Underwood." He nods politely. "Is this Felix?"

"Yes, these are our new students, Felix and Maverick Wright." She smiles, her extra-white teeth practically glowing for everyone to see. Maverick is also smiling, his freckles and dimples somewhat endearing. He drinks the classroom in, his eyebrows disappearing into his nut-brown hair that falls a little too far into his eyes.

Almost the moment that Felix sits down, he begins pushing the deck of cards away with his hand.

"Heyyy!" Andrew frowns as a classroom aide sits next to him to calm him down.

The tingling starts at my scalp. The itches travel along my elbows and make my fingers curl into balls. I try to rub my shoulders against my soft hoodie, but it isn't working. Higgins offers his paw once he senses I'm uncomfortable, so I rub his magic fur with my fingertips.

"I don't like new things," I bark at Felix.

"That's not nice, Dinah." Mr. Peterson scolds me quickly, but I stare at the table. I don't like looking into people's eyes. They're fascinating, but I grind my teeth when I have too much eye contact.

Felix grabs my headphones off the table and observes them with interest. Twinges strike every nerve in my body.

"Those are *mine*!" I bellow and snatch them from him. I shove them on my head and prepare to run away from my seat and out into the hall. Before an aide can ask me to wait, Maverick grabs my forearm more gently than I expect. Higgins growls at the boy as he cuts me off from leaving the room.

Maverick pulls me back toward the table. "It's okay. Felix will warm up once you get to know him. He has autism."

I stare blankly over at Felix, who shoves the *Thelena's Wrath* board away from him.

"No, *I* have autism," I reply reluctantly, yanking my arm away and walking back to the commotion. I choose to sit next to Mr. Peterson instead of Felix.

"I could tell by your headphones," Maverick consoles. "Felix has those too. He just didn't want to wear them today. He has autism and bipolar disorder. He doesn't talk."

"Touching me isn't okay without asking me," I state, the itches crawling all over me like cockroaches that are about to bury themselves in my skin.

I avoid his eyes, my focus going directly back to *Thelena's Wrath*. My favorite aide comes and asks to be dealt in with the magic cards.

"We'll be off, then." Ms. Underwood nods and gestures for Maverick to follow her. Maverick waves at Felix one more time and then at me. I only see it out of the corner of my eye, but it's the first time someone has been genuinely friendly to me—well, someone who wasn't an aide, family member, or a church friend who was trying to overcompensate.

Higgins woofs quietly with approval.

CHAPTER 2

WE HEAD TO ENGLISH, which is my favorite class of the day. I like to sit in the back by Mr. Clyde's desk because he'll talk about fantasy books with me. Sometimes we get carried away, and the classroom plan goes off on a major tangent. Higgins leads me to my desk, his tail wagging side to side.

I rub my shoulders against my fluffy sweatshirt to get comfortable in my chair. The school day seems to be looking up when who should sit next to me but Maverick Wright.

A jolt zaps through my spine.

"I'm glad I know someone in this class," he grunts as he tosses his backpack aside. "Dinah, right?"

I nod ever so slightly. Jenny's voice echoes in my head about engaging people socially, reminding me what is appropriate and what is not. I remember years past in middle school, attempting to make friends proved extremely difficult for me.

I opt to ask him about his roots rather than get angry at him for disrupting my schedule.

"Where did you move from?" I attempt to ask without sounding annoyed.

"Denver," Maverick answers.

"Why?"

"My mom was impressed with the state Medicaid programs and inclusiveness in the communities, so she found a job that moved us here. It sucks to start my senior year at a new school, but I'm open to new possibilities."

"I have a mom and a stepdad, Kurt. My dad lives in Oshkosh," I say without thinking.

"Oshkosh? There are some cool city names here," he marvels.

I bite my lip slightly, wanting the conversation to end. I want to chew on something so I don't have to answer his questions.

"Um, welcome to Milwaukee," I say as politely as I can.

Higgins lies on the floor in preparation for his English-period nap. I nudge him slightly with my foot to remind him he's still on duty as my anxiety rises like a kneaded pan of bread.

Mr. Clyde introduces us to the book, *Wuthering Heights*. I like to read, but I'd enjoy it more if there were elves, fairies, or some winged creatures involved. I can muster through a classic if I pretend the main characters all have magical features.

I picture myself sitting on a throne instead of a desk chair, vibrant velvet draped all over my body. Minstrels play pleasant, upbeat music while servants fan me. Comfort is not sacrificed by fashion in this castle. The palms of my hands are ice-cold. I look at them and discover that they are dazzling white.

I attempt to warm them up by burying them in my dress, then into the royal dog's fur. My palms feel warm, like firelight, as the fur powers me like some kind of life source.

"Do you like to read?" Maverick's whispering voice pierces my wonderings. It's a little hard to hear him with my headphones on, so I place my thumb between them and my ear.

"Yes, I do, but you just broke into my story," I reply curtly.

"Huh?" He wrinkles his forehead in confusion.

"My story. I was an evil queen in my court," I explain. Higgins snores slightly.

"That sounds awesome," Maverick probes. I don't normally notice things like facial expressions, but I can't help but grin in reply to his freckly smile. "You would make a great writer with an imagination like that."

"Only if Higg can come along on my book tour," I say quietly, ruffling his fur a bit.

"He's a cool dog. That coat looks good on him."

"Thanks. He's my everything." I don't know why I say something so personal, but I do.

Maverick smiles again, opens *Wuthering Heights*, and thumbs through the pages. He doesn't look excited to read it. "I like to read, but the classics can be super boring."

"What do you like to read?" I whisper, my book obsession about to take over completely.

"Science fiction for sure. Anything with space fights."

"Any high fantasy?"

"I'm sure I'd like it if I tried. Why? Do you know of any awesome books?"

My heart pounds at an alarming rate, the serotonin

flowing freely. If everyone loved books and haunted their local library like me, I think I'd fit into society easier. I open my mouth to respond but am interrupted.

"Pay attention to the style and prose of Emily Brontë. After reading the first chapter, please write two to three statements about why you think she wrote under a male pseudonym," Mr. Clyde's voice booms. It rings in my unprotected ear, and I regret opening my safe space for barely a minute. "And put your phones away."

Everyone slides their phones into their backpacks or pockets. Since I don't have a phone, I mentally end the conversation with Maverick and begin classwork. It's a tool Jenny taught me to help me get through school. Once I focus, I'm usually good to go.

I read, my mind wandering all over the place. I shake my head and try to focus. I can already tell I'm not going to like this Heathcliff guy from *Wuthering Heights*, so I invent a few other characters to keep my interest. It doesn't take long before my brain starts itching.

Felix. Felix. I want to know about Felix.

"I do therapy too. Probably not like Felix, though," I say, to my surprise.

Maverick turns his head away from the book and looks delighted that I restarted our conversation. "Yeah? That's okay. We're just starting to meet his new therapists here." His cheeks glow slightly, probably because his muscles are sore from smiling.

"You're awfully cheerful for someone who just moved across the country," I blurt out. It came out a little louder than I had anticipated.

Mr. Clyde looks over in our direction from the front of the class.

"I mean... you seem pretty cool." Maverick leans his chin on his balled-up right fist and looks at me. "Felix opened my eyes to how amazing people's differences can be."

Maverick has kind eyes. Eyes someone could back float in. The blue is bright but at the same time gray, with sparkles of darker blue near his pupils. His eyelashes are the type that all girls are jealous of—the low-maintenance, naturally thick kind.

Jenny's voice comes to the forefront. *"I know you love to gather details but remember not to stare. People will take it as rude."*

I focus back on *Wuthering Heights* and take a slow breath in.

I'm entering unfamiliar territory. I'll have to consult Jenny about conversations again.

We make it through the rest of the school day relatively unscathed, though the day flew by in a flash. Before I know it, Higgins and I are walking home, absolutely starving. I think about how I want to have my regular soft, blueberry granola bar for my snack.

I let Higgins do his business in the front yard before we go in the house. My mom and stepdad aren't home yet, but Nattie is eating a bowl of colorful, sugary cereal bites at the table. My body trembles. I don't understand how she can eat that sandy cardboard that classifies as cereal. And the marshmallows? They're hard as rocks and taste like powdered medicine. Yuck.

"Hey, Dinah. Hey, Higg," Nattie greets us with a mouthful of mush and milk. I turn around to take Higgins' harness off but also so I can talk to her without looking at the cereal.

"Hey," I reply.

Higgins snatches the treat bone in his bowl before trotting over to his kennel in the kitchen to enjoy it.

"How was school today?" Nattie asks between bites, her hot pink bangs falling into her eyes.

"It was all right. A new student touched my headphones." I take them off my head and hang them on the hook by the door, so I always know where they are.

"Did you beat them up?" She giggles as she slurps her milk. Her black lipstick smears as she laps it up, then stops. "Sorry, I know you hate that."

A rattling sensation creeps down my spine. "It's fine. I'm trying to live with it. And, no, no beating up ensued. I tried to run, though."

"Surprise, surprise." Nattie shrugs. "Remember what you're supposed to ask me now?"

I stare at the kitchen floor, my mind a blank canvas, as if the painter in charge up there has artist's block.

I subconsciously pop my knuckles. "Um."

A knock comes at the front door, saving me. Jenny is right on time. Only this time, she brought a friend. Sometimes Jenny's supervisor visits to observe therapy sessions, but this isn't her. It's a tall, thin woman with curly red hair. Her hair is brighter than anyone's I have ever seen. It almost has a clownish tint.

"Hey, Dinah. Hey, Nattie. Hello, sleeping Higg," Jenny says with a smile. She always wears workout clothes because she never knows if she has to run after me or not. "I brought somebody with me today. I hope that's okay."

"Dinah forgot to ask me," Nattie butts in.

Jenny calmly glances at me and notices me nervously playing with my fingers.

"Dinah, it's polite to ask family members about their day when you come home, especially if they ask you first," she reminds.

"How was your day?" I sputter, like a backfiring engine.

Nattie rolls her eyes and moves around me to dump her cereal into the trash can. "Just fine," she says. I'm unable to interpret whether it's a genuine answer.

The redheaded woman waves and smiles at me like she knows me. I'm instantly uncomfortable because Jenny never has someone extra along with her.

"This is Eliza. She's going to observe us for the rest of the day, okay?" Jenny states, her tone upbeat but cautious.

"Okay," I say, but it isn't okay. This is too different from how our afternoons go. I stride over to Higgins' sleeping body to grab his fur for comfort. For some reason, I feel like bad news is on the horizon.

"Hi, Dinah! We're going to be great friends," Eliza says. Her tone is one of trying too hard, and it sets off my itchy alarm.

"What's the first thing we do, Dinah?" Jenny asks.

I groan. "Homework."

"That's right. Higgins naps while we do homework. If you get anxious, you can play with one of your fidget toys."

I nod and walk over to the table, hesitant to start on my

math. I pull my notebook from my backpack and begin working.

Eliza doesn't do or say much. She just follows Jenny around the rest of the afternoon.

"I had a conversation with someone new today," I whisper to Jenny across the table.

Her face glows. "That's great news. Did you remember to ask questions?"

"I did," I answer, feeling proud of myself. "But what if he wants to talk or ask questions even more?" One day is fine, but I can't manage two straight days in a row talking to a stranger. What if I share too much or run away? What if he changes my entire routine?

I swallow the lump in my throat.

"Just talk about little things," Jenny offers. "Books. Food. You don't have to answer every question he asks. If it gets to be too much, just tell him you'll answer when you're ready."

That seems doable. I sigh, wondering what Maverick would actually want to know about me.

When it's time for my fuzzy pajamas, Jenny says to meet her at the table when I'm ready. This is definitely not part of my schedule. I grab Higgins' fur as he lies at my feet under the table. Jenny, Eliza, Mom, and Kurt join us at the table, which is weird. Kurt is usually driving an ambulance around at this time. Nattie is off somewhere, probably playing video games without me.

My anxiety shoots through the roof as I anticipate ominous bad news.

"Dinah," Mom begins slowly, as if she's defusing a bomb, "the reason Eliza came with Jenny today is because... Jenny is getting married." There's an awkward pause. "She's going to Chicago."

Everyone is staring at me as if they expect me to implode. My eyes dart to the tabletop to avoid any eye contact.

"So, she's going on vacation?" I ask. Jenny hardly ever takes vacations—at least, she hasn't in the past six years. I can deal with it. The weeks she had been gone were hard, but I made it through knowing that she would be back.

"Not exactly," Jenny says, tears welling up in her eyes. "I'm moving to Chicago, where my fiancé lives. So, Eliza will become your new aide."

Chicago is two hours away. She can commute, but it's an awful long way. She'd hardly ever see her fiancé. Everyone is still staring at me, waiting for me to respond to the news.

"Eliza is my new aide?" I cry out, finally putting the pieces together.

"Dinah, listen. It's okay. I know it's a big change, but it'll be an exciting change." Kurt attempts to calm the dragon that awakens inside my heart.

Chills melt down my spine, like someone shoved ice cream down my shirt. I shake my hair to try to get rid of all the itches. My heart speeds up, and my breathing becomes short.

"Dinah, please try to unders—" Jenny starts, but her voice drifts away.

Time for a miraculous escape.

My feet weld together with a gross, slimy sound. I look down to see that my knees and thighs are doing the same. Pain shoots down the sides of my neck where gills pop through. My hair suddenly grows and turns a mossy color. The tile floor melts away to a sea of glass, reflecting a beautiful orange sunset. The table floats there while all the adults freeze. I dive backward into the water and swim away as fast as I can until I reach my isolated cove, leaving schools of fish in my wake.

CHAPTER 3

MY MOM ENDED up giving me melatonin so I could get to sleep. Even with supplements, I wake at 4:00 a.m. to shuffle through my thoughts. I play a puzzle video game on my handheld game console to help me think.

I know I should be okay with Jenny getting married and moving away, but I'm not. It shouldn't be a big deal, but it is. She helped me learn to tolerate a full public-school day. She helps me contain my meltdowns, even though I still try to escape each time. She is simply the best aide, and there is nobody like her on this planet.

I sigh as I complete another long quest. Jenny, Mom, Dad, Kurt, and Nattie are all counting on me to be able to make it on my own one day. I can't do that if I continue being rigid with my preferences, inevitably disappointing them.

I open my WorldVid app on my smart TV and watch videos about people moving away. People are so animated on WorldVid. I could never make videos like that, unless they were magical or fantasy oriented. Then I'd have my own kingdom, and I wouldn't have to imagine anything.

Higgins snores next to me when I lie back down, his tail twitching on my chest. The warm fur calms my steadily racing heart as I think about trying to step into the shower in a few hours.

If I can barely get into the shower, then how the hell am I going to be able to switch aides?

Jenny assures me she won't be moving for three more weeks, giving her enough time to help Eliza transition over and learn my schedule, my capacities, and all my Dinah-isms. I will revel in the twenty-one precious days Jenny and I have left.

Deep down, I desperately want to be okay with the change. I really wish I could be. But I cannot physically take it; my brain won't let me. My extrasensory issues kick in, and I get the itches. Simple changes send me into hysteria, like Eliza wearing a dress when Jenny wears workout clothes. What if Eliza forces me to do things when I'm not ready? What if she doesn't understand my thought process? What if Eliza and I aren't compatible, and I have to change aides again?

My brain buzzes. I leap out of bed. Higgins whines and licks his snout as if I've performed a criminal act against him.

"Whatever, Higg. It's not like it matters to you who bathes or walks you," I hiss at him.

I'm seventeen and can't handle the tiniest change without having a breakdown. I heave a large sigh and use my tools to stop the buzzing.

I rub my feet into the carpet and transport myself to the beach.

The sand is gritty as I wiggle my toes to make the grains go through the gaps. I slowly breathe in and out. My lungs and brain fill with oxygen. The ocean breeze brushes bliss-fully against the translucent hairs on my face, causing a pleasant sensation. I can sense the orange sunlight creeping up over the horizon through my eyelids.

Everything will be all right. Someone slips their sandpa-per-like skin into my hand. *Eliza is sitting next to me with a smile that doesn't quite reach her eyes.*

She's not supposed to be in my safe place.

My eyes bolt open and my heart races. The buzzing gets louder. I try to remember my tools, but the buzzing won't stop.

Bz. Buzz. Bzzz.

My voice involuntarily wails as my palm hits my skull over and over. My mom bursts into the room, her silk bathrobe billowing behind her in a frenzy. She grabs my wrists and pulls me into a tight hug so I can't hit my head again. I bury my face into the soft silk and let the tears flow freely. I may wake the whole house, but I can't help it.

Mom runs her free hand through my hair, calming my brain from the buzzing. "Shh, shh, shh." She consoles me like she would a baby—soft and caring but with a hint of sleep-deprived annoyance.

"I'm... sorry," I apologize through gasps of sorrow.

"No, no, honey. You're completely justified," Mom whis-pers, with a hint of sadness in her voice as well. When people whisper, it tickles my ears. The long Ss are particu-larly excruciating, but I have learned to live with it over the years.

Higgins' head forces its way between our tight hug so he can offer canine comfort. "Jenny is part of our family. This will be difficult for all of us."

I break away from the hug and fall to my knees, wringing my hands in agony. Higgins rubs against my torso.

"I just wish... I just wish I could handle the change. I just wish... I could be normal," I blubber as tears flow down my cheeks—each one following the path of the other in one straight line.

Kurt appears in my doorway, with Nattie poking her bedhead around the corner. My cheeks flush as embarrassment creeps its way up my skin. Mom takes my restless hands in hers and rubs them with her thumbs. She looks me straight in the eye, but it's too much for me. I look away.

"Look at me, Dinah. Look at me." She sighs, her patience giving out. It's too early to fight. "We love you as you are. Never apologize for who you are."

A few guttural sobs escape me. Mom takes my hand and leads me to the kitchen, knowing there's no way I can go back to sleep. A warm glass of milk can usually get me to calm down. Higgins, now alert, trots behind me, thinking he's going to get breakfast early.

Someone's in the kitchen with Di-nah...

As 6:30 a.m. comes around, Higgins eagerly awaits Jenny on the doormat. She does her usual three knocks and lets herself in. Eliza is in her wake, wearing workout clothes today.

"Good morning, Dinah-Doo. How was your sleep?" Jenny says brightly. She's always been a morning person.

Mom nonchalantly makes the "cut off" sign at her neck with her free hand, her other hand holding coffee cup number three. Jenny tucks her bottom lip in and nods.

"That bad, huh?" She pulls out a kitchen chair next to me. I pay no mind because I'm buried in a fantasy thriller novel. Eliza mimics Jenny by taking a seat. "Hey you, Dinah-Doo. Do you understand anything that's going on in that book?"

"I'm trying to get to the raptor fights," I snap.

"That's in book four, I believe. The series keeps getting stranger and stranger, but I love it," Eliza says.

I blink and stare at her. My head buzzes slightly with the surprising information.

"You read fantasy?" I spout.

"Mm-hmm, and all sorts. C.S. Lewis, Robert Jordan, Brandon Sanderson—I love them all."

"That's three, not them all." I roll my eyes at the obvious branch of friendship Eliza offered. She'll have to do better than that.

"Dinah," Jenny corrects, "remember it's okay to generalize, and don't chastise others for generalizing. It's just moving the conversation forward."

I exhale through my nose, irritated.

"You're just trying to make me like you," I state plainly, staring at Eliza's nest of red hair.

"Dinah!" Mom chokes on her coffee. "Where are your manners this morning?"

"I'm not being mean. I'm simply stating a fact." And I know I'm not wrong.

Eliza nods and tucks a stray curl behind her ear. "Well, at our company, they try their best to match the aide's interests with the client's interests. That way transitions can go smoother."

Eliza smiles, but I can tell she's nervous. I bet she's wondering if I'll test her, physically and mentally.

Probably yes to both. Being me is not easy, so I imagine taking care of me is just as difficult.

I remember how long the itches stayed the last time there was a major change in my household—Kurt joining the family. The itches wouldn't leave for months and months. Jenny was introduced to our family soon after I began having multiple meltdowns a day. I can't help it. I don't mean to be a pain in the butt, but I tested Kurt to see if he was up to the challenge of dealing with me every day. He's pretty understanding now, but getting used to each other proved difficult. Mom still knows me best.

Jenny's watch alarm interrupts my thoughts.

"Time to get ready! Shower time?" Jenny smiles enthusiastically.

I lower my face to the table in protest. I'm not ready.

"No way. Not after what you said yesterday." I lift my head and cross my arms to show I mean business and to twirl the stray threads at the ends of my pajama sleeves. "Bath only."

Jenny sighs, sounding like a pang of guilt hit her in the sternum. "You're the boss," she acknowledges. She stands and makes a grand gesture as if I'm a queen about to leave the throne at a palace.

Not a bad idea.

I pull the prodigious mink-and-velvet shawl around my shoulders and steady myself for my parade. I clasp the shawl with one hand and gently salute the large but amazingly quiet crowd with my polite royal wave. Higgins, the royal dog, follows in my wake, leaving behind the trees full of prisoners in gibbets to rot for their crimes.

"Let's talk about something exciting." Jenny tries to change the subject. "You think you'll talk to your new friend Maverick today?"

I freeze in place at the thought of that. I'm not ready. Not ready for anything or anyone or all of these changes.

CHAPTER 4

MAVERICK CONTINUES to sit by me in English. We're not particularly enjoying *Wuthering Heights*, but rather enduring it together. He's still a recent acquaintance, so my brain is on stranger-danger alert. However, I can see us becoming friends down the road if he really understands autism like he says he does. He told me that him and his mom helped organize the Autism Around the World walk every April in Denver, and they hope to participate similarly here.

The fact that he talks to me so much is highly unusual. I don't begin conversations, and I don't usually participate in the ones going on around me. Most people forget to include me because of my noise-reducing headphones, but Maverick leans over and talks just loud enough for me to hear. Sometimes he gets in trouble for it with Mr. Clyde.

At lunch, I always sit in my spot in the corner of the cafeteria where it's the least noisy. If I'm having a particularly trying day, an aide will sit with me. I face the wall so my brain isn't buzzing with so many people to watch. I don't know what's worse: walking through the halls or sitting in the crowded cafeteria.

Neurotypicals can tune out conversations going on around them and call it "white noise." To me, the noise is tumultuous. It's like a robot army has taken me hostage, torturing me to make me tell them information. My headphones muffle the noise to a more tolerable level.

I'm enjoying the smooth, cold texture of my applesauce when I'm rudely interrupted by Maverick approaching and speaking condescendingly to my dog.

"Hey, boy. Who's a good boy?" Maverick laughs as he takes the seat next to Higgins, opposite me.

"He's on duty," I say sharply, pointing to Higgins' service dog harness.

"Can I sit with you?" Maverick asks, siphoning through my headphones.

Why do people ask permission *while* they're doing the thing? Ugh.

The itches creep up my ankles. My foot threatens to involuntarily kick him since I'm used to staring at the brick wall, not a boy. While I'd prefer to keep to my routine, my inner curiosities stir like the beginning of tornado season. I kind of want to see what it'd be like being friends with Maverick and whether or not I can handle it.

"Um, I guess. There are lots of other places to sit. Usually, I just look at the wall," I confess.

"A little change can't be all bad, right?" he remarks as he opens his lunchbox. He's packed himself a grilled cheese sandwich with pesto on wheat. He also has various fruits and vegetables and a bottle of juice that looks like moss.

"Your food is weird," I say before I can stop myself.

Higgins huffs in my direction. I'm sure it's a sneeze, but I swear he knows I said something socially inept.

Maverick chuckles and nods. He rolls up the sleeves of his Colorado hoodie and digs in.

"I'm a vegan," he admits. "My mom started being vegan a few years ago, and I caught on. It gives me the energy to help out with Felix."

The cheese is driving me insane. I have to ask.

"But... the cheese?"

"Tapioca starch, arrowroot, coconut oil, and potato protein isolate. My mom and I make our own fancy cheese. Cheese *substitute*."

My stomach gurgles, and not in the hungry way. I decide to change the subject while the itches crawl to my knees.

"Where is Felix?"

"Oh, he eats in the disability classroom. I ate with him yesterday, but the teacher says that I need to give him his own space." Maverick takes a bite of his cold sandwich and shrugs. "I guess sometimes I'm more of a hindrance than a help."

The itches reach my torso. My brain keeps replaying an SOS message that reads: *Remove boy, must look at wall. Remove boy, must look at wall...*

"You were told to stop eating lunch with your autistic brother, so you come sit with an autistic girl instead?" I ask as Higgins leaps off his chair to come brush against my legs. He can tell I'm getting anxious.

Maverick takes a long sip from his veggie juice and nods. "I hope you don't mind. I feel pretty comfortable around you. Everyone else is so boring."

"That's... kind of ableist," I retort, annoyance joining the itches.

"Oh, shit. I mean... sorry."

While the cafeteria is still uproarious with noise, there seems to be a ringing in my ears surrounded by silence.

"It's okay. I mean, it's not okay. People say stuff like that all the time." I sigh, looking at my food.

"Really?" Maverick says sloppily after biting a chunk of his rabbit-food sandwich. "Well, if I ever need correcting, please don't hesitate to. I don't want to offend anyone, especially you."

The itches abruptly stop. A strange feeling erupts from my chest—warm, soft, welcome. My mom's words from this morning float back to me.

We love you as you are.

"Also, I've been waiting for that book recommendation list," Maverick quips with a wink. Does he have something in his eye?

I gasp, dropping my fork, and fish in my backpack. "Oh, I forgot!" I snag a pen and squeeze it.

"You don't have to do it now." Maverick's hand closes around my wrist. A different kind of itch spreads from his touch—a tingle. "I'm just teasing. Take your time and give it to me whenever."

I shake off his hand as if his touch electrocuted me. "Mr. Handsy. I *said* you need permission to touch me."

"Right, I'm sorry." Maverick slams his eyes shut and looks as if he's in pain. I'm sure he's just feeling an emotion, but I'm in no mood to guess which one. "I'm so socially awkward and used to catching Felix before he hurts himself."

"It's okay." I pause and watch his face scrunch. "Just please don't do it again." I don't know what to say other than that. I resume eating my applesauce.

After a few minutes of conversation-less chewing, Maverick scares me with a sudden question.

"Hey, where did you get Higgins?"

Who does this guy think he is? The questions just don't stop with him.

"I got him when I was twelve. Mom brought him home to me after he was trained at a special service dog nonprofit." I pack up my lunchbox into my backpack, not really understanding why he would ask such a random thing. "Why?"

"We're thinking of getting a service dog for Felix. I love Higgins' temperament." Maverick scratches my dog's ears again. "My parents are divorced, too. It was super hard on Felix. I can only imagine how hard it was for you."

I try not to think about Dad moving to Oshkosh, probably relieved that he doesn't have to deal with my antics all the time. It makes my eyes burn, like a scream is waiting behind them, bursting at my tear ducts.

"I don't know exactly where Higgins is from. Some foundation," I say quickly, looking for an excuse to remove myself from the conversation. I glance at my smartwatch that Dad got for me last Christmas. It has soft alerts that buzz on my skin to remind me of my schedule. It's about time for me to leave, thankfully.

Standing up in anticipation of the bell, I walk away and holler back, "You'll have to ask my mom!" I don't like being late for anything if I can help it, especially classes.

I find it difficult to concentrate the rest of the day because of Maverick. He's thrown me completely off my schedule, so much that I'm not excited at all to go home and see "the Deserter" (Jenny) and "the Fraud" (Eliza). I've given them both appropriate new nicknames.

Higgins leads me through the gate and in the back door, where I drop my stuff and proceed to run to my room. The itches are so bad that I want nothing to do with my aides tonight. Higgins attempts to cut me off because he knows I'm supposed to follow my schedule. I pull a treat out of my pocket that I have been saving the whole school day and distract him with that. He graciously lets me in my room and follows me to my bed.

The itches. They need to get out. Out. *Out!*

I bury my face in my many blankets and let out a blood-curdling screech. Higgins howls along until my sobs drown him out.

Why does Jenny have to leave? Why is Maverick talking to me so much?

Why do the smallest things send me into a meltdown?

Why do I have to be this way?

Why does my bed feel so light and airy?

My fingers clutch at my blankets only to grab fluffy material that slips through my fingers. I sniffle and open my eyes to behold a peach-colored cloud. The blubbering, screaming, weak Dinah is no more. I am a sky-rider. My soft leather catsuit hugs my thighs perfectly. Shaking my silvery hair, I reach deep into the cloud and grab it by its gossamer reins.

The wind in my ears is cool but surprisingly quiet. No need for noise-reducing headphones here! I dig my heels into the cloud, the bottom surprisingly sturdier than the misty top. I'm a fierce warrior disguised as a floof of cotton candy.

A deafening roar nearly shatters my eardrums. The

cloud's path deviates with sudden winds, whipping peach fog into my face. My body shudders, and the itches begin in my toes, electrifying my skin in seconds.

The itches aren't supposed to be in my whimsical worlds.

I angrily snap the cloud's reins to speed up and away from the impending doom pulling up beside me. Thunderous, rhythmic beats accompany the enormous beast inching into my peripherals.

A dragon rider.

Shifting my attention for a split second, I spy sleek black scales along massive wings. Fear spikes inside of my chest, but I quickly squash it with a mere pinch of my intimidating presence. A sky-rider is always courageous and strong, and I will battle whatever comes my way.

But not this.

The dragon rider resembles Maverick. Hero or villain, I don't care.

I snap out of my imagination immediately.

Opening my eyes, I bury my face into Higgins' golden fur, wishing it would swallow me whole. The warm fur fuzziness on my face is one of the few comforts in the world that can calm my speeding heart rate.

Nobody ever shows up in my imaginary worlds. I'm supposed to be alone. In my space. Safe. By myself. Higgins is allowed, but he doesn't come very often.

My meltdown exhausts me. I hear a knock at my door, but I ignore it and sink into a much-needed nap.

CHAPTER 5

MOM EXCUSES me from school for the rest of the week. She and Jenny discussed how the transition needed to be handled. They agreed that I needed a few days to stim.

Stimming is when I self-regulate by rubbing Higgins' fur or feeling the carpet between my toes. Feeling different textures helps me try to silence the itches and buzzes. Sometimes the itches get too out of control, and there's nothing I can do about it but take a day or two off from my regular schedule.

Stimming is different for everyone. Last year in the disability classroom, we had a boy named Deshawn who stimmed by picking at his cuticles. Mr. Peterson had to work with him to shift his stims because he was hurting himself. Without Higgins, my stimmings were self-destructive. Before he came along, I'd chew my nails raw, bang my head against the wall, and pick at my skin until it scarred, to make the itches go away. I have to stim to help me endure the day, or even the hour, without a meltdown.

Sometimes I use a paddle brush to stimulate my skin, but

I prefer if someone else does it for me, to free my mind. It feels like the bugs beneath my skin unleash calmly and quietly through my pores. I don't know why it makes me happy, but it does.

Today, Nattie is brushing me before her friends come over to play video games. We're lying on the squishy love seat in my room, and I wish nothing would disturb this moment. This pivotal point is the first time I've been able to think and breathe for days.

What have I done to deserve my family? They love and understand me better than anyone else. Of course, I realize I'm also very frustrating to them. Parents and teachers have expectations of children, and if they don't meet those expectations, their patience thins. I wonder if the thinning patience of the adults in my life has to do with them having so many responsibilities that they don't possess unlimited time to try to walk me through my difficulties.

That's what Jenny is for.

Nattie continues to brush my arms with one hand and runs her fingers through my hair with the other. I'd like to think it's therapeutic for her as well. I clutch Higgins' fur, rubbing it between my fingers. My last meltdown was a few days ago, but I can't seem to escape my state of constant anxiety. Sleep-aids are used to help me sleep, and stimuli distract me all day. Jenny helps me with menial tasks, but she hasn't forced me to work outside of my comfort zone in fear of a meltdown. She never forces.

Sometimes Jenny will let me borrow her phone and scroll through WorldVid. I don't care much for reaction or unboxing videos, but the ones that are genuine, soul-baring, confessionals on what it's like to be different: those ones strike a chord in me. Jenny said once that we could record one if we wanted to, but I never gave it a second thought.

I find that WorldVid is a marvelous distraction for the in-between, the state of calm and readiness and panic-mode lizard brain. I'm not quite ready to slip into my safe space, but I'm also not a hundred percent comfortable with what's going on around me. I already have a playlist of some of my favorite creators. I've gone down quite the neurodiverse rabbit hole of WorldVid.

Maybe Jenny can still be my aide but through videos.

I sigh heavily, letting precious oxygen swirl around my lungs and flow to my brain, reveling in the soft waves of the brush on my arms.

A quiet knock comes at the door. I ignore it, the sweet stimulation calming me at last. Nattie continues to brush but softly responds, "Yeah?"

Mom peeks her head around the corner. I close my eyes, drinking in the dopamine my brain is finally releasing. "Hey, sweeties. I came to ask Dinah if she's still okay with the group coming over tonight."

Group. The parents of autistic kids support group. I breathe deeply and sigh through my nose, letting the carbon dioxide answer for me.

"You don't usually have a problem as long as they're quiet," Mom says, translating my sighs. She delicately closes the door.

The sweet brushing bliss carries on until a beeping comes from Nattie's watch. I grip Higgins' fur a little tighter while she glimpses at the time, her neon nail polish reflecting the soft light.

"You're going to be okay, right?" she asks in an affectionate tone. "I've got plans to play games with my friends." She shifts her bony butt in what I think is anticipation, and I realize my stimming has ended.

With my eyes still shut tight, wishing she could brush me all night, I shrug and faintly reply, "Go on."

If they could see me through my eyes, they would see someone in survival mode. Something simple for them could be something I have to hyperfocus on and may even take several steps to accomplish. Higgins and my headphones are like blinders, pointing me in the right direction and blocking out as much distraction as possible, but they don't always work. Sometimes I need the stimuli. Sometimes I need absolute silence.

Nattie doesn't hide her pleasure at being free of me. She bolts out the door faster than Higgins at breakfast time.

My soul is fragile, ready to shatter at any moment.

Higgins decides now's a perfect opportunity to lick my face, grounding me while bringing me back to reality.

Jenny only stays for a little while on Friday afternoons to help after school. Since I didn't go to school today, she took the night off. I don't like breaking my routines at all. My body won't calm down. I'd rather lie here and mope than accidentally have a meltdown and break something or hurt someone.

A few years ago, the buzzes got to me, and I punched Jenny in the nose. She was trying to persuade me to sort a jigsaw puzzle during therapy. I had had a particularly rough, unplanned weekend visit from my dad. Her nose wasn't broken, but I'll never forget the amount of blood that flowed and the despair I felt. The shock of realizing my body was out of control and had completely taken over my brain was something that will stay with me forever.

I work hard every day to brave the buzzes and the itches so something like that will never, *ever* happen again. I'm going to have to try with all my might to get used to Eliza.

Higgins nuzzles my cheek and huffs dog breath in my direction. I know it's out of love, but bleurgh. I push him away gently as I stand, my knees popping from the lack of use.

"You're a smart dog, but you're dumb." He wags his tail as his tongue hangs out, hoping to play.

I'm in comfy sweats, but I wonder if I should bathe. That might help relax me. I take a few steps and place my hand on my doorknob before I remember that Mom is busy with the group, and Nattie is battling her friends on the television downstairs.

The buzzing begins.

Because I'm not getting my way.

I take two deep breaths and practice what Jenny preaches.

Use your tools.

Just because my brain wants me to do a particular thing doesn't mean I can't change my mind. I can be flexible.

Maybe.

I peer at the stack of library books staring at me on the floor, Higgins' tail wagging enthusiastically behind it. I don't have enough energy to play with him, and for whatever reason, I don't feel like reading.

My brain is retaliating with a headache.

Out the door I go.

Ramen sounds delicious right about now. I tiptoe, carefully, in my socks to not disturb the group. I stop under the archway to the kitchen when I overhear my name spoken in a flurry of other words. I press my ear against the door to use my super-human hearing.

"Sounds lovely. There's already an Autism Around the World walk here every April, but I'll give you their volunteer information," I hear Mom say.

"Fantastic! Maverick and Felix will be all for that," says a new voice.

Maverick's mom is here?

Higgins' tail wags against the wall, giving us away. I count about nine different parents chattering and laughing before footsteps approach me.

Mom opens the door.

I stare at the ground.

"Feeling better, hun?" she asks, running her gentle fingers through my fine hair.

I shrug.

"Do you want to come and meet the new people tonight? I think you've met their son, Felix. He's in one of your classrooms."

"He touched my headphones," I mumble, not looking up.

Delicate laughs patter against the walls in the living room. Mom puts her hand in mine and leads me into the dimly lit living room. People treat it like a book club, but I know it's for people struggling to raise their kids. Kids like me.

I stare at the meticulously vacuumed carpet. From my peripheral vision, I spot a pair of crossed legs on the floor.

He's rocking back and forth while clicking his tongue, his headphones securely in place.

"Hi, Felix," I say, softly enough that he can't hear. He seems preoccupied with his stimming anyway. I raise my chin and examine two women sitting next to him, one of them with a loving hand resting on his head.

"Hello, Dinah. I'm Sherri, and this is Trish. We're Felix's moms," the one with tons of freckles and glasses says politely. My ears begin buzzing, trying to process the fact that Maverick and Felix have two moms. It's clear that Sherri is their birth mom, as Trish has a darker complexion with shiny, flowing, dark hair. I remember Maverick saying his parents are divorced.

"And Maverick's too," I blurt out. *Thanks, brain.*

The parents' laughter ensues. While gentle, it sounds like nails on a chalkboard.

"Yes, Maverick's too," Trish says. The bangles around her neck and wrist jingle slightly. I don't like the sound of them. I imagine Felix doesn't either, unless he associates them with comforting sounds, like the pages of a book turning for me.

Higgins steals the spotlight, naturally, when he receives many good-boy pets from the regulars. An alert goes off in my brain.

"Mom, tell Felix's mom where you got Higgins," I blurt before I decide to excuse myself and run out the door, through the hallway, and back to safety. Forget ramen. I'm going to stay in my room all weekend.

Traitorous Higgins stays in the living room for ten minutes, reveling in all the pets and praise he can. When he whines at my door, I hesitate for a second before letting him in.

I sigh and grab the fur on his head for comfort. I bring his neck up to my face and let him give me a big bear hug, my train of thought melting into a haze.

Higgins' heart beats louder and more menacing. His fur becomes rough, coarse, and painstakingly warm. Hot breath and snorts linger above my head as I almost freeze in a panic.

I'm face to face with a grizzly bear.

The dense fog upon the forest floor swirls around the bear in an alien-like way. I'm in imminent danger, that is for certain, but my heartbeat pounds with determination instead of fear.

My silver armor reverberates as I swiftly pull my sword from its sheath. Brandishing it bravely, I call out a warrior's cry as loud as I can to intimidate the beast. The bear takes a swat at me, like I'm a pestering fly. I jump backward and form my stance again, looking the grizzly straight in the eye. It rallies on its hind legs and lets out a deafening roar, a signal of lost patience. Claws are coming at me from every angle, but my decades of training block every attack. I will take it down, as with any other enemy—be it bears, dragons, bandits, sorcerers, or the like.

The bear finally hits its target, knocking my helmet off. Golden hair spills out of my armor down to my waist. My head is pounding. My eyesight blurs a bit on the left. I present my sword once again, its weight balancing my elbows and giving me a more menacing stance. I draw it back, breathe, and thrust it forward before the beast can hit me again. The sword penetrates the fur and skin, hitting the heart. It's another deafening roar accompanying the wound. The bear drops back to all fours, and I witness my golden opportunity to finish this fight. I draw out my blade and keep slashing at the bear's body, every inch that I can reach. With each swift movement, I wound its head and neck until the terrible grizzly falls onto its side, causing the fog to upheave like a massive rock penetrates the sea.

I'm shaking with adrenaline. Sweat pours down my brow in triumph. My breathing is more like wheezing as I drain every last bit of energy I possess. I plop myself next to the defeated bear, my armor protesting the flexibility I demand of it. I rub the fur gently, and its magical powers of calming wash over me. Staring upward at the stars, I revel in my mighty triumph.

I sigh as my head sinks onto my pillow, still stroking Higgins' fur. The soft, twinkly lights that hang above my bed give the illusion of the outdoors, and they're strangely calming.

"I would never hurt you," I whisper in my dog's fluffy ear. His body raises and falls steadily, exhausted from our duel.

I drift off, hoping that nobody will ask me strange questions tomorrow.

CHAPTER 6

MOM'S KNOCK is barely audible, but she underestimates my super-hearing powers. Higgins jumps off my bed, eagerly rushing to the door. His tail wags, and his legs dance a bit. He needs to go out.

"Come in. And let Higg out." I groan, pulling my covers up to my chin. I don't have any intention of getting out of bed today. I'm sure Mom has other plans.

The door squeaks open, and Higgins bolts like lightning through Mom's legs. She chuckles while brushing her wet hair. She knows I despise that—I don't want wet or strange hair on my carpet.

She does her makeup first and then her hair. People give me a hard time for always wanting routine, but they should take a closer look at their own strange rituals. She's still in her plaid pajama set, so I gather it's before nine in the morning.

A long sigh escapes her nostrils. That's a giveaway she's going to try to run something by me in the hopes that the schedule change won't freak me out. Here's hoping.

As she slides a claw clip into her hair, she asks, "Did you sleep good, hun?"

"Mmm sure," I mumble before disappearing underneath my comforter. I create a little cave for myself with a tiny hole big enough to breathe out of.

"I take this as a sign that you plan on continuing the hermit life today?" she asks, a little annoyance barely tainting her sweet voice. "We need to kick this depression so you can go back to school on Monday. I think you did great last night with the group."

Kick this depression? What am I, a soccer player?

"I lasted a whole minute. Yay, for me," I reply curtly.

Mom ignores my sassy comment and plows on. "Anyway, I was wondering if you'd be okay with the Wrights coming over today. We're going to brainstorm fundraiser ideas for Felix to get his own therapy dog. They'll be here for lunch and most of the afternoon."

"They were just here last night," I state through the hole in the blanket cave. The last person I want to talk to is Maverick, although secretly, the thought of him in my house warms my cheeks.

"Yes, I enjoyed their company and want to help them through the tedious process of getting an autism therapy dog. There are lots of hoops to jump through. It always helps to have someone who's been through it to help you." The annoyance in her voice is a little clearer.

I say nothing while I contemplate there being more people in my home, my one place of comfort in this absurdly loud world. Higgins struts into the room and jumps onto my back, forcing a whoosh of breath and coughing fit upon my lungs. Mom strolls nearer and pulls the cave entrance down until she sees my face. I'm unprepared for the rush of cool air. The itches start immediately.

"Would you be okay with that? You don't have to join us; however, I'd rather you would. Time to break you out of this cave. How about a bath? I'll put citrus in it." She smiles and ruffles my hair with her soft touch and the comforting scratch of acrylic fingernails. "This cave has become a little ripe, if you know what I mean."

I'm normally not up for sudden changes to my schedule. Jenny has told Mom about that plenty of times, but she tries to bring me around to her natural impulsiveness at least once a month. On Saturdays we mainly do chores, go on walks, visit the library, and that's about it. I stim on Sundays to comfort myself from the week at school and therapy, but I've been stimming for days while being out of school.

The tension in the air between my mother and me becomes peanut-butter thick.

"Whatever! Have your friends over, just leave *me* alone." I sink deeper down toward the foot of the bed and pull the comforter over me once again, making sure this time my cave is airtight.

I swear my mom's temper is rising like the pressure in a boiling teapot.

Jenny often tells us to pick our battles. I don't understand what the saying means, but I think I'm in a battle with Mom right now. I wait for her to counterattack.

What's her strategy?

"How about," she reproaches, choosing her words as carefully as a miffed mother can, "We have your favorite dessert tonight? I'll make pumpkin pie."

Oooh. Bribery. I like the sound of that.

"I still get to go to the library." I bargain, my voice comes out muffled from underneath the hot blankets. I state my terms firmly, testing the waters to see if she will fight or comply. She usually complies because, really, I'm the boss of this house.

Well, when Jenny isn't here.

Mom sighs in an exhausted defeat, her metaphorical white flag waving.

She doesn't try to force me to do anything out of my comfort zone in fear of a meltdown.

Once I get up and into the bath, the water soothes me. It's nice she doesn't rush me to get out of the bathroom, and she doesn't insist I dry my hair with the hair dryer when I oppose. I dress in purple leggings and a soft gray hoodie. Higgins appears very hopeful once he notices that I'm actually getting ready for the first time in many days. His eyes widen and make that beautiful "Pleeease?" look that means he wants a walk badly.

"After breakfast, Higg," I insist. I tuck my fingertips inside my hoodie pocket and rub the stray fraying material between them as I walk toward the kitchen.

Someone's in the kitchen with Di-nah.

Someone's in the kitchen I know.

"Mooorn-ah! Good morning, Dinah." Nattie yawns as a greeting. Her disheveled hair is in braids, presumably at the hands of one of her friends last night. She's finishing up her disgusting colorful rock-solid cereal at the end of the table. My sister looks comfy in a yellow shirt from some anime show and pajama pants with skulls on them. She's beginning to define her style. My style has one requirement: comfort.

"Morning, Nattie. *I know, I knooow,*" I sing as Higgins

hangs on my heels, desperate for a walk. I snatch my regular apple juice and yogurt from the fridge, newly stocked. Seems like Mom took an emergency grocery shopping trip last night.

"Morning to you too, Dinah," Kurt calls from behind his newspaper and coffee.

"Yep, yep," I call back. Let me finish my damn song. The itches initiate in my lower back this morning. *"Strummin' that old ban-jooo."*

Higgins heads toward Kurt for his morning pets, flying fast through my legs. My knees buckle and I tumble towards the ground, my juice soaring midair toward the kitchen table. I crash onto my elbows and hips. The bruises will be screaming at me later. As if in slow motion, the glass that once held apple juice lands on the tile and shatters into dozens of pieces. The noise bursts through my forehead and into my brain, ringing through my ears like a multi-car crash pileup on the highway. My eyes water as a shower of glass flies into my hair.

Higgins yelps, realizing his mistake. He runs back to shelter me way too late.

"Oh no, Dinah!" Kurt calls as he leaps from the table to my defense. Mom rushes from the living room—her hair halfway curled—and grabs the broom from the closet to hurry and sweep up the glass.

Itches.

Ringing.

Buzzing.

They're all there.

I forget how to breathe. My limbs are frozen in place,

hips and elbows throbbing in protest. A few sharp shards cut into my hands.

I scream forbidden words, using the last of my breath in my lungs. I lash out at Higgins and push him away forcefully. If he did his job, which is taking care of me, instead of trying to be Mr. Center of Attention, this morning would've continued swimmingly.

"Dinah!" Mom scolds, sweeping up glass as Kurt picks fragments out of my hands with a blood-covered tissue. The pieces tinkle along the tile loudly, echoing in my eardrums. Mom runs behind the table, carefully avoiding the sharp floor, and grabs my headphones by the front door. She tosses them to Kurt, who shakes the glass shards out of my hair and puts my lifesavers on my head, checking carefully for more glass. He's an EMT, so he's accustomed to staying calm around blood.

Nattie continues crunching her cereal, acting like it's any other Saturday.

I avoid Higgins' sad eyes. "He's a dumbass! I don't want to look at him."

He's whimpering, well aware that he has made a huge blunder.

"Come on, Di, he's such a good boy. He just wants love, like any other dog," Nattie insists and goes to comfort Higgins in the corner.

My entire body shakes. The tears flow freely as Kurt guides me to the living room, keeping a firm grip on my forearm to make sure I don't run away back to my room. I want to, so badly though.

This morning was going fine. I was even ready to face an

impulsive change in my schedule. I sniff loudly and bury my face into Kurt's shirt.

"Nattie, the kit," Kurt calls softly over the distant tinkling of swept-up glass being thrown in the garbage.

The sniffs turn into cool, sharp breaths. My chest and throat tighten. Every pore of my skin is buzzing. I'm frozen. The world seems to swirl around me like a tornado, its powerful winds roaring in my ears.

"Dinah?" Kurt grabs my other forearm and looks into my eyes.

I break away and see Higgins' distraught face as he sits in the doorway, too ashamed to come near me.

Stupid, stupid dog.

But I love him. And I need him.

The sharp breathing continues, accelerating, but not bringing any oxygen in. I'm hyperventilating. A panic attack is rearing its ugly head.

Kurt attempts to wrap my hands in gauze, but I nudge him away with my knees.

Everything's swirling. I can't stop.

Mom runs to me. I kick her in the shin.

Higgins deems it the appropriate time to start howling, sounding the alarm.

So many things are happening at once, my lack of oxygen being the foremost concern. My family surrounds me, and it isn't until Jenny comes to my rescue that I'm able to take deeper breaths. She runs her fingernails in my hair and then on my face like with a baby to help them fall asleep. My breath shudders, but at least sweet oxygen is flowing freely to my brain.

I know Jenny isn't here right now. I've dissociated and

am picturing my comfort person in order to not cause harm to my family. I'm sure it's my mother running her nails along my skin, but I keep my eyes shut tight and imagine Jenny is here, calming me.

I can't shower. I can't laugh at myself falling down in the kitchen. I can't wear anything outside of my comfort zone. I can't handle different people like Eliza taking care of me, or people trying... no, *wanting* to be my friend. I can read and retain at an amazingly fast pace and get acceptable grades, but I don't know how I'm going to be a functioning adult. Life can go from zero to sixty in a nanosecond.

It's in desperate times like these when the only outlook I see for my future is bleak.

I refuse to spend any time with the Wrights today or ever. In class, I'll sit in the corner and avoid talking to Maverick.

To my satisfaction, Mom calls the Wrights to let them know it'd be better to visit next weekend. I'm somewhat relieved but also guilty for being the reason for them having to cancel their plans. Maverick was probably looking forward to brainstorming fundraising ideas.

I hope he can forgive me. Maybe I can make a list of ideas for him.

Jenny rubs my shoulders with soft palms. Peaceful humming accompanies cello music flowing from her phone. Cello always makes me feel at ease for some reason. The bow against the smooth, reverberating tones of the instrument is like comfort food to my ears.

I inhale the flowery scents of her lotion while my toes happily play with my blanket. I don't care if I have to sit still for a while—that's how relaxed I am. I can literally feel the many cuts on my hands beginning to heal.

I think about Kurt and Mom's discussion I overheard yesterday after all the glass got cleaned up. They heatedly talked about how Higgins has become lax in his duties and how he needs to focus on me. He is a service dog, not a family pet.

He's so much more than either of those things to me.

"How's that, Dinah-Doo? Are you ready for yoga?" Jenny asks sweetly.

"I'm glad you're here and Eliza's not," I blurt out.

Jenny gives me a glance of mixed emotions that I can't read—somewhere between resentment and agreement. She sighs. "Eliza couldn't come in today because it's Sunday. She's religious and likes to give her Sundays to church. I, on the other hand, can't resist a good emergency weekend." A smirk appears on her face. "Otherwise, she would be here."

I can't look into her eyes. There's so much pressure that mine feel like there are moles burrowing into my lower lids. I stare at my twinkle lights to force my watery eyes to dry out, only to fail.

"I'm sorry you had a bad weekend. However, that doesn't change the fact I have to move to Chicago," she states as tears escape my eyes. "Something I've been trying to teach you for seven years is that change can be awesome if you let it be. It's like an adventure or a really big surprise."

Adventures are okay only if they're in my mind or on a page.

I hate surprises.

I hate change.

Itches shiver down my back, but the meditation session puts my body in a semi-permanent state of unwind. Higgins barely leaves an inch between my leg and his fur—he's been on me like a rash since my meltdown.

Jenny introduced me to yoga four years ago when I started high school. My muscles are fond of stretching. Plus, I'm nice and composed afterward. Best of all, she puts silly yoga cartoons on WorldVid that make the routines slightly more fun.

"The goal here is to keep you relaxed throughout your sleep so you're ready to return to school tomorrow. Remember, the world won't wait for you." She smiles and clicks on my TV.

The world won't wait.... Jenny's fiancé won't wait....

"Why can't he move here?" I ask in a low, desperate whisper.

Jenny pulls a soft pajama onesie with a makeshift narwhal horn on the hood out of my drawer and lays it on the bed. She absently looks at her phone while I dress. Pulling on the silly pajamas, I rub my eyes on the sleeves.

"He's taking his father's company over. It's headquartered in Chicago. Unless I want to commute two hours here and back a day, I have to go, Dinah-Doo." She gives this explanation in a big, long breath, like her words are coming up too fast. She strides over to her yoga mat next to mine and gestures for me to do the same.

I obey by slowly dropping to the ground, but I stab her with my fluffy narwhal horn on the top of my head in defiance.

Yoga stretches all my muscles out like taffy, pulled and

relaxed to sweet perfection. The warm, bubbly bath I had earlier combined with yoga and topped with fluffy jammies is a near guarantee I'll have a good night's rest.

I promised Mom and Jenny I'd return to school tomorrow and that I would use my tools whenever I encounter any emotional triggers. If I continue to regress, Eliza may have to sit with me in school and help me throughout my day. That's the last thing in the absolute universe I want. That's Higgins' job.

So, I will put my nose to the proverbial grindstone.

My glistening horn shines in the moonlight upon a sea of glass. I exhale excess water through my blowhole, scattering droplets amongst the stars. The playful splash of my giant body hitting the calm, flat sea fuels my adrenaline toward my blanket of seaweed. The narwhal sleeps tonight.

My white noise machine exudes sweet, fuzzy bliss to my brain. The combination of the comforting noise with Higgins' snoring is practically perfect. I welcome the unconscious oblivion.

CHAPTER 7

DESPITE THE NOISE-CANCELING headphones over my precious ears, the bell always sends a small shiver down my spine. The noise runs wildly through my nerves, banging on every corner of my vertebrae until my brain says it's safe to proceed. I can't fathom how other students deal with such an atrocious sound.

Higgins leads me on his leash through the hallway. The students form their everyday maze around me. The maze would crush me if it weren't for Higgins. His golden coat shining in the old, buzzing fluorescent lights always makes the short trip better. Every now and again I hear students say "Aww!" but Higgins is a good boy and does his job, ignoring distractions to take me from point A to point B. Like English class.

One student has such pungent rosy perfume on that I almost throw up in the science hall. *Hurrrk.*

Another boy with a letterman jacket whoops loudly, cheering on his friend poking a classmate under the ribs to see if he can take a bruise like a man. Higgins leads me onward. If I didn't have him, I'd probably be running off to hide in a closet to escape the unnecessary noise.

I am grateful for him and feel bad for yelling at him. Change is hard. Expected change is harder. Unexpected change that injures me is unbearable.

I let out a slow exhale. Having Higgins lets me attend school, and having aides help me does mean a lot to me. I yell and complain because I hate the thought of my routines going awry, not because I want everything to go my way. Though I do want control, I smile in appreciation that I am able to have comfort in my privileges.

The world won't wait for you... Jenny's voice echoes in my mind.

I'm grateful to reach Mr. Clyde's room in record time so I don't have to interact with anyone. As I take my seat, I'm tempted to leave my headphones on the whole class period so I can have an excuse to not respond to anything and just read. Higgins stares with a disapproving look as if he knows what I'm thinking, so I roll my eyes and shove my headphones in my backpack. Every time the door opens, the sounds from the hallway cause my eyes to twitch and my nerves to shudder.

My fingers dig around in my backpack for *Wuthering Heights*. I stare down the boring cover and sigh reluctantly. Maybe I'll find it enjoyable if I imagine Heathcliff as a nymph and Catherine as a woodland elf.

"Good morning, Dinah," a cautious voice says. Maverick sits next to me with a concerned smile on his face. "How are you today? I'm glad you're back in school. Heard you had a rough weekend."

I almost forgot all about Maverick, the overly friendly

new boy who interrupted my dragon daydream. Almost. My nerves fizzle, and I forget how to think for a moment. His smile reminds me of how he has disrupted my routines and caused chaos in my safe place, and yet nothing completely catastrophic has happened yet. I think back to seconds ago when I was basking in my privilege, realizing that something as small as a person with a calming aura can completely change my perspective.

Not just a person, a friend.

"Yep," I reply, still imagining a woodland fairy-tale version of classic literature.

"I'm sad we didn't get to come over Saturday, but we understand completely. It happened to us a time or two. Or a hundred." Maverick smiles, a careful tone to his voice. The voice he uses to talk to Felix.

My eyes dart to the open book. "Thanks. I'll ask my mom if you can come over again soon. I want to help Felix find a Higgins for himself," I say.

At the sound of his name, Higgins noses my elbow to signal me to lower my arm. He licks my hand with a big slobber.

"Awesome!"

My mouth goes dry as I try to hold back my words, but, of course, they come bursting out before I can do anything about it. "Can you not sit with me at lunch today?"

Maverick looks confused as the lights go down and Mr. Clyde starts today's presentation. "Sure..." he says, seemingly disheartened.

"No, it's... I like your friendship. I do," I whisper, trying to avoid getting in trouble. "It's just that a lot of changes are happening all at once. My lunch routine is how I reset and make it through the rest of the school day. So, it won't be forever. Only until I get used to the idea."

"The idea that we're friends?" Maverick's smile eats up his whole face.

Don't stare.

"Um..." Earlier, words were coming out before I had realized what was happening. Now they won't string together to form a simple sentence. The itches start at the back of my neck, like the words are trapped there and I have to gargle to get them out.

I rummage in my backpack to grab a notebook and write down a few sentences.

The idea that I have a friend who wants to talk to me at lunch. It's usually my time to think. Change is hard for me to get used to.

I rip the paper out of the notebook and set it on Maverick's desk. I act like I'm paying attention to the presentation about the last few chapters, but my mind is racing a million miles a minute.

The itches at my neck stop abruptly, but my head buzzes with anticipation as he scribbles back a reply. Writing down my thoughts feels easier.

My paper arrives back on my desk. I gulp, trying to moisturize my drying mouth, reading the reply.

Totally understand.

The buzzes are gone, but my heart thumps out of my chest. Higgins notices and puts his head in my lap for me to scratch, but I'm not anxious. I slowly inhale and exhale—just like in yoga—to calm myself down. I don't know if this is the start of a meltdown or if I'm going to lose my mind in the middle of English class.

The warm feeling that happened last week once again erupts in my chest. I can't quite describe it fully, only that I feel... safe.

I imagine pain bursting from the top of my ears as they grow and point up toward the ceiling. The classroom dissolves into a dark forest full of corrupted spirits, constantly spewing harbingers of death and destruction toward me.

As the elf queen of the dryads, my magic warns me that the nearby trees have been turned against me by a tremendous evil. The great beast of the woods is at my feet, comforted by my healing touch. A bonfire sparks next to us, crackling in the darkness to give us warmth. Through the fire, I visualize clear, bright blue eyes staring me down.

The nymph warlord is playing a pacifying tune on his lute that releases magical protection into the air, keeping the corrupt forest at bay. I listen with calm intent and allow the music to take me over. The smell of the burning wood is comforting, and knowing the nymph lord is near, protecting me, satisfies my previously troubled heart.

I blink, realizing I've been staring off into space with my mouth open like a fish. I scribble back a quick reply, my handwriting quality suffering.

Do you like to play video games?

I hold my breath, hoping that he will accept my subtle invitation.

Maverick grins when he reads my question. Immediately following, he gives me a single nod.

My smile grows, and I think about him in my house. This time, I can't wait to have him ask me questions.

I'm going to give Eliza a chance.

If I can give Maverick a chance at being my friend, then I can certainly give her one too. She's no Jenny, but I need to accept that change is inevitable, no matter how much it hurts.

No matter how much it gives me the itches.

A slight chill in the air bites at my legs on the way home from school. I enjoy a brisk walk with Higgins, but October shouldn't be this chilly already.

Maybe I'll be a vegan like Maverick.

I stop in my tracks and double over from laughing. I can't try a new dinner dish to save my life, and I just had a passing thought about becoming a vegan. Higgins takes the golden opportunity to go do his business on the Harrises' lawn.

An ambulance with its siren on shoots through the neighborhood, speeding like the driver has their foot all the way down. I ram my palms on both sides of my headphones to squish them hard over my ears. Shutting my eyes tight, I wait for the ungodly noise to pass. Higgins howls at the ambulance like he's somehow helping.

"I know! No need to alarm me. I can hear it," I yell, my own voice muffled through my headphones.

As the wail of the siren passes my body, my teeth rattle. My brain wants to burst through my skull and plummet to the ground. As my heart pounds in the pandemonium, I use my meditation tools to breathe slowly and empty my emotions to tell my body to stop holding my senses hostage.

Breathe in and hold, breathe out. Breathe in and hold, breathe out.

I fall to my knees.

Higgins presents himself so that I can cling onto his fur and bury my face.

Breathe in and hold, breathe out. Breathe in and hold, breathe out.

Higgins' slobbery tongue gives me a comforting lick on my cheek, and I find myself smiling. My heart rate slows to normal much quicker than it usually does. A whole new wave of emotions hits me as I realize my gigantic triumph.

"I did it... I did it, boy!" I laugh, hopping to my feet. I can't wait to tell Jenny and Mom about how I used my tools and didn't have a meltdown.

I remember Kurt saying something about how sirens aren't allowed in the neighborhoods, only on busy streets and highways. I make a mental note to tattle to Kurt about the ambulance.

I practically float the rest of the way home and burst in the side door. "Mommm!" I squeal at her behind the counter, where she is chopping up vegetables for dinner. She always takes care to cut them precisely and quietly, unlike the loud TV chefs.

"Hello to you too." She laughs and walks toward me to see if I will give her a hug. Sometimes, an embrace is the last thing I want. Today, I'm so happy that I wrap my arms around her first. Ordinarily constricting, her hug is like a cocoon of wholesomeness. I wait a whole five seconds to break away.

"Mom, an ambulance with its siren on went past me, and Higgins helped me through it. I didn't cry or anything." I remove my headphones with such vigor that a few hairs on my head are caught and split. I ignore the pain on my scalp. My knees won't stop bouncing until I've told Jenny.

"Oh my gawd, Dinah! That's fantastic." Mom smiles. I think I spy her lower eyelids well up with fluid. Either she is so proud she's crying, or her eyeliner got in her eye, or... I crane my neck over to the counter. Nope, she isn't chopping onions!

"I know! *I know, oh, someone's in the kitchen with Dinaaah!*" I sing and chuck my backpack on the ground. It's supposed to go in my room, but after my victory, I don't feel like following any more rules. I guarantee Jenny will make me pick it up later, even though I had a breakthrough moment.

"I'm so glad for you, honey," my mom says, wiping her eye on her blouse. She continues to chop vegetables that are presumably for her, Kurt, and Nattie. I usually have a grilled cheese sandwich or something light like an orange or string cheese for dinner. "Wait until Kurt, Jenny, and even your father hear about this."

I glance at the calendar hanging on the refrigerator with a magnet. I forgot it's the first week of the month—our weekend spent with Dad. When I was younger, Mom used to drive us to Oshkosh, but now he comes to town to hang out with us. We usually see a movie or go to dinner. Trial and error concluded that Dad's house just didn't feel as safe as our house in Milwaukee.

"Also, I invited Maverick to come over on Friday," I blurt while rummaging in the pantry for a snack.

The chopping stops.

"Wait, who's Maverick?" Mom asks, narrowing her eyes in my direction.

"His moms were talking about coming over for the fundraising ideas," I say between mouthfuls of brown sugar toaster pastry.

"Ohhh. I thought his name was Felix for some funny reason."

"That's his brother."

Mom surveys me with a smirk on her face. "How very nice and thoughtful of you to invite them over again. We can discuss fundraising ideas for their service dog."

I'd better invite the whole family over, too. Mom would probably be so overenthusiastic if she found out that I was having a friend over, and only that friend. Her eyes would leak like a garden hose. It's not that I don't like praise from others, but if I receive too much praise, I'm highly disappointed in myself if I regress.

"Sure, you can text their moms," I reply on my way out of the kitchen. Higgins follows behind. As I jog to my room, I feel like frolicking. I'm like a farm girl, running through a field of wildflowers.

Of course, I'm no ordinary farm girl. I can manipulate the elements around me.

Wind billows through my hair without whistling in my ears. The sun shines on my porcelain skin—the beating heat absent from its life-giving light. My fingertips graze the blooms, and I breathe in the scent of nature, none of it stinging my senses, all of it sweet. Higgins bounds in and out of sight, his fur getting lost in the thousands of tall stems.

I continue running toward the pond at the end of the field. Ripping off my dress, I jump right in, not fearing if the temperature is too cold or if there's sticky mud on the bottom. The water is like a blanket of silk around my skin. I open my eyes and marvel at the wonder that is the world under a sheet of water. Fish swim past me, plants glide gracefully, and they all scatter as Higgins arrives in a considerable splash of bubbles.

The bang of the front door in the distance announces the arrival of Jenny and Eliza. I break through the surface of my daydream and arrive back to reality. The "pond" was my pile of fluffy blankets on my bed. I decide to hide here, knowing what is coming.

"Dinaaah," Eliza calls down the hallway. "You forgot to bring your backpack with you!"

Higgins' tail bats my desk, his collar jangling in anticipation of pets. I cautiously peek over the pile of fluff at the figure in my doorway.

"Where's Jenny?" I ask.

"She's talking to your mom." Eliza's smile curls up, but I don't allow the warmth to reach me.

Then I remember I'm supposed to give her a chance.

It's been an exceptional day so far, but a tiring one.

Successfully using my tools wears me out. Maybe if I can get to sleep early tonight, I can continue having a good day for Eliza and not be a cranky-pants in the morning for her.

"I don't think I have any homework," I concede, propping on my elbows to see her more properly. "We finished *Wuthering Heights*, finally."

"Do you mind if I look to make sure?" Eliza asks, already unzipping my backpack before I can say no.

She doesn't trust my word.

Which I find incredibly annoying.

I sigh and plop down again into my fluffy blankets, to which Higgins gives a disapproving snort.

"Whose side are you on, traitor?" I whisper into his fur. He exhales happily, his breath coating me in a cloud of fumes.

Eliza flips through my disorganized papers and sighs with defeat. "Looks like you're right. So, what should we do tonight?"

I look around. My room is already spotless, no thanks to me. Mom says I'm too rigid in my routine, but she should look in the mirror. I swear she vacuums and picks up my room every day while I'm at school.

"How about a video game?" I ask hopefully.

Eliza smiles with what seems to be sincerity. "Well, video games are more of a reward."

"I freaking made it home today with an ambulance in my ear!" I bark, rolling into my blankets more so they cocoon me away from this awkward conversation. I reach inside my brain to the newly created folder with Eliza's name on it, color coding the traits and interests about her that irk me.

The small squeak of the door can only mean that Jenny has finally poked her head in with her high pony swinging behind her. I tune out her and Eliza's "aide talk" while I scratch Higgins' fur in my hidey-hole. I wouldn't mind chilling here for the rest of the night, doing absolutely nothing. That never flies with Jenny, though.

I think hard to try to come up with something that doesn't involve much effort.

"How about some WorldVid tonight?" I suggest with hope in my voice.

Eliza and Jenny look around the room, noticing that between my bed, my desk, and Higgins sprawling on the loveseat, there's not much room to maneuver. After a short debate, we agree to go downstairs and watch WorldVid in the basement, as long as I bring my fortress of fluffy blankets with me.

I usually like to watch my favorite creators, but after today's adventures I feel like something more mellow. All three of us listen to meditation music while watching sensory visuals with the occasional funny pet video.

I think back to my safe place where I was running through the field of flowers and how free I felt in that moment. I felt free after inviting someone into my home, into where I feel the most at ease—and I'm strangely okay with it.

I find myself drifting off while Jenny and Eliza are watching a puppy video and laughing together.

My eyes are closed, but I'm awakened by hushed voices and movements. Kurt is lifting me up in his arms, whispering with Jenny. I debate revealing my awakened state, but I decide on keeping my eyes shut so he will carry my lazy butt to bed. I've done enough work today, and every muscle in my body aches and buzzes.

Eliza hastily marches up the stairs, undoubtedly trying to be quiet but failing. Kurt begins his ascent with Jenny's voice in his wake.

"I can't believe you're leaving in two weeks," Kurt says in a hushed tone. His words strike my heart like a dagger, swift and unexpected. I know they wouldn't dare bring this up if I appear to be awake, so I keep up the façade.

"That's not true. I'm never leaving," Jenny says, ending in a sniff. "I'm trying *not* to think about it." Her voice shakes as they ascend the steps slowly, trying not to wake me.

"Putting your happiness first can be very difficult, but for love, it's worth it," Kurt whispers. Surprisingly, his wisdom is correct in this case instead of what it is usually on a daily basis: annoying.

Jenny isn't leaving me because she has to. She's leaving me because, ultimately, her fiancé brings her the greatest happiness.

I usually scoff at happily-ever-afters, but Jenny wants her happily ever after, and she's willing to sacrifice her dream job for it.

The rest of the whispered conversation flies over my head as it buzzes with the newly acquired information. My cocoon of blankets and I make a landing on my bed. Higgins jumps up after me, his collar clinking with the force of the jump. When Kurt and Jenny tiptoe out of the room, I grab onto Higgins' fur and give him the good-boy scratches he deserves. The comfort of his soft fur flying everywhere as shedding season nears brings me all the feel-goods. The feel-bads are tossed out the window as if flying to the clouds.

I want my happily ever after, too. I'm not sure what I want or who I want it with, but I want it. For that, I have to get used to change. That means thinking about Maverick and how tomorrow is going to go.

I've never related to Heathcliff from *Wuthering Heights* more.

CHAPTER 8

MAVERICK and I are in the backyard sitting on the trampoline. A blanket is wrapped around my lap in case I get cold. I'm between my furry boy and my friendly boy. The wind isn't so chilly today, but the cherry tree leaves are turning an exquisite shade of red.

Usually my Friday schedule is simple: school, home, a little bit of time with Jenny, video games, books, bed. Today, the Wrights are over in between Jenny time and video games, and I'm dealing with it the best I can.

"Ah!" A juicy piece of orange squirts on my cheek.

I wipe it off in a single swipe and giggle.

Oranges are my favorite fruit, possibly my favorite food. People are surprised when they discover this fact because oranges are citrusy and have a certain bite to them—and peeling them can be frustrating. Over the years, I've perfected my peeling technique and can peel in a flash. For whatever reason, I enjoy the tingle on my tongue. I like how it hydrates and feeds me at the same time. Mom makes sure to purchase oranges on every grocery store trip, even if we have a few left. She never forgets. If she picks up a bad batch that for some reason isn't as tasty, she will almost always drop everything and go get some from another store.

Today's orange is savory. Tangy citrus juices between my teeth force a smile out of me as I offer Maverick a slice. He obliges.

Maverick and I exited our moms' conversation in the living room when Felix started yelling. I wish I had my headphones on at the time. My ears are still ringing.

I realize he can't help it, and I feel bad because I can't help running away.

"Hey, you *can* smile," Maverick says, swallowing his orange piece.

My face rests back to its normal, resting position. "You smile enough for the both of us. How do you do it? Don't your cheeks hurt?"

He shrugs and leans onto his back, his hands supporting his neck. "Not if you're well practiced. I have a resting happy face, I guess."

My mind races a hundred miles an hour with so many questions for Maverick. I squint my eyes and try to pin one down as a thought comes rushing out of my mouth.

"I don't get how you can be happy all the time. Really. You're in a blended family, have a brother that doesn't make life easy, and you moved across the country your senior year of high school." I express my thoughts in one breath. It's like a freight train of words plummeted through a mine shaft of explosives.

Maverick's smile fades ever so slightly. He sighs before asking if he can pet Higgins. I tell him it's okay because he's home and not on-duty.

He extends his arm past my lower back to scratch him. Higgins jumps up and sits so close to the good-boy pets that he's nearly on Maverick's face. He laughs and props up on his side so he can look at me and pet my dog at the same time.

He has eyes I could back float in. They are the perfect blend of blue and gray.

"I can sense that you've come to a logical conclusion that I can't possibly be happy in my current life situation," he starts, making direct eye contact with me, which I usually hate, but I can't break away. "The truth is, I'm not a good person, Dinah. I acted horrible to my dad and moms. I acted like Felix was a burden, and I didn't want to deal with him. I was your average douche nozzle."

"Douche nozzle?" I ask in a stern tone. I don't know what one is or why it's average when I've never even heard of it.

"It's a word one of my friends called me back in Denver, and I deserved it." Maverick sucks in his upper lip, causing his face to be more severe than I have ever seen it.

A small breeze blows through the backyard, sending the smell of pine dust to add to my ever-growing list of stimulation.

"They don't sound like much of a friend, then," I respond.

"Nope, they were the best friend I could ever have, and I ruined it, like I ruin most things," he reminisces, as if reliving something unbearable.

I shake my head, unable to process the conflicting pieces of information. Maverick is the nicest person I know. His descriptions of himself don't match the behavior I've seen from him. How he sees himself and how I see him are at war in my head, brandishing swords of truth and clashing shields of opinion.

"Moving away from Denver was a chance for me to make a new start. I decided it was now or never to change. A chance to not be a crappy person forever." He scratches Higgins' ears and begins the "who's a good boy" routine.

My head swims with a myriad of thoughts, drowning in the mountain of socially acceptable conversations we could be having. Instead, it settles on:

"I hate change."

Maverick chuckles, nodding. "It can suck, but I choose to see these changes as an opportunity."

I chew on my right cheek, sucking out the last of the orange juice in my mouth. My mind wanders in no particular direction, but I want to clear the awkward air.

I dig into my hoodie pocket as soon as I remember that I prepared for such an event. I wave it in front of Maverick's face, the movement bouncing us on the trampoline ever so slightly. Higgins sniffs it to make sure it's not a treat.

"What's this?" he asks, clasping it between two fingers like scissors.

"My list of fantasy recommendations," I say and flap my hands a bit. That can happen when I'm a little excited. I have energy zapping through my nerves. The hand flapping can help it escape.

"Oh, sweet!" Maverick replies, unfolding the paper. "Wow... it's, uh... long."

"Yeah, well, the Foes Without Hate series has fourteen books total, well, not including two prequels and a companion novel. Then there's the Frontline Descendants which have seventeen, then the Scourge of Utopia books are always awesome, but that series has over a thousand pages in each installment."

My smartwatch buzzes, interrupting my hyperfocus. It lets me know it's time for Jenny and Eliza to leave. Jenny's been doing some on-site training with Eliza while the rest of the family discussed therapy dogs. Beneath that reminder is another mentioning my dad is coming to town for miniature golf tomorrow. A sigh escapes my lips. I don't want to face Jenny's last week, and I certainly don't feel like miniature golf.

It's been a stress-filled week. It started out fine, and I've continually put in the effort to have a satisfactory week. I want to send Jenny off on a high note, not crying and wishing she didn't have to leave. She deserves happiness, and I don't need to be a... douche nozzle about it.

"That's a cool watch." Maverick's voice invades my thoughts.

I rock back and forth slightly, bouncing the trampoline. When I'm anxious, rhythmic movement helps calm me down, or what Jenny calls it: lizard brain. It refers to the fight-or-flight response from our brain stems, but I have no freaking idea why it's called lizard brain.

"My dad gave it to me. He's coming tomorrow. I don't know if I feel like hanging out with him," I explain. I feel like an undeserving daughter for a fraction of a second, but Jenny's lessons about people-pleasing come floating back to my mind. I don't have to do anything with anyone if I don't want to. I'm a human being, not a robot.

Maverick shrugs, his silhouette against the setting sun bouncing a little with my swaying. "Sometimes we have to do what we don't want to do. Even neurotypical people have a hard time doing that."

I should be panicking.

I should be crying in my bed.

I don't want Jenny to leave. I don't want to hang out with my dad. I certainly don't want to alter my schedule by hanging out with Maverick in my backyard. Hilariously, I don't want to move. Being around him is comforting, almost as much as my pile of fluff on my bed.

I have no control over this moment, and yet I'm okay with that. We were supposed to play *Animal Brawl* and come up with fundraising ideas, but the idea of inviting others into my routines intimidated me, hence the escape to the backyard. I've enjoyed being outside with him under the chilly sunset far more than I anticipated. This change is weird because I kind of like it.

The back door bangs open, causing Higgins to yelp, which in turn causes my ears to ring. Itches begin in my ears and vibrate down to my toes. I cling to my blanket and wrap it tighter around me.

It's only Jenny and Eliza leaving for the weekend. They both wave in our direction. Eliza calls, "Have a nice weekend, Dinah! See you Monday." While both ladies are in their regular gym clothing, Eliza has cranberry-red lipstick on, and Jenny has glittery bronzer around her forehead, which means they both have plans tonight.

I don't say anything back to them. I wonder how I'd look with cranberry-red lipstick.

They look at each other and smile as they walk toward their cars, as if my aides know a secret I don't.

Extra weight atop my shoulders and back means

Maverick is adding to my safety cocoon, putting his arm around me. I do an inner check for itches, only to be surprised that I come up empty.

"You okay?" Maverick asks.

Only then do I do a double take and realize Maverick Wright has his arm around me like it's no big deal.

My brain is swarming with intrusive thoughts about how I only trust my family to touch me.

This person is new.

I don't handle new things well.

A shiver of fear shakes my spine. I leap from my blanket and his arms. I dive from the trampoline, risking broken bones on the off chance of a hard landing. I speed up, my feet barely touching the cool, autumn grass.

Higgins trails behind me as my second-in-command, but I don't anticipate how quick Maverick's reflexes are.

"Hey!" he calls.

There's a pounding of another pair of feet directly behind me. He has the advantage of longer legs, so his calm walking strides catch up to me in no time. I almost run into him as he puts his hands up in front of me like he's ready to catch a flying basketball. Though Maverick's voice is soft, my ears pick up his tone like a foghorn. "I'm a friend. I'm only trying to help. You don't need to run away from me."

One glance of his cerulean eyes makes me sidestep and stare at the ground while he speaks. "I need friends, you need friends, so let's be friends."

He talks like being friends is the easiest thing in the world.

I frown, nod, and slowly back up. Maverick stays put, giving me the space I need. At least he's figured out not to touch me without permission. A text message buzz comes from his pocket. I assume it's from his moms, saying they are ready to go home.

Perhaps his drown-worthy eyes against the tangerine sky complementing the red cherry tree should be a scene enjoyed. To me, it's overstimulating. Friday nights are video game nights, and I haven't played with Nattie yet.

What's the polite social protocol here without running away? I dig toward the back of my brain for an answer buried deep, somewhere between unicorn lore and fairy life expectancy.

Thank him for hanging out or use a farewell greeting and leave it at that?

A or B, 1 or 2. Choose. *Choose.* Choose!

"Thanks for, uh... I'll see you at school," I mutter and turn toward the screen door.

Maverick brushes my forearm, gentle but firm. Higgins is long gone through the doggy door. Dinner is more important than anything right now.

"I said... you need to ask *permission* to touch me," I growl, yanking my arm away.

His face immediately changes to instant regret. "I'm sorry, Dinah. I'm so used to holding on to Felix that it's hard for me. I do it to everyone."

"Not me, please," I say through gritted teeth. "What do you want?"

"What's your number? Why don't we text? Maybe I can help you through this weekend with your dad," Maverick says.

"I don't have a phone. I have my smartwatch that tells time and has a calendar. No texting, no social media," I reply, swiftly backing up into the house. I close the screen door, staring at the ground.

Mom says social media will only give me anxiety and is a waste of time. Apparently, people my age use pictures for validation of their attractiveness and the "likes" they receive as self-worth.

"It might be easier to communicate. You know, like how we pass notes in English? It's just like texting." He smiles again. Genuinely or out of habit, I'll never be sure now.

I try to make eye contact one more time, making it only to his ears. They're cute and not too chunky in the lobe. If his ears were pointier, he could pass for a woodland elf. At this thought, I decide to pick my *Animal Brawl* character. My Supersonic Rabbit Hustler is totally going to take down Nattie's usual Giraffe Neck-Breaker.

"Have a fun weekend, then." I hear Maverick's quiet sigh behind me as if in defeat.

He follows me inside but heads to the living room, no doubt to tell his moms he's ready to get away from me. Awkward, socially inept, idiotic me.

CHAPTER 9

I PROCEED DOWNSTAIRS, not caring how long Maverick, Felix, and their moms stay. I try not to dwell on what just happened, psyching myself up to kick Nattie's ass.

After we both win one match and tie for third, I agree to be done for the night because it's getting late, and I still want to read and prepare myself for close encounters of the Dad kind tomorrow.

Nattie switches off the TV and throws a weird question at me from out of a black hole.

"So how is Mr. Wright, aka Mr. Handsome?" She smiles her toothy grin at me. I have no idea how her mind works or why such torture brings her pleasure.

Because I'm programming my alarm for tomorrow on my watch, it takes me a few moments to register her question. My brow furrows and eyes widen. "How should I know how Maverick and Felix's dad is or if he's even relatively favorable looking? Plus, he's over forty. You're nasty, Nattie."

I don't know why she snorts and throws her head back in

a giggling fit. The sound of her laughing can brighten a room and even warm my lifeless heart.

"Sorry for being vague." She gasps amidst her laughter. "I meant Maverick. I saw you two on the trampoline talking. You know, *alone*." She wags her eyebrows at me in some sort of amusing way. I'm not sure if it's meant to be sarcastic or sincere.

"How dare you! Higgins was there too." I upturn my lips in a soft smile, rubbing Higgins' neck affectionately.

I doubt Nattie would want to know how Maverick was, as she doesn't really know him, and if she cared so much, why couldn't she ask him herself? A simple "Hi, how are you?" is all it takes. Greeting strangers comes easily to her. Concluding there's context I'm failing to grasp, I go along with appropriate conversation.

"He's fine. He's Maverick." I jump up from the couch, and Higgins leads the way up the stairs for reading time.

Nattie gets up and follows as well. Sometimes when she has nothing to do on the weekends, she follows me around and teases me. I don't mind unless I'm on the brink of a melt-down, which I'm not currently, but I have had a long week. Anxiety is nearly at the next leg of the relay race, ready to pass the baton to panic.

"He's cute, Dinah, can't you see?" Nattie hisses when we close my door. She sits on my love seat while I stand at my bookcase, looking longingly at the stack of library books that need to be read before next weekend.

Of course I can see that. I look at Maverick and see his tall stature, broad shoulders, and freckled face.

More pressing issues come floating to my frontal lobe.

"Why do I have to go miniature golfing with Dad? Why

can't I stay home and read?" I whine, picking up a high-fantasy book and falling onto my bed covers.

"Because you chose the activity and were feeling particularly brave that day."

"I don't wanna anymore."

"How come?"

I shrug, but I know the real reasons. Pick one. Because next week is Jenny's last week of work? Because Dad's visits poke uncomfortable holes in my structured schedule? Because I want a phone to text Maverick all weekend?

Wait. Back up an inch.

Apparently, thoughts of Maverick are not only invading my safe places. They are also interrupting my regular thought processes. I shake my head to let the rogue thought of him fall right out of my ear and hit the floor.

If Nattie notices my neurotic movement, she doesn't say so. She's busy giving Higgins bedtime scratches. She sighs and looks up at me. Her smile fades.

"Ugh. Are you having a brain fart?" she asks.

A large yawn escapes my face before I register the question.

"Di-nah," she snaps.

"Oh, uh, sorry. What were we...?" I blurt.

"Earth to Dinah. I can't read your mind."

A pang of guilt hits me in the chest. "I know that."

"Geez, I don't know why I attempt conversation sometimes."

"What? Why are you acting like this?" My emotions strike me like a meteor in my stomach.

Higgins whines his "something's wrong" whine.

I exhale slowly through my nostrils, my finally-winding-down thoughts abruptly revving to top speed again. I've done so well this week—I can't give up now.

"Listen, I know my limits, and we're pushing them. I'm sorry for whatever I did to make you upset. I don't think I need anything more stimulating this weekend," I admit in defeat, sticking my hands in my hoodie for protection.

"And Dad will understand that if you just phrase it that way. Com-MU-ni-ca-tion, Dinah. We've told you thousands of times." Nattie's words bite, and she throws her hands up in the air, turning to leave.

I won't, though. For whatever reason, communicating with my dad is like swallowing nails for me. I can't help but have traumatic memories of when he finally left, unable to deal with my mother and me at the same time.

"Do you think Mom would let me have a phone?" I ask carefully, testing the waters.

Nattie stops with her hand on the door handle. "Excuse me? If you get to have a phone, then I certainly have to have one too."

"We're teenagers. Why shouldn't we have them?" I agree, trying to get the outcome I want out of Nattie. "What if we... don't go miniature golfing tomorrow?"

My sister slowly turns on her heels, intrigued.

"What if we 'convince' Dad to take us phone shopping tomorrow?" Nattie says with a sly look.

Now we're talking.

CHAPTER 10

I CURL up in my bed-cocoon in disbelief at the luck I've had today. At first, Dad wasn't on board with our request for phones, but he gave in after he hurt my feelings. I don't think he meant to; he just isn't around me enough to know what my triggers are. He doesn't understand when I'm anxious about something like miniature golf and its accompanying unknown loud noises and people. His voice rose, and so did my panic-induced adrenaline, bringing on the waterworks. Situations like these make having three parents a living hell. To top it off, Mom and Dad got in a shouting match upon our arrival home, probably over him purchasing phones without a discussion with her. So, I'm in my room with my headphones on while blasting cello music to avoid it.

After the argument dies down and I'm safe to remove my headphones, I begin playing with my new toy. Nattie and I send funny cat GIFs to each other, and I can hear her laughing in her room. My favorite is a white cat chasing after a toy mouse up the walls. I snort and nearly pee myself.

I don't often get people's diverse sense of humor, but I'm

willing to bet that because Maverick and I seem to get along, he'd appreciate a few sassy texts. Then I remember I don't have his number. Crap.

Once Mom cools down, I send her a text to ask Maverick's mom Sherri if I can have his number. I think Mom is more surprised that I have someone I can call a close friend, so she texts it to me about twenty minutes later without question.

I plug his number in. My heart thumps in my chest, thinking about how to form our first conversation.

> Me: Guess who?

A thrill shivers down my spine as I send the text.

Higgins snores next to me while I wait. The trip to town with Dad apparently wore him out. I remember when he was a newly trained puppy and rarely napped during the day. He almost had as much energy as me. Higgins is about six now, and the five years we've had him has made all the difference in the world to me.

A ding from my phone chases the thought from my mind.

The text reads:

> Maverick: Please don't tell me you're a murderer sending me on a scavenger hunt to save my life. I'm in no mood!

I knew Maverick and I had similar senses of humor. I can't help but smile and quickly type out the next message.

> Me: It's Dinah Finlayson.

The three dancing dots at the bottom left of the screen are incredibly satisfying to watch as he types.

> Maverick: No need for last names. I only know one Dinah ☺

My cheeks hurt. No human being should be able to smile as much as Maverick does.

> Me: We went phone shopping instead of miniature golfing.

> Maverick: I'm glad. How did your day with your dad go overall?

This text comes much faster than the others. I can hardly keep up with where the numbers and letters are.

An interrupting ding indicates Nattie has found another cat GIF to send me from the other side of the wall. I can't be bothered. The conversation is going exactly how I desire, and I don't want anything to mess it up for me—even my sister.

I text Maverick about how my day was, how Dad hurt my feelings but apologized with a phone, how Mom wasn't excited about it, but she came around with enough persuasion. I leave out my parents arguing. It doesn't seem like the type of thing I should share, according to Jenny's teachings. I also tell him how Nattie and I are sending cat GIFs to each other from either side of a wall to which Maverick reacts with a cry-laughing emoji.

My chest flutters like I swallowed a bucket of sparkles. Communicating without talking—without the social expectation of eye contact—is a beautiful thing. I'm confident I can carry on a conversation in text much better than I can in my day-to-day life. It's like I've pushed through a towering, invisible barrier a heroine must break through in order to become who she is truly meant to be.

Warmth spreads from my rib cage to my toes. Dormant coals in my soul are suddenly ablaze, free to dance in the night among the stars.

A loud bang on the wall cracks my skull and rattles my brain.

"Hey! Reply to my cat GIF, dammit!"

Sunday is spent planning Jenny's surprise goodbye party, which is a few days away. My heart sinks to my ankles and drags along the wooden floorboards. I'm dreading the week ahead. While my phone ensures Jenny and I will stay close, I'm still grieving her departure from Milwaukee. I ask Mom if we can go to the wedding. She says she has already asked Jenny about that and that the ceremony is apparently intimate and exclusive—only a handful of family members are included. Which is okay, I guess.

It's a fair reason. If I ever get married, I don't want hundreds of people staring at me, daring anything to go wrong. The universe is rarely fair when it comes to planning and executing grand events.

I want my nuptials to take place in a weeping willow forest with branches so thick they block out the light. A thicket with a small waterfall and fairy lights will swallow the nearby trees whole. Limited seating will be covered in woodland greenery to give the guests a thorough, immersive experience. Cellists bowing a gorgeous tune will be the only sound to accompany my delicate walk down a stony garden path to meet my love at the end of the aisle and the beginning of eternity.

Nattie laughs at my decorative vision, but we'll see who's laughing when I make her wear a flowy fairy dress as my maid of honor.

I let Mom do most of the planning for the party since the only thing I want control of is for things to stay the same, and there's no chance of that happening. I don't see what the big deal in planning everything is—the affair is just going to be everyone yelling "Surprise," giving her departing gifts, serving a cake, and the adults enjoying alcohol.

Itches. Wiggles. They need to get out. Anxiety bubbles up like a newly awakened volcano, dormant for thousands of years.

I jump up and grab my headphones and Higgins' leash on the hooks next to the door. He bounds forward immediately, as if the jingle of the leash is the call of his people to arms.

"Going on a walk, hun?" Mom asks, staring me down through her reading glasses. I hold in the staggering desire to push them up the bridge of her nose. Her hot coffee steams her lenses. "You don't want to help us plan the cake?"

"Jenny likes lemon cake," I say like I have somewhere important to be. In truth, I just need out. The air in the house is forming a net, which is trying to trap and suffocate me. I latch Higgins' leash onto his harness, and we're out the door before Mom can reply.

A funny thing about the Midwest is that the weather is indecisive—does it want to rain or not? The Wisconsin sky is mischievous that way. Sometimes, the clouds cover the blue sky and water doesn't pour down. It just hangs in the air like a hedge maze with no entrance, but soft and transparent. Everything appears wet, but you're not. You can feel the mist on your face, but it isn't too thick. It's a perfect, endless string of pearls you can walk through.

"Lazy Sunday" is a term that only applies to some of our neighborhood—divided against the churchgoers and the sleep-inners. Around midmorning is the perfect time to head on a walk and clear a head, especially in the mist. Not to mention, when Wisconsin football season starts, there's not a soul to be seen because everyone is inside watching the game on TV. The wide-open air is fresh to my lungs and spreads oxygen around my organs so I'm able to escape the itches.

Higgins' bushy tail noticeably needs a trim. His tail knocks the leash on his harness back and forth from overexcitement. I love how happy he is to lead me around the block.

With no particular destination in mind, we wander over to the park at the end of the road and across the street. It isn't so much a park as it is a picnic table and a set of swings. It'll do for a makeshift thinking spot. I wait until absolutely no cars are on the adjacent road before attempting to cross, something Higgins also takes very seriously.

Once I park myself on the old rubber swing with semi-rusty chains, I rock back and forth slightly. Swinging is one of my favorite ways to stim, particularly with my headphones on so that the changing wind pressure doesn't soar through my ears. I experience the weightless reaction that is so intoxicating. It is priceless. Freeing.

Higgins sits and waits for me, no need for me to hang on to his collar. He's trained so he will never run away or even leave my side if we're outside. His head bobs back and forth, following my swinging adventure with great interest.

My phone dings from my pocket. I'm surprised I hear it over the creak and swoosh of the swing. The mist hits my face at a velocity that makes it hard to peer down and check my messages. I dig my heels into the wood chips to slow myself. A few scatter, causing Higgins to break his gaze.

I pull my phone out of my hoodie pocket and swipe to unlock it.

> Maverick: Whatcha doin this sabbath day?

I giggle because I've never been to church a day in my life.

> Me: Definitely not worshiping anything. Just on a walk with Higgins.

The toes of my sneakers dig into the dirt under the wood chips as I sway my leg in anticipation. Maverick types fast but not fast enough for instant gratification.

> Maverick: Sounds fun. I was just thinking about fundraisers for Felix's therapy dog. I think a silent auction on Halloween would be awesome. Spooky themed

A silent auction. I like the sound of that, or lack thereof, whatever it is.

> Maverick: Will you help us organize it?

Bile lurks at the back of my throat. The thought of being in charge of something seems over my head. It sounds like something that's going to take a lot of effort and time. Not to mention, I've never so much as organized a birthday party. I can't even help plan Jenny's going-away party, and I know her better than I know myself. There are so many things that could go wrong. That's why I appreciate my mom for always taking care of those moments. I never realized how grateful I am how Mom manages events when things go awry. Next time, I'll try to help her with them the best I can, instead of having a breakdown.

Maybe if Maverick takes the lead, then I can try to take a small task on. Organizing the food and beverages seems simple enough. Thinking I can somehow do it all on my own feels satisfying as well.

Leaping off the swing, I stick my phone back into my hoodie, grab Higgins' leash, and start my way back towards home. The mist now feels more like a sheet of plastic wrap I can't fight through—its translucent substance sticks to me with every step I take.

I warned Maverick not to spring things on me. I told him I have to get used to big ideas and changes, and too many are happening at once. Some of them are welcomed, like my phone. Most of them are negative, threatening to snap the strings of the stable schedule I've had for the past seven years. I break into a jog so the mist finally wets my hair without the impact of water pressure like rain or a shower.

Higgins breathes heavily with his tongue out as we jog up the street toward home.

Bounding through the doorway, I don't stop until I reach my room. I slam the door, peel off my damp clothes, and lie on my bed in my bra and underwear. My fluffy sheets enclose me. Whining and scratching reveal I've locked Higgins out of the room. I'll let him back in once he's dried off a bit.

Ding.

I reach over my bed and grab my phone out of my hoodie.

> Maverick: Only if you want to, that is

Well then.

First it sounded like he really wanted my help. Now it sounds like—after thinking it over for fifteen minutes—he's not particularly excited about inviting me. It sounds like I'm a tag-along burden, not someone he genuinely wants to spend time with.

A heat rises in my chest like molten lava hardening my shell. I knew I shouldn't have gotten a phone just for a boy. I'm enraged at myself. I want to punch myself in the face. Ridiculous. All the negative energy in my body exits through my legs, not my fists. I start kicking my blankets and let out one short, frustrated scream.

Nobody knocks at my door. My family is probably willingly ignoring me.

Whatever.

I pick up the nearest book from my library stash to lose myself in it, determined to shut the world around me out for at least the next few hours.

The setting of this book involves magical realism and a late 1800s circus. The protagonist is a performer who dances ballet on top of an elephant. She is investigating her mysterious yet cunning ringmaster, who she is sure is up to something.

The lights come back up as our show has ended. Higgins the elephant and I are ready to call it a night. I pat his trunk, straighten my tutu, and saunter over to my part of the dressing room while the animal caretakers direct my massive mammal to his dinner.

Cool evening air on my sweating face greets me like an old friend. A performer's high soars through my veins. Adding wine to my blood shall be the perfect concoction for a restful night. My plans come to a halt when the ringmaster cuts me off in my path, tipping his hat.

"Fantastic show tonight, m'lady. We would be lost without you," he quips in his charming voice. His ocean-blue eyes gape at me from under the brim of his top hat in a perplexing way, as if his thoughts are completely different from the subject matter he is speaking of.

"Thank you, although Higgins deserves all of the praise," I state, well aware of my bare shoulders and thighs. I'm in need of a cloak as soon as possible to hide from his wandering eyes. I motion to walk around him, trying not to cake my ballet slippers in mud.

The ringmaster pulls me toward him using his magnetic powers, practically throwing me into his arms. I'm being touched. I start to panic, but I look up into his eyes, which instantly calm me for some odd reason.

"I thought we could celebrate by going into town, possibly getting a drink." He smiles slightly, looking directly into my eyes. I can't help but blush; his invitation is quite forward. Perhaps one drink with him will satisfy his thirst for my company, and he'll move on to a more interested young lady.

He lets me go and I step back into a slippery puddle of mud, nearly losing my balance. What a sight I would have made of myself.

"Only if you want to, that is," he says, extending a gloved, gentlemanly hand.

My eyes widen as the illusion ends and a question pops up in my head.

Forgetting I'm barely dressed, I jump out of my covers, fling my door open, and barge into Nattie's room. As usual, Higgins is right at my side.

"Yo! Knock much?" she yelps, tugging down a sweater she just threw on. Her hair is askew, half of it standing on end from static. I'd laugh, but my question pounds against my forehead, threatening to break free from my skull.

"Nattie, what does Maverick mean by this?" I point a shaking finger to the phrase in the book I just read.

Maverick: Only if you want to, that is

She stares at me with a look like she's about to make fun of me. "Wait... Maverick texted you in a book?" she asks, a giggle at the end of her breath. "And why are you in your undies?"

Annoyed, I crane my neck to the ceiling. Why wasn't I born in the day and age where mind reading is a perfectly normal superpower? Then I wouldn't struggle with communication as much.

"No! He texted 'Only if you want to, that is,' after asking if I'd help with a fundraiser for Felix's therapy dog."

"Did you answer him?"

"I don't know what the hell he means, Nattie!"

"Okay, okay. Calm your tits." She'd never say that around Mom. She skims through the page of my mystical circus novel from the library and nods, her bottom lip jutted out in concentration. For a moment, all I hear is Higgins panting.

"It looks like the ringmaster asks the girl to do something, and he adds that last little bit, so she doesn't feel like she has no other choice." She swallows and puts her hands on her hips, looking at me square in the face. She still has a laugh behind her eyes that she's dying to let out.

I stare blankly.

"Look," she continues, moving her hands to my bare shoulders. Her cold fingers send shivers down my spine. I can't move. "It sounds like Maverick wants to involve you in the dog adoption process because he likes being around you, but he doesn't want you to be uncomfortable. So, if you don't want to, tell him no. If you want to, tell him yes." My sister's voice starts to have a sharpness to it, indicating I'm getting on her nerves.

I shrug my shoulders to get Nattie's grip to loosen. I stare at the wall, concentrating hard.

"So, he's not being a douche nozzle," I finally state.

Nattie can't hold in her laughter anymore. She snorts, gasps for air, and almost falls face-first into her closet.

My nose crinkles, missing the joke.

"I love you, you blockhead." She breathes, bringing me into a forced hug against her scratchy sweater. I pat my fingers on her waist twice and quickly jump back. I don't feel like being strangled at the moment. "And no. He's just trying to be nice."

He's just trying to be nice.

"Like... nice-to-the-autistic-girl nice or nice-to-a-friend nice?" I ask, afraid to hear an answer either way.

"Nice-to-a-friend nice. I'm positive." Nattie smiles, the static in her pink hair returning to normal. "Mom might be afraid of you getting hurt. But I say it's your life, and you deserve every experience."

Whatever she means by that.

Goose bumps pop up all over my skin, except for my feet, where Higgins is sitting to keep them warm. I better put some clothes on before Kurt comes walking around the corner.

"'Kay, thanks," I say and shuffle back to my own room. I don't bother picking out different day clothes. Instead, I gravitate to my onesies of comfort in the pajama drawer. Once I am cozy from head-to-toe in one of my personal favorite pajama onesies (panda, with little puffball-like ears on top of the hood), Higgins goes to chew a toy on my love seat while I plop back onto my cloud-like bed of blankets.

I'm a relieved happy ball of fluff.

I grab my phone and open it to find no recent messages. I finally type a response to Maverick.

> Me: To keep you in suspense, I'll let you know my answer at school tomorrow.

CHAPTER 11

I PLAY with my headphones as I await Felix's arrival to Mr. Peterson's class, hoping to see Maverick dropping him off so I can give him an answer to his question. He kept sending texts yesterday that were silly and insistent on me telling him sooner. This is one surprise I like hanging over his head. Usually, I spit out secrets faster than lightning. Not this time.

Blood roars through my ears and my heart thumps at a tiny glimpse of Maverick standing at the doorway. I smile ear to ear, but it quickly fades when I see Felix having a hard time getting to class.

He slams the door shut, whining and rejecting Maverick's help. Mr. Peterson and another aide run to help, their voices calm and pleasant instead of alarmed, which is what neurotypical people usually emote in an escalated situation. I think back to a few of my past meltdowns in public places—the mall, hospitals, etc.—where neurotypical people began backing up and yelling for help. Just the thought of the petrified looks on their faces sends some itches up my spine.

I glance at Andrew, who is already setting up a new game of *Thelena's Wrath*. I insisted we restart after my untimely loss last week. I yank on my headphones, tell Higgins to stay, and promise Andrew I'll be right back.

Striding toward the door, I feel confident I can help Felix. He knows me and my family a little better now. Hopefully the sight of me will give him some comfort.

He's wearing pajama bottoms and an anime sweatshirt, his hair askew beneath his headphones.

"Hey, Felix, we've got your favorite candy today," Mr. Peterson coaxes from the doorway. Maverick has a hold of Felix's shoulders, mumbling into his ear to help him over the threshold.

The new aide—whose name I can't remember because she doesn't work with me—is trying to bribe Felix with the promise of watching fun videos on a classroom tablet. That isn't working either.

I whistle below a whisper, and Higgins is almost immediately at my side.

"Hi, Felix, do you want to pet Higgins today?" I call in what is hopefully a calm but not overly sweet tone.

Felix's body stumbles forward a foot or two when he's distracted by my dog. The aide grabs his hand gently and lowers it to Higgins' fur to let him experience the softness. I glance up to send Maverick a smile, but he's gone.

I try not to worry since the bell is about to ring. He probably doesn't want to be late.

No point in getting upset, I tell myself. Still, my heart sinks and my back itches, threatening to spread the madness throughout my entire body.

If things don't go a hundred percent according to your

plan, it's no excuse to not smile and move on. Life hardly ever obeys our schedule, Jenny's voice says in my head. *Life's a suckfest.*

I exhale my anxieties through my nostrils and turn my lips upward at the sight of Felix hugging my dog. He's on the floor, arms superglued to my good boy's fur, but Mr. Peterson seems satisfied. He got Felix in the door. Getting him to his seat might be too much to handle. The aide takes a nearby chair and sits by him near the door, offering the tablet when Felix is ready to start working.

"Thank you, Dinah." Mr. Peterson approaches me. "It's generous of you to help Felix by letting him bond with your service dog."

I'm uncomfortable with the praise and eye contact. I turn away, but I gain a beaming sense of something close to pride spreading through my chest. I shuffle over to my regular table, where Andrew is bouncing in his seat, the game set up and ready to play. I smirk when I see that his thick glasses are sliding on and off his nose.

I roll high numbers throughout the game despite my discomfort. Felix hogs Higgins almost the whole entire hour. I'm making myself be okay with it. At least I can take my headphones off because he isn't screaming anymore.

A pang of feel-bads hit my neck, and I think it might be a twinge of jealousy. Higgins is *my* dog. It's hard to be grown-up about sharing, even though it's a concept that everyone usually learns in kindergarten. What if *I* have a meltdown? Higgins is only one dog; he can't clone himself.

There's a reason his harness says: "AUTISM SERVICE DOG DO NOT SEPARATE FROM HANDLER."

That's when the realization punches me in the gut. Felix

needs a therapy dog. ASAP. Higgins is mine, and I don't want Felix getting attached to him. I promise myself to be extra enthusiastic about fundraising efforts for the Wrights from now on. I want Felix to have just as good of a boy as I have.

When my smartwatch buzzer goes off for my next class, I pack up and get ready to go. I'm grateful for my headphones as Felix begins crying. Higgins tries to escape his grasp to aide me. I pat my leg and hold out his leash. He somehow breaks free of Felix's prying fingers and arrives at my side, visibly disgruntled but still quite proud of himself. He shakes his furry ears as if to rid himself of the essence of Felix.

Blood rushes to Felix's face, his sea-blue eyes the same color as his brother's, welling with tears. I sputter a feeble apology when I pass him sitting on the floor to proceed to the hallway. All signs point toward a terrible Monday at the Wright house. I struggle to recognize the commotion going on in my heart. My heart is like a cactus, prickly and harsh. I know I've had rough days like Felix is having today. I was so excited to come to school that I gave Eliza no fuss this morning. She helped me pick out a cute outfit to find confidence in—a gray hoodie with floral leggings and red sneakers.

I think I'm empathizing with him.

As we walk through the hallway to English—my heart flutters with anticipation—I can't help but think about Jenny and me talking about empathy many months ago.

"Empathy is the ability to connect with someone who is going through a feeling or an event you have experienced for yourself," Jenny explains.

"How do you know when you're empathy-ing?" I ask.

"Empathizing," she corrects.

"How do you know when you're... empathizing?"

"You'll see someone struggling and think of a memory you have that's similar to what they're going through." She rubs my hand warmly, as if calming the bad memories that threaten to surface. *"When you're faced with a friend going through a hard time, if you know what it's like to feel that way, you can say, 'I know how you feel.' You can connect emotionally with them."*

Connect emotionally.

Emotions aren't really my problem—it's more like keeping them in check under social circumstances.

I arrive at English and almost sprint to my seat. Higgins curls up at my feet. I glance around at my fellow students with their normal senses, their regular hearing, their lizard brains fully in check. Usually, I don't pay neurotypical people much heed unless I interact with them on a daily basis, like my family. Today, after witnessing Felix's meltdown and empathizing with him, I'm finding it difficult to escape this emotional state.

"Phones away!" Mr. Clyde says.

I tuck mine into my backpack for safekeeping.

My fingertips tingle. The skin between my bottom eyelids and cheekbones hurts like volcanic pressure is building under the surface. My wisdom teeth grind together, surely causing rot and damage that will need to be addressed when they are taken out. Every joint in my body tenses, ready to explode into a million pieces.

"Good morning, Dinah," Maverick whispers when he comes closer. He puts his hand on my desk and whispers, "Are you okay? You don't look so good." He's wearing a black-and-orange Denver football shirt—a highly punishable offense here in Milwaukee—and dark wash jeans. He is sporting fashion seemingly thrown together at the last minute.

His fingertips near mine shoot electricity through my body, recharging my human batteries. I swallow hard and nod, trying not to stare at his face. It isn't his usual smiling look—more expressionless. It's either a look of concern or cunningness. Paired with the question, I'm going to go with concern. Maverick sits next to me and lets his backpack fall to the floor with a groan.

Mr. Clyde turns the lights off and wheels out the overhead projector.

"How did Felix do in class?" Maverick asks, his voice low.

I pull a piece of paper and pen out of my backpack to instigate our usual communication method. I write:

Fine until I left. He hung on to Higgins all hour.

Maverick leans over and smirks at my response. This time I allow myself to stare. He has bags under his eyes, and his hair isn't styled as usual. I have to ask:

Rough morning?

He nods but doesn't write any details back. All he writes is:

Thanks for your awesome therapy dog. I can't wait to get one for him.

A jolt rings through me as if *The Hunchback of Notre Dame*'s Quasimodo himself is pulling on a rope to ring my bell. I sit upright, causing some of the students to glance in my direction, their expressions unreadable. I pay them no mind, as I have an impulsive need to do the thing that pops in my head. I completely forgot about telling Maverick my answer for the silent auction. I bend over and scribble swiftly.

I'm totally up for helping with the fundraiser, by the way. We could do a bake sale or a video game challenge. We can talk more about the Halloween silent auction.

His smile returns in full-force, and it does major damage to my insides. My chest crumbles as a deep-sea monster breaks through my defenses—but the sea monster is warm and friendly.

Mr. Clyde clears his throat, and we both look up to his slightly furrowed brows. The rest of our conversation will have to wait. Maverick scrawls when our teacher turns away.

Until lunch then?

Throughout the rest of the morning, I try to wrap my head around the fact that Maverick will be eating with me again. It'll be years before I forget the massive meltdown that ensued last time, causing three days of missed school. At least this time, I have about two hours' notice to mentally prepare myself. I have gotten more familiar with him.

By the time the lunch bell rings, I'm already leaving Mrs. Engleworth's history classroom with Higgins, determined to get to my spot and finish talking with Maverick. My phone is burning a hole in my backpack, but I don't want to lose it to a teacher. Not having my phone to text anytime I feel like it is hard to get used to, and I've only owned a phone for two days.

I'm almost to the lunchroom when the pain hits me.

I double over in crippling pain. My uterus is about to claw its way out of my body and unleash the apocalypse. The evil spreads from my pelvis to my lower back, then up my spine to implode inside my brain. The sharp pain is so excruciating that I fall to my knees in the hallway. I would be embarrassed, but I'm currently being eaten alive by my organs. The world is spinning. So many students are staring, expressing their disgust. I can't remember my last thought when I sink to the floor, clinging to Higgins. I'm unable to stand.

Having my period is the worst. Last month I asked Mom to be on birth control, but she has been stalling. Each time I bring it up, she says we need to see a doctor first. I get it, putting pills into my body can have side effects, but according to Nattie, half the girls at school take it.

It's not like I want it for sex.

Only time will tell if Mom lets me take it. I can't even think about Maverick or how many people are staring at me. I just need this to go away. All of my attention is on the pain pulsing through my veins.

There's a gasp from a staff member, and before long, I'm taken into the nurse's office. Waiting for my mom to pick me up is torture. The large clock ticktocks each second like a hammer strike on my uterus.

CHAPTER 12

THE GIRL in the car window reflection looks exhausted. I gaze at myself and think of a multiverse-me that's trapped between the glass. I wonder if she also has to deal with problems like debilitating cramps and bleeding. Since she's made of glass, I highly doubt it. She only worries about the inevitable shattering of her world in one form or another. Will it come in the form of a car accident? Crushed into a cube to lie in a junkyard for years? Or do people in the glass multiverse have their own pending apocalypse?

Upon my arrival at home early from school, Mom helps me out of the car and into my room. She's already let Eliza know to cancel therapy because of my embarrassing "emergency," so that's one less headache. Mom encourages me to change into comfy clothes and my magical period panties. Instead of using uncomfortable hygienic products, these panties are extra absorbent and much easier for me to deal with. She insists I stay in bed and text her when she needs to bring me more pain medication. I'm glad she recognizes that I need alone time. Nattie gets in trouble for muttering something like "overdramatic" under her breath as she walks by my room.

When I'm finally devoid of humans in my personal space, I lie on my bed of fluff and grab my phone from my side table where Mom left it. Higgins' soft hair cozying up to my face quiets the pain.

After giving him a kiss, I swipe my phone open.

I have a myriad of messages. I swipe in a single motion, remembering I left Maverick hanging at school today, leaving our conversation unfinished.

> Jenny: FEEL BETTER! I will see you soon!

Jenny's party is in two days. I sigh, thinking about how I'll dread the day with or without a heating pad on my abdomen.

All of Maverick's messages are of a more concerned nature.

> Did you go home halfway through the day?

> I hope you're okay, whatever is going on. Let me know

> A girl in my gym class says you threw up and passed out. Dinah, I'm so worried about you

> Here if you need to talk. Or text

Rumors travel fast. I did *not* throw up, but of course everyone in school has to think that I did.

Too exhausted to reply, I lay my phone down on my chest and finally let it all out. The overstimulation of the day hits me head-on.

An emotional meltdown is about to erupt inside of my skin.

I don't want Jenny to go.

I don't want Maverick to grow close to me. If he moves on with his life like Jenny—running off to chase his happily ever after—I won't be able to take it. I've never had a best friend before, and maybe life is better that way.

Closing my eyes, I sink into my safe place.

I ascend the rocky ridge as gracefully as I can, lifting my skirts of fog so they don't catch around my ankles. Behind me, my veil of darkness casts over the kingdom, everything falling under my spell as I climb higher. My shadow of sorrow will drape over the earth, and all will suffer at the consequences of the king who cursed me.

My breath comes short in my lungs, I finally pull myself over the peak to achieve my dreary performance. Dusting myself off, I sit on a stump of a long-dead tree to catch my breath. The shadows curl up at my feet, then hide behind my skirts as a wall of light bursts through the clouds.

He descends, his brightness beyond all beauty. His ornate cloak and translucent skin transfix me, but I must focus on my objective at all costs. The crown on his head magnificent, his hair blowing effortlessly, he immediately puts a spell on me. I can't comprehend how I reasoned with myself to come out of banishment, thinking I could resist his prowess. All I want is to throw myself into his arms, but that would result in instant death.

"I begged you not to do this," his voice echoes beyond his

shield. He sounds unwavering, but there is a hint of sadness in his tone.

I stand my ground and find my stubbornness. "Darkness is all I have left now, thanks to you. You brought this upon yourself!"

His eyes stare at me, and I stare back through my veil. His jawline is so pristine. I open my hand and flex my fingers, conjuring up the darkness in my palm if a weapon is needed. I don't see his sword yet, but I can't be too careful at this point. I must proceed.

I glare at him, partly with disgust, but the larger part of me wants it to be over. If we can't be together, I don't want to live. Light and dark cannot coexist; we are the paradox that will never be.

"I loved you!" I scream through black tears that have escaped my eyes. "I loved you, and you banished me to the other side of the world for it!" The ball of darkness in my hand is growing in power, ready to strike whenever I will it.

The king presses his shield forward as if puncturing jelly. The darkness doesn't attack; it recoils against him. He struggles against the dark forces to put one foot in front of the other to come toward me. Slivers of light dance toward me like lightning strikes, and I fear for my life.

"Stop!" I wail. My magic falters and fizzles away. His power is overtaking mine—light penetrating the dark, succumbing to the physical elements as only opposing forces can. His sword stays firmly at his side, his shield nearly in front of me. My veil of darkness is now my only protection as my magic utterly fails me.

He is now so close to me that I can see the pools of blue in his bright eyes. I would be blinded, my eyeballs burned in their sockets, if not for my veil. My heart nearly stops. I forget how to breathe, but I know I'm alive by my blood roaring in my ears. His arm is around my waist... and I'm not dead.

"You... you sent me away," I whisper, my voice crushing against the forces of light.

"Only because you were too afraid to find out what would happen," he whispers, the powers clashing between us like a roaring wind. My skirts fly everywhere, and his cloak is billowing behind him. The resulting lightning storm on the mountain is tumultuous, life-threatening in and of itself.

I shut my eyes tightly and prepare for the sweet release, death's friendly touch.

Only it doesn't come.

The king throws down his shield, rips the veil off my face, and kisses me so passionately that the very world erupts in tremors. I'm completely consumed by the blazing light, my dark powers sucked from their source and seemingly evaporating. The very peak we stand on is crumbling, but our feet are lifted up as we merge into the greater power of light combined with darkness, gods of the sky.

My eyes fly open in shock.

Oh no.

I need a *cold* shower.

I still haven't texted Maverick by the next morning. He has probably asked one of his moms to check in with mine. If he really wanted to find out if I was dead or alive, he has resources. I simply don't feel brave enough to explain what happened to him.

Plus, there's the little snag that I apparently think he's attractive. He's shown up in my safe place enough times that I had to make a difficult call. I have concluded that I indeed have a crush. Hormones are now the bane of my entire existence.

The anger that rises from my stupidity combined with my abdominal pain sure makes for a cranky Dinah. I try to be helpful to Mom with the final preparations for Jenny's surprise party tomorrow night, but she'd have more success if she asked Higgins to help. I'm holed up in bed with a heating pad on my lower stomach, plenty of water bottles on the floor, my library books near, and my handheld video game console on my table. I can be happily cranky here all day.

Eliza and Jenny arrive at their usual time to check on me, but there isn't much to be done. I'm in no state, physically or mentally, to perform exercises. However, Eliza piques my interest when she says she can show me some yoga stretches that help relieve menstrual pain. That could come in handy.

Other than that, I dismiss everything she says. She doesn't know what it's like to be me. Her trying to make me step outside my comfort zone is not something I'm willing to do, at least for a long while.

Too many changes have happened. I am over them all. The universe can suck... whatever it doesn't like to suck. I'll sit here on my bed of fluff for years.

I do like how Jenny rubs my hands. She's teaching Eliza so that she can do it once she leaves. My lower eyelids sting at the thought. I try to brush it away, but now it's suffocating me. I drown in the horrible thought.

"I'm glad you're feeling better, Dinah-Doo," Jenny says, smiling at me with her glistening eyes. She's trying to show no emotion, I can tell. I would rather her lay it all out with me so I can understand her thoughts.

"Are you sad?" I whisper, shifting my heating pad around on my bed. Higgins really likes to sit on it when it isn't occupied.

Jenny sighs and gives a slight nod. "I'm torn. I'm incredibly happy to marry Brendon, but of course I'm sad to leave my job and you."

"It'll be tough at first, but you'll see. We'll become great friends," Eliza butts in.

I shut my eyes so I can roll them without getting in trouble.

"Remember, we'll always be friends. Whenever you want to talk to me, I'm always a text away now. I'm so excited you got a phone." Jenny smiles and wipes one of her eyes on the sleeve of her upper arm. "I can't wait to hear all the amazing things you'll accomplish. Like the day you heard the ambulance and didn't melt down. I did a dance—I was so happy! And you know what an awful dancer I am."

I much prefer being the cause of Jenny's happiness instead of frustrations.

The rest of the evening consists of mindless chitchat until we do yoga to prepare for bed. I attempt a few poses before the pain makes my eyes water. Eliza shows me a back stretch that's supposed to help. It doesn't do anything earth-shattering. I crawl back into my cocoon and bid good night to my aides, knowing that tomorrow is my absolute last day with Jenny.

Ever.

The irrevocable void erupts in my chest and swirls like a whirlpool, leading to the depths of the earth. Pure sadness coats my heart and overtakes my emotions. I take a shuddering breath and lift my phone off my side table. I need an out. An escape. A safe place.

I text Maverick.

> Me: I'm alive.

The three dancing dots appear almost instantly, to my astonishment.

> Maverick: My mom heard from your mom. I'm glad you're okay. Are you feeling better?

How much did his mom tell him? One crisis at a time. I hyperfocus on the bigger problem at hand. I can always gloss over embarrassing moments at school later. Or never.

> Me: Yes and no. My aide of seven years is moving away after tomorrow. ☹

The dots dance again.

> Maverick: That's got to be so hard. Felix has a hard time when his regular aide is sick or he has a substitute teacher, so I can't imagine what you're going through

The sadness fades away, replaced with a new feeling so convoluted that I can't possibly define it to one emotion. Frustrated? Annoyed? Hopeless devotion? Angry at myself?

I can't take his Mr. Nice-Guy façade anymore. I type furiously before I can stop myself.

> Me: Why are you so nice to me?

My heart thumps like I'm running an uphill marathon. My usually comfortable blankets are suddenly hot and scratchy. I kick them off while Higgins whines with inconvenience. I loathe social norms. Why can't everyone say what they're thinking or what they're feeling, so I can navigate through life easier? I just want every answer out of Maverick's mouth to be straight with me. I've barely known the guy for a few weeks, and our friendship has done nothing but prove that having friends is too anxiety-inducing for me. Communication with him is like a drug. I need my fix every day, but I don't want to look at him. I want to hear his voice but not hold a conversation where I'm expected to participate. I want to know about his past without revealing any of mine.

Is it too much to ask?

The dots keep dancing and disappearing as if he's deleting his message and starting over. I take the time between his response to do some breathing exercises to calm myself before the bubbling puddle of emotions sets off a geyser.

> Maverick: Because I like being around you. You are interesting to be around. I'm not faking being nice to you to score brownie points in heaven. I truly consider you a friend

> Besides, I like having a source for fantasy
> book recommendations

Can't he be someone else's friend and stop invading my thoughts and dreams? Shouldn't he be spending time with neurotypical people instead of chatting it up with me? I figure since he already has a nonverbal, autistic brother, the last thing he would want is a friend like me.

> Me: I'm atypical. Having me for a friend
> may not be very fun.

My heart thumps in my chest as I feel my self-esteem drop. The three little dots on the screen dance for some time. Maverick replies with a long paragraph.

> Maverick: There's more to you than a
> diagnosis. Living with Felix for fourteen
> years, I thought I knew everything about
> autism, but you have proven me wrong.
> You're fascinating. I like how you dip into
> your fantasy worlds. I like how you see
> the world we live in. I like your
> bookworm-ness. Like I've told you before,
> other kids our age are boring and
> predictable. I used to be exactly like
> them, the worst of their kind. I hate
> predictable

A sensation flies up my spine, but it's not chills, and it's not the itches. It's... warmth, spreading to my heart. The despair floating in the air flutters away, sweeping my worries out the door and replacing the space in my room with a bowl of warm soup I can swim in. My body shudders. I've never felt like this before, but damn, I like it. Breathing deeply, I exhale and pull myself together before I melt into a giant puddle for Higgins to lap up.

I try to think of a socially appropriate response. I remember talking with Jenny about "breaking the ice" when a conversation takes an awkward turn. I decide to try my hand at humor.

> Me: Good, I thought you were just using me to get to my dog.

I snort at my own joke. Hopefully he grasps sarcasm easier than I do—I'm a newbie at it.

Maverick sends a cry-laughing emoji.

> Maverick: You figured me out

> Me: I hope you enjoy the books I recommended more than Wuthering Heights.

> Maverick: ANYTHING IS BETTER THAN WUTHERING HEIGHTS

I send laughing emojis.

It's as good a time as any to use the conversation starters Jenny has taught me.

> Me: If you could be any animal, what would you be?

> Maverick: A Rottweiler dog. Think of the adventures they have!

I bury my face in my pillow to keep from laughing.

Another ding comes with a question.

> Maverick: What about you?

I'd want to be a human that can shapeshift into any animal, but that doesn't seem like a fair answer.

> Me: Anything that can fly.

> Maverick: You wanna be a bird for Halloween?

I giggle.

> Me: No! I'm going to be a magical elven.

It's been on my bucket list since last year.

> Maverick: I can't wait to see how gorgeous you are

My cheeks flush at his compliment. Before I can dwell on that too much, I ask him what his costume will be.

> Maverick: It's a surprise

I hate surprises. There has to be a way for me to pull it out of him.

The guessing-game continues back and forth until well after my bedtime. I'm no closer to guessing his costume than I was when the conversation started. He'll either be a nail or an old man. We keep texting. My heart pounds with the adrenaline of having a real conversation. I'm both proud of myself and slightly aghast that I'm being a wild child—staying up late talking to a boy.

CHAPTER 13

I FELL asleep with my phone next to my pillow last night. Unfortunately, Mom saw it when she threw back my covers to give me painkillers and water. Now she assumes I was up all night talking to Maverick. On any other day, I'd be worried about the repercussions. Today, I don't give two rat turds. I'm happy I was up late talking to Maverick.

Higgins bounds off of my bed and heads out, presumably to do his morning business. With Mom's help, I'm able to sit up a bit to swallow the bitter painkiller pill, which tastes like rusted metal. She thought ahead and brought me a mixed berry yogurt to wash it down with so that it will absorb faster. She sighs and sits on my blankets next to me, cradling my face.

"I know I don't say this enough, Dinah, but I love you, and your persistence amazes me. Come what may, you face it head-on." She smiles, her crow's feet disappearing rather than growing deeper. Long-lost laugh lines replace stress lines, and her freckled forehead only makes her look more beautiful to me. Mom looks like she has already been up for a few hours prepping for the party. Her brow is sweaty, her hair in a messy bun, and she's wearing a dirtied apron. Her hunched posture gives off a stressed vibe.

I stare at my sheets and pull my heating pad over my lower stomach. "I love you too," I say softly, unable to meet her brown-eyed gaze. "I wish I could help with the planning. I really want to try to be more independent."

"We'll make it through today, okay?" She lifts my chin, checking for tears and giving me a feeble smile. "And after today"—she stands up and brushes off her apron—"we'll book an appointment with your doctor to discuss birth control options. Seeing you like this breaks my heart."

"Mom! It's just birth control." I roll my eyes so hard, I might possibly dislocate them, if that's even possible.

My head buzzes with a thousand thoughts. This is all too much to process. I need to be able to handle one thing at a time. Today I only want to handle my favorite aide leaving for good—not my health problems, not school, not anything else.

Ding.

Mom spies my phone in the bed and raises an eyebrow at me. She grabs for it teasingly, but I clutch it like it's my most-prized possession. I'm about to yell at her when I catch her smiling. Sarcasm.

It's a text from Jenny, containing nothing but a single heart emoji. Sometimes when I can't find the words, symbols are more effective. The dread in my heart is sprinkled with affection for a moment but overall remains morbidly bleak. I sink back into my dark hole of blankets, unable to come up for air.

"Text me if you need me, honey. Eliza will be here soon," Mom calls affectionately on her way out.

Higgins is back, burrowing his way down to me with his freshly fed breath. I spoon him and hold him tightly, my phone gripped in my hand. I breathe in the sweet scent of his fur—lavender. Kurt must have given him a bath yesterday. I breathe in again and imagine miles of lavender fields blowing in a beautiful sunset. It's where I long to be—somewhere without any physical or emotional pain.

Before I can transfer myself there, another alert comes from my phone. My heart does a feeble skip. Maverick is probably the only person I'd tolerate texting with right now.

> Dad: Heard you weren't feeling well.
> Thinking of you. Love you.

I haven't texted my dad since he bought me my phone. Whoops. I send a heart emoji because that's all the effort I can expend.

Numbness overtakes the pain, which is a relief, but the emotional distress remains. I lie perfectly still in my bed, as if sealed in a coffin. An invisible force is weighing me down like a demon pushing my shoulders and daring me to try to escape. I succumb to my depression and fall back to sleep. Unable to ambulate, unable to emote—it seems like all I can do is surrender.

I know Eliza is in the room before she tries to stir me awake. Nothing sneaks past Higgins. His head perks up. He sniffs as soon as the door creaks open, whipping an ear across my face. Part of me wants to lift my middle finger in greeting once she pulls my blankets back, but that would start the day off on the wrong foot, and today already sucks enough.

"Good morning, Dinaaah," she says in a soft, singsong tone, like how one would wake a toddler. I try to shove my annoyance to the back of my brain and forget about it.

I stretch my arms out so they poke through the hole at the top of my fluffy blankets. Eliza gently pulls them down to reveal my face. Higgins sits up, ready for duty.

"How you aren't sweating to death, I have no clue," Eliza states in genuine disbelief. "My guess is you're not feeling ready to go back to school?"

The last thing I want is a bath. Or to put regular clothes on. Leave me to rot in my depression hole. I stare at the ceiling to avoid her gaze and shake my head, no.

Yoga is the only thing that can coax me out of bed because I do need the exercise. I have plenty of energy pent up from my three-day bedridden adventure.

After we both stretch and pose, Eliza talks me into some other activities. Nothing hardcore, just a board game or two to try to keep my mind off the party. Lunchtime passes, and we have a picnic in my room, which is kind of fun. She's staying longer today because the party is tonight, which I guess is fine.

Eliza pushes the limits when she asks if we can take Higgins on a walk. I'd have to put on actual clothes.

"It'll help the cramping. Lying still can make them worse." She picks out a white sweatshirt with sparkles on the front and black leggings that are decorated with constellations for me, and hands me my hairbrush, implying that my hair looks a mess.

I take it, performing a huge eye roll for her in the process for her to witness.

My soul is dragged out the door kicking and screaming, but I do as Eliza asks so Jenny can have a good last day. Tomorrow, no such promises will be made or kept. The brisk walk is quite nice, despite the involuntary origin of it. The bright orange leaves on the tree are a sight to behold, like a myriad of monarch butterflies resting on the branches. One of my favorite things about autumn is crunching acorns under my feet. There are plenty on the sidewalk for me to indulge in today. Higgins leads the way on our usual route down the street to the park, turning right to go around the block.

Eliza asks why we don't go left, and the itches begin.

"Because we always go right," I answer. Jenny has also tried to convince us to go on different walk routes to no avail. I like this way because we walk by the park, the one house with the funny hedges trimmed like different animals, and the house with too many garden gnomes.

I hate to admit it, but walking around does ease the pain like Eliza said it would. Maybe Jenny's cake tonight will ease the emotional pain.

Ding.

Or a text from Maverick might brighten my day.

I dig my phone out of my jacket and notice Eliza eyeing it warily. "Don't you want to finish your walk?"

"I can text and walk," I insist, even though I'm unsure if I can. I hand Higgins' leash over to Eliza and use both hands to text.

> Maverick: I hope you feel better soon.
> English is not as fun without you

Happy flutters flood my chest and spread out over my

skin. I grin from ear to ear and happily stomp on acorns as I text back immediately.

> Me: Am doing better. Will try to make it tomorrow.

Eliza smirks at me when I replace my phone back in my jacket.

"What?" I ask, taken aback.

"Are you texting the boy that was here last week? The one you were eating oranges with on the trampoline?" she asks in an inquisitive tone. I sense this is pure curiosity rather than sniffing out trouble.

I say nothing until we arrive back at home. What is everyone's interest in mine and Maverick's friendship? Sure, he's cute, and I have a tiny crush. But for some reason, I can't help but be protective about this part of my life. I finally have a real friend. I want to keep that fact close to my chest and cherish it for as long as I can.

It's almost party time, so I wash my face and hands. I'm relieved the pain is finally subsiding. Three days of uterine hell was more than enough for me. I peer at my reflection in my floor-length mirror and wonder if anyone has ever had a crush on me. I don't think I'm terrible looking, but I'm no Grecian goddess either.

I snap on my headphones in anticipation of the loud shouts of "Surprise!" and then examine myself again. People have often asked me before what music I'm listening to or if I want to be a helicopter pilot when they see me with my headphones on. I give the girl inside the glass world a small smile.

Moments later Mom, Kurt, Nattie, Eliza, Higgins, and me are hunched behind furniture in the living room. When Jenny knocks on the door, Mom calls for her to come in like she usually does. The second we all jump up and yell, "Surprise!" tears flood her eyes.

She hugs us through streaked makeup and smiles. She shares details about her new downtown Chicago apartment and how she can't wait to start decorating. She gushes over her lemon buttercream cake and insists it's all too much. Mom hands her an envelope and says it's her wedding gift. I have no idea what can be inside there besides a card. Maybe money?

When it starts getting dark and we have laughed, wiped our eyes, and had two helpings of cake each, the first yawn appears, and the depression consumes me. Jenny walks over and gives me the longest, warmest, and saddest of hugs.

She lifts one side of my headphones and speaks softly in my ear, "I have something for you."

"What? No, it's *your* party," I protest, aghast that I didn't get her anything personal to remember me by. I figured the party would be enough.

"I had to." Jenny reveals a prettily wrapped box with my name on it like it's my birthday.

I gape at Mom apprehensively, asking permission to open it. She gives a nod while wiping her face. I tear open the purple ribbon, the glistening silver paper, and the pristine white box underneath to find a stuffed animal. A stuffed dog that looks exactly like Higgins.

"I found a website that makes stuffed animals personalized to look just like your pets," Jenny exclaims.

"Oh, oh wow," I blurt, letting out all the air in my lungs

in surprise. "Now I have *two* Higgins to snuggle with at night!" I jump into her arms and wrap mine around her neck. I hug Jenny so tightly that my muscles scream in protest.

The tears start. The sobs follow, and the wailing leads to a complete breakdown.

While looking in the mirror earlier, I traded lives with the girl in the glass. I was pressurized in a sea of cold, solid-looking glass for the past two hours, safe and sound. When Jenny hugs me for the last time, the glass girl shatters and falls into a thousand pieces on the floor, blowing away into sparkling sand. That girl will return one day, in the form of the mirror or the car window reflection, but for now, she sails away upon the wind. No emotions to feel, no tears to cry, and no one to tell her it is going to be all right when she knows that it isn't.

CHAPTER 14

I TEXT Jenny right when I wake up to say good morning, I text her right after school to let her know how my day was, and I text her right before bedtime to let her know how therapy was. So far, there have been no meltdowns since we implemented this schedule. It's a good thing that by the time Jenny moved, I was used to Eliza, but that doesn't mean I don't unintentionally give her a hard time.

My brain is comfortable with Jenny, like how your butt makes an indent in your favorite spot on the couch. It's like saying, "Okay, we took your old couch to the dump, but here's another one," and it has no imprint. My body reacts without my input sometimes when it doesn't like change. I'm doing the best I know how, and somehow, Eliza is okay with that. She says that one day we will get to the point where I'm a hundred percent comfortable with her, but I doubt it.

Eliza, Higgins, and I passed out the Halloween auction flyers on our walks to the park, and I took an armful to school to pin up on announcement boards and tape to the plastic-like brick walls. I wish I had a talent to donate, but instead I decide to donate some books that are gathering dust—either I have lost interest in them, or I didn't like the writing style. My hope is that someone with a different literary taste can enjoy them. Maverick has offered to donate some of his video games, and Felix wants to show off his anime collection.

I'm certain Felix will come as something comfortable because he lives in his sweats, but Maverick has left me clueless. He continues to tell me his costume is a secret. I wish he'd just tell me instead of teasing me. My mom and both of Maverick's moms put in a lot of time, effort, and phone calls over the next two weeks. The community center was booked, so they called local businesses, friends, churches, and anyone that would be willing to donate a service or a talent to the silent auction on Halloween. My mom works from home for the local paper and she knows just about everyone who owns a business in the area.

Today I woke up both anxious and excited. The silent auction is finally here, and that means I get to spend extra time around Maverick and Felix to help them raise the money to purchase a therapy dog. I sigh and look up at my twinkly lights on the ceiling while still lying in bed. I'm glad Halloween is on a weekend this year—school and the auction would have been too much.

Eliza is well-prepared for everything. We groom, do yoga, she does my nails, and we do some face masks together. We had to chase Higgins out of the room so he wouldn't eat the cucumbers for our eyes. She brought over a card game about manners. It's actually very helpful in scoping out social norms and explaining the hidden rules that everyone understands but me.

I get ready for the hectic evening by getting in the

shower, which I'm trying my hardest to implement into my routine. While everything I do with Eliza is fun, I still can't help rubbing my feet on the carpet to calm the itches. It's soft, but the rawness of my skin from the sudden movements is something I crave. The stimming helps me focus, and it helps me multitask. I keep thinking about the silent auction, how many people will be there, what Maverick will be dressed up as, who will buy my books, and how I'll look in my elven princess costume.

The water is more tolerable if it's colder instead of being hot. I sing "Someone's in the shower with Dinah" to muscle through it.

When I get out of the shower, Eliza asks, "What's Maverick dressing up as tonight?"

A shock zips up my spinal cord. I throw her a "why would you ask that?" look. "I don't know. He says it's a secret," I say, gazing back down at my feet.

We stay silent as she blow-dries my hair and teases it to give it some volume.

"You hate secrets," Eliza says through a toothy grin. Her red curls fall into her face.

"No, I hate *surprises!*" I raise my voice a little.

Higgins jumps off the love seat to come to my defense, his hot breath on my face a welcome comfort.

"Well then, you're going to hate what comes next," she says, texting someone on her phone. I hear a chime out in the hallway, Mom's alert tone.

"Knock, knock! Delivery for the elven princess!" Mom's super-cheesy tone comes around the door. She presents me with a plain box.

I stare at her.

"Thanks for the box?" I say in what I hope is a thankful tone instead of a sarcastic one.

"Open it, Dinah. Goodness." Mom sighs, slight exasperation in her voice. Her cheeks are rosy, and her pupils are dilated. I wager a guess that whatever is in the box is exciting for her.

I approach the box carefully, not knowing if it will explode or melt when I touch it. I gently take the top off. It's full of packing peanuts—one of my favorite things to touch.

"Oh yay! Thank you," I exclaim, immediately clearing a spot in my schedule later to play with their squeaky, soft plushiness.

They burst into laughter, and I know I've missed some kind of social cue.

"Look through the peanuts," Eliza says, shaking the box a little so that the squeaky stuffing rustles aside to reveal something sitting at the bottom.

I hold the box with one hand and dig through the peanuts with the other. What I feel is an awkward shape and multiple textures. I pull out a new pair of headphones. They are the prettiest I have ever seen. Pointy ears are glued on either side—elven ears. The actual muffs are jewel-encrusted patterns intertwined with dark hair ringlets that will blend in with my hair. On the headband is the most gorgeous tiara made out of crystal quartz. I can see my glittering reflection in each crystal staring back at me, astonishment in my eyes.

"I... I...." I don't know what to say. I go numb from my scalp to my toes. I had planned to wear my plain old everyday headphones for the auction tonight, but with these I'll look magnificent.

For a moment, the only sound is Higgins' bushy tail pounding against the floor.

"Well?" Eliza rubs her hands together.

"Thank you," I say quickly.

"I'm glad you like them. I made them myself." Eliza smiles. She puts them on my head, ruffling my hair around them as gently as she can, though a few hairs tug at my scalp.

I turn to look in the mirror, uneasy about what it might reveal. There stands a stunning elven queen with more confidence than I've ever held in one pinky finger. The way Eliza teased my hair makes it look fuller, so I don't look like I have headphones on at all, just a magnificent crown and pointy ears. My lips upturn slightly, in a regal sort of way.

"Elven queens don't wear hoodies and leggings," I state, putting my hands on my hips for added dramatic effect.

"Nope, they sure don't," Mom agrees, and we all wander into my closet.

She grabs a hanger on which hangs my velvet, renaissance-like dress with long sleeves that flare and almost cascade to the floor. It's a gorgeous maroon. I remember a few months ago Mom had it custom-made with soft materials, no tags, and no rough inseams. Just because I'm not a fan of knocking on strangers' doors for candy doesn't mean I can't dress up for the holiday.

A few hours later, I'm feeling more beautiful than I have ever felt. Who needs to escape to a fairy-tale safe place when I can be stunning in real life? I'm super hyped to show Maverick my fantasy costume come true.

I bounce up-and-down in Eliza's car on the way to the community center. She's not dressed up very much, only the generic black top and pants with cat ears on her red curls—aka the classic no-effort costume.

Fashion is subjective; that means everyone has their own tastes. No need to comment on what you think is ugly. The person wearing it might love it. Jenny's voice pops into my head. I quickly take a selfie of my elaborate headdress and send it to her. I can't wait to read her reaction.

Mom went over earlier to help set up the tables.

Nattie is an undead ballerina. She did a hauntingly good job on her makeup. Even Higgins won't let her scratch him—he didn't recognize her at first and now has trust issues.

I try to quit bouncing, containing the hyperactivity in my knees. I'd probably be shooting off every angle of the car's interior if I wasn't restrained by the itchy seat belt. While the dress is comfortable, I have a pair of leggings under it. Letting my legs roam free in their own skin just feels wrong.

"Tonight will be fun," Eliza says while making a right turn. "I'll give you guys your space, okay? I'm just there to observe."

When we finally arrive, I practically fly out the car door. Usually, I'm apprehensive about entering strange places, but I practically run through the ice-cold autumn air and burst through the community center's doors. Lake Michigan teases its wintery bluster by blowing my long sleeves and hair everywhere.

I find my way through the lobby to the hall entrance, where a large poster of Felix stands with big purple letters that reads: "FELIX WRIGHT FUNDRAISER FOR AUTISM SERVICE DOG."

A sign-in book stands on a table with instructions to write my name and email so I can participate in the raffle. I scribble down my contact information and emerge into a spooky sight that is pleasant for both my ears and eyes.

Fake spiderwebs and cute pumpkins dot the tables while fake waxy candles hang from every corner. In years past, Mom has tried to take me to Halloween carnivals where there were too many kids, bright flashing lights, creepy crap that jumped out and scared me, and music that rattled my eardrums. Here, the eerie music is soft, the lights are dimmed, and the cute pumpkins are scattered everywhere instead of in horrific decor that traumatizes young children.

Trish, dressed up as a beekeeper, greets me at the entrance. "Hello there, Dinah! I'm so happy you're here. We have plenty of sensory-friendly activities in the corner while the auction is going on." She points to the far corner of the room where some chairs are set up. There appears to be stickers on the floor with numbers. I assume that means an autism-friendly cakewalk is going to take place. I can handle that.

Along the walls are the items or talents being auctioned off. Baked goods, toys, books, babysitting, gift cards, cleaning services, and hotel bundles—my mom really went all out. I love how people can write their name and bid instead of shouting it out or having a loud auctioneer steer the numbers.

I wander over to the sensory-friendly corner, picking up my skirts so I don't trip over the hem. I notice Felix sitting there with Sherri, who's dressed up as something a little more cutesy: a flower. She's in a tight green onesie with a hat that resembles daisy petals, and her makeup is done with luscious eyelashes and freckles. She even painted a tiny red ladybug on her cheek. Her hair is tousled in wavy curls, and she simply looks stunning. Felix is dressed in yellow comfy sweatshirt and sweatpants with black stripes on them, which is probably all he can stand. He's got on black headphones. I assume he's supposed to be a bumblebee.

"Need some pollen or honey?" she asks me.

I know she's just acting, but a slight twinge of annoyance hits me. That's not how you're supposed to greet people, but whatever.

"No," I say, promptly taking a seat. "So, you're all dressed as a family?" I look for Maverick, wondering what he could possibly be dressed as.

"We usually do a theme every year as a family," Sherri answers, her smile wide.

I spot Mom in the corner filling refreshment cups. Nattie painted Mom's face as a skull earlier to go with her glow-in-the-dark skeleton suit. I also see Nattie chatting with her friends, whom she convinced to come, as well as their parents. A warmth spreads in my chest for Nattie despite her brattiness. I'm filled with a funny sensation I decide to pin down as gratitude.

Felix startles me with a bout of raucous laughter. Higgins whines and tries to tug his leash out of my hands. Although, he sits firmly, remembering his elite training, his snout twitches, and his eyes turn glossy as if frightened—something is definitely bugging him. Flapping his hands happily, Felix gapes beyond my shoulder. I cautiously turn my head to see nothing but a big ball of something green behind me.

Maverick is dressed as a jolly garden gnome.

My cheeks are raw by the time I'm done laughing.

Bushy, white eyebrows and a white beard decorate his face, as well as a squat green hat, and a stuffed blue button-down shirt. The best part of the costume are the stubby legs hanging by his side as he wears a tutu-like red-and-white mushroom around his waist, topped off with green leggings covered in strips of construction paper that resemble grass.

"Mock all you want. I chose this costume voluntarily," Maverick says from somewhere inside the bearded monstrosity.

Sherri wipes her eyes; her mascara has run a little bit from the laughter.

The chuckles, the costume surprise, and Maverick's presence contributes to the heightening of my senses. I'm suddenly aware of how many people are in the room, what temperature it is, and an irritable itch on my hip coming from somewhere in the dress. I guess the seamstress didn't sew *everything* perfectly.

"You look fantastic," Maverick says to me. Blood rushes to my cheeks. I stare at the floor in response. "Those are *so* cool. Where'd you get them?"

"My aide made them," I answer warily. A few more people arrive at the sensory corner. I feel abruptly claustrophobic.

"Do you want to walk around and look at the auction items?" Maverick asks, sticking his thumb in the direction of the auction tables.

"I'm going to start the cakewalk soon, Dinah, if you want to stay here," Sherri says.

I don't want to seem rude. My brain and my heart have an internal struggle about social norms and what would be the most appropriate response. My blood pressure rises slightly—I can tell by the vein pulsating in my neck.

Why can't I choose both?

"We'll come back," Maverick answers his mom, as if I've already said yes.

I smile as we begin walking toward the tables, leaving Felix laughing happily behind us. Higgins whines but hesitantly pads along beside me. He glances back at Nattie as if he wishes he were her therapy dog for the evening.

When we arrive at the first table, he says, "Really, you've outdone yourself. I love your elf costume."

I'm careful not to bump into his bulbous mushroom top. I try to cling to every word he's saying. I'm doing my best, but despite the carpeted community center, the dimmer lights, and the softer music, it's still a lot to take in.

"And so have you. I truly didn't expect all of... this," I say with a giggle.

I take a look at the first item up for auction—a three-tiered cake from a local Milwaukee bakery. "Are you going to bid on anything?"

"Are you going to give me a job?" Maverick asks.

I assume it's sarcasm, so I laugh and shake my head. "I'll take that as a no," I say, sashaying behind him toward the next item: my books. I look at them in awe, even though none of them are my favorite.

"Donated by Dinah Finlayson, local student," Maverick reads. I can tell he's smiling by his voice, even when it's deep inside a ridiculous costume.

"Yep, that's me." I check the auction sheet, but nobody has bid yet.

I must be frowning, because Maverick says, "The right person will take them home."

"Sure hope so." I sigh as more and more people begin to pile in. I try to focus on the positives of this event for Felix instead of how panic-ridden everything makes me. Crowds of people. Endless buzzing conversation. Everyone else breathing my air.

"I had no idea this many people would come," Maverick says, his bearded head staring at the door in awe as a line of people are signing in. "We're so new to the community that it blows my mind."

Higgins' wet nose bops my hand, letting me know he's there.

He senses my heightened anxiety.

"It's for a good cause, and my mom knows everyone," I say, nodding. Only I can't stop nodding. My fingers tap against each other, and my knees keep bending. I'm getting overstimulated.

"Dinah?" Maverick's voice calls through the fog and reaches my ringing ears.

My body feels like I'm twisting side-to-side. My bones and joints feel like splitting from the overload of everything. Everything is too much; my muscle fibers thin against the pressure. I need something soft to ease my discomfort. I need something to brush my skin on.

Frustration joins the list of heightened senses, even with Higgins trying to help. Desperation comes along, and I wonder why all the yoga, the chilled-out therapy, and the preparation for this is failing.

I need to rub my toes on the carpet. I need fresh air.

Breathe.

I can't. Immediate escape is unavoidable. This door will do.

"It's too much," I tell Maverick and run back behind the

tables. I open a nearby emergency exit, causing a blaring alarm to rain down on the event.

I'm frozen in place with the door open as I realize my grave mistake. Every person is covering their ears, not just the ones on the autism spectrum. Flashing lights from high up on the wall by the exit sign light up the dimly lit room. Chaos ensues.

Felix screams. Every autistic kid is freaking out, and it's my fault.

The next thing I know is that I'm in the car with Eliza heading back home.

CHAPTER 15

I WAS SO embarrassed by my meltdown at the silent auction last week that I avoided Maverick's texts for days. If we talk, we keep it to Dickens, as we are now reading *A Tale of Two Cities* in English class. Not a bad book per se, but it could use some dragons.

Every morning in November seems to begin with my skin crawling, followed by my body's inability to get out of bed. When meltdowns begin happening daily, a counselor from school calls Mom and suggests I try to do half home-school, and half public school until after the Christmas holidays. The homeschool will be online and something I'm highly interested in. It means never having to leave the comfort of my own room. I realize that's the opposite of what Mom and Kurt want—me to be comfortable enough to not be independent one day.

I'm not ready.

Who would brush my skin? Who would help me calm down if I have an anxiety attack? Who would help me out of bed if my body won't let me? These thoughts of hopelessness and dread cause my new therapist to put me on a small dose of antidepressants.

My senior year is turning out to be a drag.

Mom says a different kind of therapist—one that deals with traumatic changes in life—will help me through Jenny's departure. After hearing about my stunt on Halloween and Jenny leaving, Eliza's boss recommended I talk out my feelings with a professional counselor who specializes with people on the spectrum. Apparently, it's common for autistic people to have roller-coaster behaviors—like when I do well one week and ghastly the next. I'm not excited to try to establish trust with another person besides Eliza.

My first session with Jason isn't terrible. His deep voice is comforting.

He picked the perfect career for his voice—the man could make butter melt in the freezer by talking to it. His deep brown eyes welcome us into his cozy office where I plop on the squishy couch immediately. His round glasses and closely cropped, graying black hair gives him the look of someone you can trust with your darkest secrets. It makes him the ideal best friend and even more sinister personal enemy.

He asks me a few questions about how my days usually go and about Higgins. I dip my fingers in purple kinetic sand while we talk. I like the smooth, grainy feel of it. The sand makes me stay present instead of flying off to my safe place. I know it's a trick on my senses, but I can't resist.

One Friday afternoon in mid-November, I'm curled up at the foot of my bed in the fetal position, fighting an internal battle of hormones versus my newly prescribed birth control mixed with anxiety meds, when I hear a ding.

> Maverick: I missed you in school today

Yeah, well, my body apparently hates me.

Footsteps in the hallway announce Eliza is coming back from writing on the laptop, so I don't text back immediately. I tuck my phone under my pillow.

The door squeaks open, and I know she has come to say her goodbye for the weekend. "Hey," she says with a chuckle when she pulls back my blankets. "You text me if you need anything. Okay?"

"Yep," I mutter. Higgins hops down for a goodbye pet. Once he gets one, he abandons me for dinner. "Bye," I say to both Higgins and Eliza as they walk out the door.

I throw my covers up over my head again, free to shut out the world and hide. I grab my phone under my pillowcase and swipe the screen open.

> Maverick: I want to see you before Felix and I go visit my dad in Denver for Thanksgiving. Are you free tonight or tomorrow?

I can't seem to escape sudden, sprung-on plans that keep messing with my schedule. I want to, but I don't want to. Then I think of the mood swings and meltdowns I'm currently experiencing. Are they worth fighting through to see Maverick?

His blue eyes and smile come back to haunt me. I can't lie, I miss him too. I've only seen him in school a handful of times since I humiliated myself on Halloween. If he really is a true friend, he won't mind my antics—depression and all.

> Me: You'll have to come visit. I'm not up to going anywhere. Sorry.

An hour later, Mom answers the knock at the door and is surprised to see Maverick. I distantly overhear her telling him about the final numbers from the fundraiser—just barely five hundred dollars. Not even close to the thousands of dollars that are needed, but at least it's a start.

I hear his footsteps following hers toward the stairs. I've managed to creep downstairs to play video games to get my mind off Maverick's inevitable arrival. Now, he's here. My hair is probably a mess, but I don't care.

My heart does a backflip as Maverick circles the couch with a cautious smile, his face a little shadowy with stubble. He's wearing a superhero hoodie. He slides the hood off and shakes out his hair. He needs a haircut, but I'm liking how his hair falls into his eyes.

He takes out his phone from his hoodie pocket and taps it, little *tick-ticks* accompanying his fingertips. To my surprise, another set of footsteps come down the stairs, and I realize he's also brought Felix over.

Ding.

> Maverick: So, do we talk in your house or text?

"Come sit down," I say, gesturing him forward with my outward palm.

Higgins whizzes past his legs and jumps up on the couch to protect me. We both laugh at his silly gesture because he obviously hasn't figured out that Maverick is also a walking safe space for me.

Felix lets out a little moan of hesitancy when he approaches the couch, his green headphones on, his hair askew, and his trusty tablet in hand. Maverick reaches his hand out to beckon him forward, directing him to a seat on the edge of the couch.

"So, what are you playing?" Maverick asks. He sets himself up on the other side of Higgins and looks right at me.

I glance at the controller in my hands and then back at him.

"*Animal Brawl*, as per usual," I reply, unsure where to navigate this conversation. Should I ask him to play with me? Should I continue to play solo while he watches? Should I include Felix? Or should I turn it off so we can talk?

An alert pops up with our last text discussion attached to it. "So, you're leaving for Thanksgiving?" I find myself asking.

Maverick sticks his hands in his hoodie pocket again and nods. "Yeah. I'm not excited about it. Felix will do okay on the plane if he has a fully charged tablet. It's just... upsetting, his schedule will be horrible. It'll take weeks for him to get back to his routine."

Felix makes a few noises when he hears his name, pointing to the game he's playing on the tablet.

I sigh. "Sounds like me."

Higgins wags his tail impatiently as if telling us to hurry and reach the point.

"Mind if I join you?" Maverick points at the pause screen on the TV after a few seconds of silence.

Crap. I knew I should've asked him. Itches climb up my arms in response. He grabs the second controller before I respond.

Maverick chooses Mr. Manatee, a sea mammal that has a big mustache and tattoos. "This guy looks like he'd win in a gang fight," he convinces himself. He'll probably mash buttons in the hope he'll knock me over. He's *so* wrong. I'm going to counter with Jumpin' Jane Kangaroo. He'll cry when I'm done with him.

"So, I guess we can't always hang out at school anymore," he says as I choose an arena.

My chest tingles in anticipation of an ending to his sentence, but it never comes. I assume he's talking about my partial homeschooling until after Christmas break. I cling to his every word to make sure I understand the things that aren't said.

When people speak, they always seem to say sentences that mean two or sometimes three things other than their original meaning. Like if their point were a layered dip, I would only scoop the shredded cheese onto my chip while everyone else scoops to the bottom. People pick up the beans, guacamole, sour cream, tomatoes, and queso, and I miss all that. I only comprehend the toppings.

"Guess not," I reply, hoping he will get to his point soon. Itches start at the back of my neck. Being around him outside of school is awesome, but it doesn't mean I'm not anxious about having an actual friend over, let alone a cute boy that I regularly daydream about.

The hairs on my neck stand up at the end. They pulsate

as my brain sends signals screaming down my nerves. Say. What. You. Came. To. Say. *Say it.* Saaay iiit.

I press the pause button before the fight begins.

My eyes go a little blurry when I realize I'm staring at the TV unblinking. "I'm sorry," I say, apologizing for whatever horrendous thing my brain is going to make me say next. "Can you just come out and say what you couldn't say in a text? I'm dying over here trying to interpret everything you're saying and not saying."

He lets out a short laugh, clearly taken aback but still smiling. Felix laughs along with him in a very rehearsed way, not looking up from his tablet. "Very well then. I thought we could see a movie together before I leave for Denver."

"A movie? Like, in the movie theater?" I ask, my eyes widening. I only enjoy movies in the safety of my basement on the TV. For a movie I really want to see, I sometimes can suffer through with headphones on, but it's incredibly over-stimulating. Too many people, too many smells, too many loud noises, etc.

Maverick nods and smiles again. I swear he's going to have wrinkled dimples by the time he's twenty years old if he keeps it up.

"I had a feeling you would want to see that fantasy film that's adapted from the book *Kingdom Delivered*, right? Have you read it?"

"Have I *read* it?" I exclaim, nearly jumping off the couch. "I live and breathe *Kingdom Delivered*! It's only one of my favorite series ever." I squirm in place, too excited to worry about hidden meanings and social norms.

"Then it's a date." Maverick winks.

Inside me, endorphins dance the tango with serotonin.

My knees won't stop bouncing. Higgins puts a paw on my thigh to remind me what's going on around me. I clear my throat and focus on the TV.

"Ready to die?" I ask with a malicious undertone.

"Bring it." He smiles. "But, first, could you please explain the rules?"

I snort and laugh involuntarily. I had no idea Maverick was such a noob.

"You said you like to play video games!" I accuse.

"Well, yeah! But I've never played this one before."

"Okay." I put down my controller, preparing to go into hyperfocus mode. "Our characters are different creatures of the animal kingdom with cute little characteristics and stylized moves unique to each of them. See?" I point to my kangaroo. "We each pick a character and beat each other up until the health bar runs out."

Maverick beams at me. "That's so morbid. I love it."

Felix is still enveloped in his own game.

I start the fight.

We're in a small arena, so I work Jumpin' Jane's air space to my advantage. I could be a douche nozzle and just spam my kick attack, but I try to go easy on him.

"Who is my guy anyway?" Maverick asks, causing me to gasp.

I break focus for one second to answer. "An underwater mob boss."

"Wait... I picked a *bad guy*?"

A tornado of emotion whirls inside of me. The adrenaline of possibly beating Maverick at my favorite game, plus the astonishment of his lack of game knowledge, and the realization that my best friend just asked me out combine in a power combo attack. I unleash all my secret moves and knock him off the edge.

"Dinah!" Maverick yells in accusation.

My heart jumps in fear that I've done something wrong. Higgins perks his ears up in preparation, but on closer examination, I realize the boy on the other side of the couch is laughing.

Maverick doesn't win one match, no matter who he chooses as his fighter. He keeps picking large characters who I can easily counter with light and speedy ones. Classic noob mistake.

We laugh until our sides hurt. I can't remember when I've had this much fun and felt this at ease. Higgins sensed I was fine forever ago, so he fell asleep between us, his legs up in the air in a compromising position.

Of course, I want to keep going after ten rounds, but Jenny taught me to look for body language the best I can to determine the end of an activity. When Maverick stretches and sets his controller down, I copy him.

"Accepted defeat?" I ask, my cheeks aching.

He laughs. "Hail Dinah, Queen of *Animal Brawl*."

There's an awkward pause where Higgins' snores fill the silence. Maverick studies me like he's trying to find a person's eyes behind a mask. My eyes burn.

I turn away and softly scratch Higgins' belly, his leg twitching in his sleep.

Maverick lifts his hood and jingles his keys in his pocket. I know those signals for sure. He's ready to leave. Felix whines in protest, and Higgins' ears perk up. To my surprise, he leaves my side to help another autistic teen in distress.

"Aw, Higgins likes you, Fel." Maverick laughs, bending down to scratch his ears.

Felix tears his eyes from his tablet for the first time since the Wright brothers arrived in my basement. He greets Higgins with a smile and pats him on the head.

Maverick looks back at me, and I hope I'm smiling.

Higgins is helping someone else besides me, and not for the first time. He's just the best dog that anyone can ask for.

"You really need your own dog, don't you, bud?" the older brother says affectionately to the younger. Maverick fiddles with the keys, jingling them in his pocket once again.

I try to prolong their departure.

"I'm doing mostly homeschool right now because my meltdowns are out of control. I had to be put on antidepressants when my aide moved away." Personal information spills from my lips easily. The words escape me like a burst dam, pressure spreading everywhere the syllables can reach. They splash up against Maverick, who doesn't drown but sits erect like a mighty wall to contain the flow of information.

"Shit, that sucks," is all he says.

I'm satisfied with the answer. He rubs his hands together in his hoodie pocket. I can hear the skin colliding with my superhuman hearing.

"I'm sorry, Dinah."

At his words, I'm as light as a feather. Talking to Maverick is unique—once we have a conversation going, it ebbs and flows effortlessly. I've preferred texting so that I don't have to spit out something senseless, but over time, he has become easier to talk to. He understands my social inabilities.

"I'll be okay. I hope. Eventually. Maybe." I can't pick the right word to say.

"Can I touch you?" he asks.

Everything stops. The silence fills the basement with some kind of sticky yet thick tension. I find myself nodding before I have fully processed the request through my brain. At least he remembered to ask. I nod once.

Maverick's fingers slide under my chin. His hands are on my skin. I don't know how to react to the rough yet pleasant feeling.

"I'm only a text away, okay?"

I'm still processing the jumble of seconds that just happened when Higgins puts his snout between my chin and his fingers, Felix moaning a protest that my dog is no longer available for him.

"Alrighty, Felix. Let's get outta here." Maverick's eyes catch mine, and I'm drowning. My skin tingles where he touched me. "See you Sunday?"

Sunday? Sunday! "I can't waiiit. I want to see *Kingdom Delivered* so badly," my brain speaks for me.

Maverick can't contain his excitement either. "I somehow knew the elf queen wouldn't pass up that chance." He stands up and walks a little closer to the basement stairs. "It's getting dark. We better get going. Felix is afraid of the dark and would much rather be at home under his covers." Maverick curls his arm around his brother's elbow to escort him out. Felix protests with a mean glance. "I'll check in with you later and let you know the details—the show times and all that."

I inhale deeply through my nostrils, and it catches a bit with all the adrenaline pumping through my veins. I pray to every elven God I've ever read about that Maverick didn't hear that. Normally, I'd be under my blanket dying of embarrassment. Now, I can't help but hold Maverick's gaze. It's like he has the magic touch to love and accept people.

Blood rushes to my cheeks. Higgins licks my face to make sure I don't have a fever. I break Maverick's gaze. He said they were leaving, but he isn't moving. Better nudge him out the door before the itches start. "Drive safe," I say.

Maverick nods and meekly smiles. "I will. I bring the van when Felix is along for the ride. I hope your meltdowns calm down soon." His face stops smiling and molds into one of concern or anger. I'm going with concern. The blood flow in my throat does a loop-the-loop at the thought of my friend truly caring about me.

He reaches out and pets Higgins on the head, who hesitates at first but gives in. He can never resist good-boy pets.

"Bye," Maverick says, finally exiting.

I hold my breath until the front door closes. I let gravity overtake me and freefall into my gaming blanket, which in my head turns into a bed of yellow peonies. Their petals rise upward with my bodily force and float steadily back down to earth. Soft music falls upon my ears as cotton-candy pink clouds clash with the pure-blue sky. I breathe in the flowery scent and let it flow through my veins like whipped icing. Slow, churning, and enjoyable. I smile as I replay the conversation we just had.

I'm going on my first date.

CHAPTER 16

THAT NIGHT, horrific nightmares haunt me until I wake in a pool of freezing sweat.

My shuddering gasps for breath stir Higgins awake. On autopilot, he climbs onto my back and applies pressure therapy to my body. I'm wrapped in a Higgins burrito of safety while he waits through my silent panic attack. His warm, comforting weight calms the itches. My breathing returns to normal in about five hundred and fifty-three Higgins heartbeats.

To some, this might appear as a failure of a Saturday morning, but I take it as an opportunity to restart the day. I pretend to wake up all over again, dismissing my meltdown like it never happened.

When I go into the kitchen, Nattie pretends nothing happened, which I appreciate. I hadn't considered that she possibly heard me hyperventilating through the wall our rooms share. I squint at the oven clock to see that it's 6:00 a.m., much earlier than anyone should have to wake up on a Saturday.

"Good morning, Dinah," Nattie says when she sees me.

"What're you doing up?" I ask in response.

Nattie shrugs and insists she couldn't sleep. I try not to think about whether she woke up because of me.

I whisper-sing while tiptoeing to the table to sit with Nattie and her giant cup of coffee.

Someone's in the kitchen with Di-nah...

Higgins looks like he needs coffee too, but he settles for a spot to curl up in under Nattie's chair.

"What do you have going on today?" I ask, brushing some annoying hairs out of my face. My teenage hormones are causing me to grow baby hairs around my forehead to thicken my hair. For what reason? Probably to make puberty even more annoying than it already is.

Nattie yawns as she shrugs, bringing her large cup to her lips and sipping like a monk who has unlocked the secret of nirvana. "I'll probably go hang at Cheyenne's house or something. Nothing too exciting. You? Reading and *Animal Brawl* when I get back?"

"I don't really know." I try to find some way to break the ice so she won't freak out on me. "I have a date tomorrow and—"

"You *what?*" Nattie yelps, jumping so hard out of her seat that coffee spills like a fountain onto Higgins' fur.

He howls. It echoes off the kitchen tile onto my heels, vibrating up my nervous system. My teeth grit as I shut my eyes tight, willing myself to breathe properly. I can fight the sudden burst of sound—I know I can. My heart fills with horror that my precious dog has possibly been burned, so I rush to his side.

"Nattie!" I yell. "How could you?"

"I didn't mean to," Nattie snaps as Higgins tucks his tail underneath himself and whines. "I can't believe you didn't tell me you have a *date*."

I exhale through my nostrils. My heart beats loud enough that I swear Nattie can hear it too. She jumps up from her seat to grab a towel from the hall closet while I console Higgins, making sure the heated coffee only got on his fur, not his skin. I'm relieved to see that he seems to be only shook up, not injured.

As Nattie dries Higgins off, I smile slightly and say, "I guess that wasn't the best way for me to tell you."

"You think? Why didn't you tell me sooner?" Nattie tries to whisper, but her voice comes out as a quiet shout. "Is it Maverick? Oh, hell yes, it's Maverick." She's bouncing on her rainbow-painted toes at the news.

A robed Kurt enters the kitchen, his eyes still shut. Higgins whines and runs to Kurt's feet, his tail between his legs. His whimpering is enough for Kurt to fully gain consciousness, as he slowly opens his bloodshot eyes.

"What's wrong, boy? What happened? Who tortured this poor guy?" Kurt groggily asks in our direction. He stumbles over to the coffeemaker to pour himself a large cup congruent to Nattie's spilt one.

"He accidentally got a hot shower of coffee," I say, patting my leg for Higgins to come near. My heart hurts for him. He did a spectacular job with my panic attack this morning, only to be rewarded with burns. I hug him around the neck, to which he responds with a tail happily thumping on the floor. It's as if he's totally forgotten his own pain.

We don't deserve dogs.

"So that's what the loud noise is about?" Kurt asks,

scratching his salt-and-pepper hair, a chunk of it in the back standing on end. He squints at me with concern. "Are you okay, Dinah?"

I nod, giving off the idea that I'm perfectly fine. Never mind the panic attack, the ringing in my ears from Higgins' howling, or the fact that I have no idea how to prepare for my first date tomorrow.

"We have big plans today, Kurt. Do not disturb," Nattie says in a stern tone. She grabs my hand and tugs it, a signal that she wants to go back to my room and meticulously plan. I'm not sure what for. Last time this happened, we both ended up with phones.

"Okay, then I guess I'm stuck with bathing the dog," Kurt mutters in a cantankerous tone.

Nattie treats me to a day of pampering. She gives me a manicure, a pedicure, a face mask, tries to shape my eyebrows (I put a quick stop to that), and begins giving me dating advice as if she's twenty-five, not fifteen.

"I don't like the movie theater because of all the loud noises, but I told him that I would kill to go see *Kingdom Delivered*. I think we're probably going just as friends," I say, more to myself than Nattie. I don't want to get my hopes up or any of my other emotions. I silently pray to whomever is listening that I will sit through the movie like a lifeless statue, my emotions safely enclosed in stone.

"Huh. You'd think he would know that, having Felix as his brother," Nattie wonders aloud, still brushing. She knows exactly how to make my hair softer without tugging my roots, and I love it. I exhale through my nostrils, relaxed from stimming that I didn't have to do myself.

"What would you do if I couldn't talk?" I ask, the

thought forming seemingly out of nowhere. Sometimes my brain throws darts with off-topic conversations taped to them —if one of them hits the bull's-eye, I can't help but go with it.

"Like Felix?" She pauses her brushing and bites her lip, apparently thinking hard. "I mean, it'd be very stressful sometimes, but your personality would shine through and still bug me." Nattie makes a face at me in the mirror.

I never for a moment considered the thought that Felix has a personality under his silence. I internally shame myself for not thinking of him the way I want others to think of me: as a human being.

I crumble a little on the inside, realizing that I might have some ableist thoughts. As a disabled person, I need to do better.

Nattie's phone buzzes—the signal of the end of our sisterly fun. I marvel at the rare instance in which my sister actually wants to spend time with me, not roll her eyes and go do something else. I appreciate it, but I know from experience she'll probably switch moods again by tonight.

Once Nattie is out the door to head to Cheyenne's, a lavender-scented, extra fluffy Higgins trots through, strutting his stuff like a show horse performing dressage.

"Look who's so handsome," I say, welcoming his fluffiness into my arms. Soon I'm absently stroking his fur, thinking way too many thoughts—they scroll by like the extra-fast credits at the end of a movie.

My vision becomes a blur and smooths out to a savannah that stretches for hundreds of miles. Billions of stars twinkle down from the azure sky, getting help from the full moon to light my countenance.

Higgins' breath becomes more expansive, his rib cage

sounding ten times larger than normal. Air gets captured in his chest, and it rolls around until it makes a rumbling noise that shakes my skeleton. He's purring. He backs away from me to shake his giant, regal mane and bows, offering his servitude to me.

I rise from the ground, my skirts falling back into place—their white linen so free and light they blow in the midnight breeze. I'm barefoot, and my toes wriggle into the soft clay, some of it has stuck in the cracks of my arch. I bend down to place my hands on either side of the lion's head to give instructions to take me throughout the wild kingdom, but when I open my mouth, no sound comes out.

My brain is signaling for me to speak. My voice box vibrates, but still nothing happens. I look to my lion, worry in his primitive eyes. His hot breath bounces off my distressed face and into the starry night, waiting for his queen's desires to become known.

I struggle with every ounce of my weight I can to will my lungs, larynx, and mouth to work together, but nothing comes out. I accept that I must rule through other communications.

Ominous drum music pounds the ground, and I prepare for the worst. The enemy has arrived. Without verbal instructions, my animal army won't be able to protect their queen. I dig my fingers into my lion's fur and bury my face as well. The drums magnify, thumping their way inside my brain.

The drumbeat is my own beating heart, blood roaring in my ears, pumping adrenaline throughout my body. Twisting Higgins' golden fur between my fingers, I continue to hold him close.

What a terrible friend I am.

This must be what empathy feels like. Sympathy? Empathy? One of those.

Felix has a much harder life than me. Maverick has a much harder life than me, and all I do is think about myself. Maverick could be suffering. I haven't asked one question about him or Felix—I answer questions about myself or ask stupid nerd-related questions.

I'm learning empathy, and through it I'm learning that I'm a very self-centered person—unfeeling and basically an unstable robot. I dig my phone out from under my pile of library books to shoot Maverick a quick text message. I type quickly, hoping he's not busy so he can send a response right away.

> Me: Who is Felix's favorite superhero?

To my relief, the three dots dance less than sixty seconds later.

> Maverick: Hello to you too... lol. It's Black Panther. It reminds him of my dad's cat, Poe. Why the random question?

I smile at the thought of Felix loving a cat, but then frown as it appears the cat is in Denver. No wonder Felix needs a service animal. He's probably missing his cat.

> Me: I realized what a crappy friend I am and how I hardly know anything about you two, yet you know lots about me.

I swallow impatiently, wondering what Maverick will reply.

> Maverick: You're not a crappy friend at all, Dinah! You're just so interesting that I prefer to talk about you

Blood rushes to my cheeks uncontrollably. Higgins begins to lick my right cheek out of concern. The dots are still dancing, so I wait, rocking back and forth to pass the time.

> Maverick: Excited for tomorrow

I hurriedly type back.

> Me: I'm excited too. Don't try to change the subject. I want to find out more about you.

I don't expect the dancing dots to linger, but it's well over five minutes before Maverick's next message comes through. It's not terribly long, so I imagine he either got distracted and had to prioritize something over texting me, or he was struggling to figure out what to say. Either way, I know I'm over-analyzing, and that never leads to anything good.

> Maverick: Before I moved to Milwaukee doesn't matter anymore. I told you I was a horrible person, a real douche nozzle. Believe me, you don't want to know

I didn't expect that answer at all. It sounds like Maverick has some self-loathing issues, same as me. Only his loathing is his past self.

CHAPTER 17

I CAN DO THIS.

I can go on a date with my best friend.

I can go on a date with my best friend who has a mysterious past that I'm too scared to dig into.

I can go on a date with a boy I'm developing feelings for.

Crap.

The knock on the door tells me that Maverick has arrived. It isn't until Mom expresses her surprise at him coming over that I realize I forgot to tell her to expect him, let alone ask if I could go out with him today. It is just lunchtime, so maybe she won't think it's that big of a deal.

I fly around the corner, singing, "*Someone's going on a date with Di-nah. Someone's in the house to pick up Dinah.*"

It doesn't help that his first words upon seeing me are, "It's too slushy for my dad's old motorcycle, so I borrowed my mom's van. The Felix-mobile. Plus, I didn't think Higgins would fit on the bike."

Mom raises her eyebrows at the word *motorcycle*, but so do I.

The gray T-shirt under a black zip-up sweater gives him a distinguished look. He's shaved and styled his hair like he does for school. I hope my eyes aren't dilated so I don't give away any unspoken details to my mom or, worse, Maverick.

My safe place wants to imagine me riding off with a bad boy on the back of his motorcycle into the sunset, but I chase it out of my brain and hide it somewhere between princess trivia and juice flavors. I'll come back for it later.

I move over to the side of the door to grab my headphones off their hook. Mom grabs my hand and interlocks our fingers—her way of getting my attention to focus on her a hundred percent.

"Where are we going?" Mom asks sweetly with a pinch of concern.

Maverick glances at me, a little stunned. "Oh, sorry, Mrs. Allen. I thought Dinah would've told you."

I grit my teeth and try to make my eyes look apologetic, but I don't know if I'm sending the right signal. Body language is not my forte.

"Dinah said she wanted to see *Kingdom Delivered* with me."

Mom, not used to hearing "Mrs. Allen," (or maybe it's me who's not used to it) raises her eyebrows so far up they might disappear into her hairline. I forget that Finlayson is my dad's name, even after all these years. She purses her lips into a kind of duckface and peers at me, either with a pleased look or a shocked one. Either way, I can tell she's not mad.

"Well, that sounds like a lot of fun. Though movies can be hard on you, honey. Do you want some of your anxiety medication?" she asks, letting go of my fingers one by one.

My cheeks burn with embarrassment. Maverick doesn't

need to know that I have to take pills before every major event.

Don't be ashamed of who you are, be unapologetically you, Dinah-Doo, Jenny's voice reminds me.

I nod while grabbing Higgins' leash. He bounces all over the living room in excitement when he hears it jingle. Maverick laughs his contagious laugh, and I can't help but grin.

I'm in so much trouble. Before the movie is over, I bet my skin will change to a permanent pink tone from all the blushing I'm already doing.

Maverick helps put on Higgins' vest and leash while I get my meds from my mom in the kitchen. I whisper, "*Someone's in the kitchen with Dinaaah.*" She pours out a pill, and I can't stop the words from coming. "Quit smiling, Mom. It's just a movie with my friend."

"A very handsome friend," Mom states, not as quietly as I'd like her to. I throw the pill in my mouth and run away from her.

"Is your phone charged?" she calls after me.

"Yes," I grunt and shove my headphones over my ears.

"Will you be back for dinner?"

"Yes," I spit, shooting her a "geez, Mom" glare. I dart out into the slush and arrive at the van before Maverick does, desperate to drive away from here.

Higgins and Maverick follow, a grin still on his face. He unlocks the door and opens it for me. I'm used to having a lot of things done for me, but this act is different. Like a gentleman of yesteryear in one of my historical fiction books. I breathe in and out, trying not to feel overwhelmed. I don't know how to feel about this act of kindness just yet, so I log it away in my brain for later.

Once Higgins is safely in the back seat, my seatbelt is on, and Maverick climbs into the van, I cringe. The space inside the van compresses me into a cube like a trash compactor.

"All right," he says, turning the ignition. He might as well have turned a key to my heart, because it revs up in my chest right at that instant.

Wow, my imagination can be so cheesy, sometimes.

We're backing out of the driveway. We're leaving my house. The windshield wipers squeak back and forth, pushing hundreds of flecks of water aside that collide into other flecks to form pools. What do we talk about now? What should I say? How long does it take to get to the theater? How long is the movie? I wish I'd looked this information up on my phone beforehand. What if we say nothing to each other for hours? What if this is the worst first date in the entire history of first dates?

I'm suddenly aware of the sticky leather seats clinging to my butt through my leggings. My palms trace alongside the car door, the bumps in the plastic pleasing the nerves in my hands. My multiverse twin stares at me in the window, with a "What the hell are you doing?" look on her face. I whip my head around to tear my gaze away from her and end up staring at Maverick.

"Music?" he asks.

"Yes, please." Anything to break this awkward silence. He turns the radio to the rock channel but makes sure it's barely audible so that it doesn't slosh around in my brain uncontrollably.

We sit in silence for a few more minutes, only the faint

rock music and Higgins' dog breath to keep us company. Finally, Maverick sighs.

"Okay, I give. What do you want to know about me?" he asks, glancing in my direction.

I sigh in relief, grateful for a topic that I can carry on for hours. I dig through my brain files to find the drawer that is marked "Maverick" and peek at the questions I racked up last night after our texting session. They display before my eyes like a grocery list, each question color coded and bullet pointed with follow-up questions.

"Were you born in Denver?" I ask, reassuring myself that Maverick has given me the green light and is, therefore, a glutton for punishment.

"Thornton, a little outside of Denver. Denver has a ton of suburbs," he answers, his eyes on the road. Safety first.

"Felix too?"

"Felix too."

"Okay, cool. Next, why do you keep calling yourself a douche nozzle? That's not a nice thing to say about yourself," I say matter-of-factly.

He laughs out loud. Then nods and purses his lips before answering, "I guess I learned from the best, dear Daddy-o majored in douche-ism in college."

"I didn't know that was a thing," I say, astounded.

Maverick laughs again. "No, I mean, being a horrific person comes naturally to him."

I wonder what Sherri ever saw in Maverick's dad and why she agreed to marry him and even have children with him if he was such a terrible person.

Maverick takes the silence as a signal to go on, even though I'm using the silence to space out my thoughts.

"My dad isn't very understanding. It's his way or no way. He wasn't supportive of Felix's treatment and has very little patience with him. That's why I'm Felix's fiercest protector because I'm basically... his father figure," he says slowly, as if he's never spoken any of these things aloud before.

"I'm like my mom," Maverick continues, extremely focused on the rainy road now. "If I'm told I can't do something, my attitude is like 'watch me,' and I go and do it. When my dad was coming down hard on me, I should've listened to my mom. Instead, I didn't listen to either of them and ended up doing some messed up stuff."

We were getting very deep into the conversation. Kurt calls it *deep* deep.

Higgins pants excitedly when the car slows and Maverick turns into a parking spot.

"Like?" I'm dying to know but try not to show it. It's beyond my control what my emotions decide to display on my face once the lizard brain kicks in.

Maverick hesitates, peering at me, his hand still on the wheel. His look is so mesmerizing, I can't quite figure it out. It's like he's wondering whether to tell me his darkest secret or not. I have a flashback to the gods of light and dark meeting atop the highest peak, and my heart leaps again.

Later! I tell my safe place.

Maverick steps out of the van and comes around to my side of the vehicle. He lets Higgins out first, then opens my door. The silence is heavy in the air... does it mean he wants to end the conversation there? Or should I ask him again?

He hands me Higgins' leash and thrusts his hands deep in his pockets. I take that as a sign that the conversation is done. As we walk across the wet parking lot to the ticket office, my lizard brain won't shut up.

Like? Like what? Did he rob a bank? Beat someone up? Get expelled from school? Get caught with weed?

Like what? Like what! *Like what?*

"Two for *Kingdom Delivered*, already paid in advance," Maverick says to the lady at the window. She nods with a smile toward me.

He hooks his arm around my elbow and props it up like he's escorting me to a ball I'll have to run away from and leave a shoe at later.

Usually at the movie theater, I'd have physical copies of our tickets that the employees rip. I try not to focus on it, but it's out of my routine, so my brain itches.

"Um, Maverick? Are we going to grab popcorn?" I mutter. The air is still tense from our conversation in the van, but it's also eerily quiet in the theater lobby. Plus, the ushers are staring at me. A tinge of annoyance makes me reach up to take my headphones off. I put them in my purse and try to ignore the loud popcorn popper that sounds like it's cooking in my ear canals.

"Nah, I figured we'd skip it this time," he answers.

I'm confused as all hell. No popcorn? What is this, a fancy restaurant?

My annoyed mood tingles over my back, bringing up a shade of red in my eyes. I'm more than annoyed. I'm downright pissed. I'm sacrificing my comfort for a fantasy movie I'm excited to see, and it's discomforting. Higgins scampers along as an usher waves her hand toward theater number one.

Once my eyes adjust to the dark hallway, I notice the

blank screen. Usually the loud, local commercials are playing before a movie. The itches are begging my skull to let them burst through and cause havoc because everything is out of order.

Maverick turns the corner and says in a barely audible tone, "Well, look at that."

And I look.

Two trays full of popcorn, candy, and drinks are in the very middle seats of the theater. Nobody else is seated—we're completely alone.

"Oh wow," I mutter, almost out of breath from the anger that whizzes out of me. The itches burrow back into my cerebrum where they belong. Higgins sits like a good boy and wags his tail, waiting for instruction.

Maverick leads me up the stairs to our seats. I immediately grab the red licorice candy in excitement. My drink is ice water, which is perfect, because sodas make my tongue hurt. When I was younger, my mom said I called soda "spicy," and it was a sign she had brought up to my doctor. I still call things I don't like "spicy" because it's a fun way to put it.

I dig my headphones out of my purse in anticipation of the movie starting, but Maverick grabs them and puts them in the seat next to him.

"Hey! Rude. I need those," I say, smiling because I know he's teasing.

"No, you won't. I've arranged for the sound to be turned down and for the lights to stay up. And no previews, so we can get right to the good stuff." As he says this, my eyes fuzz over and my tongue goes numb. My heart feels useless and is about to fall out of my chest onto the sticky movie theater floor.

"Maverick, I...." I don't know what to say.

He cups his palms on both sides of my face and pulls my chin toward his. Usually, I'd revolt and tell him to not touch me. But I find his touch comforting. I want him to touch me.

He leans a little closer, his eyelashes tickling my forehead.

I stop breathing.

"Is this okay?" Maverick whispers.

I gulp and nod as my soul leaves my body. He plants his lips firmly but gently on mine. While every nerve in my body sets ablaze, I melt into my seat like the butter on my extra-large popcorn.

I'm having an out-of-body experience. For once, everything isn't tingling, a ticking time bomb ready to go off at any second. My eyes are watching a movie, but my soul is floating above my head, taking everything in.

Maverick rented out a movie theater room for me. He made it sensory-friendly for me.

Maverick kissed me.

Processing these sudden changes is like landing on an alien planet. I hover here and there, drowning in a myriad of feelings while my body remains an empty shell.

Maybe change isn't such a bad thing after all. Instead of resisting it with every force I possess, should I embrace it with open arms? When our lips part, his grin matches mine to the point of blushing. I glance down where he's brushing my palm with his fingernails.

He knows how to play me like a fiddle. Growing up with

an autistic brother, he's learned coping techniques that Nattie and my mom have learned over the years.

Floating here, I overanalyze every scenario that can possibly occur between the end of the movie and my arrival at home. I decide to fill the time with observations about the movie, the differences between the book and the film, and things I wish were left in or out. What happens if I run out of topics before we get home? Will awkward silence reign supreme? Will he ask if we can go out again? What if he kisses me again?

If I were in my body, I'd be freaking out. But since I'm in my astral form, I bellow into the void, letting out a silent scream to encompass all that's beautiful and wrong about this moment, Maverick sitting next to me stroking my hand.

Twenty minutes, thirty minutes, over an hour later—and his hand still hasn't left mine. It's impossible not to feel its smoothness caressing mine. It's like I'm watching the movie in front of me, and my hand is watching a movie with Maverick's hand. The itches are at bay, but I'm on high alert with everything around me. The overstimulation makes me sit at the edge of my seat, smelling the buttery scents, chewing the warm popcorn, focusing on Maverick's hand, and listening to the voices coming from the screen. It's as if I'm about to shoot off into space.

Yet time passes like a speeding bullet in my spiritual void because the ending credits roll in before I know it. When I fall back into my body, I detect two things: my heart is full and so is my stomach. Overall, my senses tell my brain that I'm satisfied. I enjoyed the movie, I enjoyed the stimulation on my hand, and I enjoyed the junk food Mom normally doesn't let me have.

Maverick turns his face towards me and asks, "Well?"

It takes me a minute to gather exactly what I want to say because I'm trying not to stare at Maverick's lips, wondering when he'll kiss me again. "I enjoyed the movie much more than any other movie. Probably because there were no heavy breathers or constant candy unwrapping." The corners of my lips curl up.

"I thought it was cool when the warrior's eyes lit up, and the field caught on fire. That surprised me." He stands up, indicating it's time to head home.

Higgins' snores cease. He gets up on all fours, shakes popcorn off his fur, and follows close behind us.

I blaze onward with my plan to start critiquing the film compared to the book. "And that sword fight? I mean, come on!"

I continue to talk about the movie, barely acknowledging that we're getting in the van.

My conversation seems to be more with the dashboard than with Maverick. Looking at him right now might just fizzle my nerve endings and cause a spark that will engulf the van in flames.

Higgins' face is as close to mine as it can be from the back seat. He's protecting me, readying himself if Maverick should try to get between us. I'm sweating from nervousness, my torso damp beneath my hoodie. Tension fills the air— thick like peanut butter between the three of us in the van's cabin. I glance at the girl in the window, her dark eyes boring into mine. Through her transparent gaze, I recognize the street that leads to my cul-de-sac. I release a silent sigh of relief, unable to control the emotions shooting at me from every direction any longer.

When we pull up into my driveway, Higgins lets out happy barks. I flick his snout and point to my headphones, to which he promptly whines, realizing his mistake.

"Higg, you can be such a dummy," I mutter and let him out.

"Bye," I say to Maverick, ready to dive into my bedroom.

"Wait."

I look deeply into his blue eyes and hope he understands how much I need to escape this van. "No, I really can't," I whisper.

"You can't?" he repeats as if hoping he heard wrong. "I was going to tell you something important. About me."

"While I appreciate the gesture, I can't handle it right now, Maverick." I turn to jump out, wishing I didn't wait for Maverick to let me leave. The itches spread—even worse, they're accompanied by the buzzes.

He examines me from the top of my head down to my shoes, then back up to my eyes. Surely, he sees how distressed I'm feeling. A few alerts go off in my head about etiquette from Jenny.

"Thank you for the lovely evening. Seriously," I say, giving him a quick glance. My energy must be released somewhere. I bounce up and down in my seat. "Everything about this day has been perfect. I don't want to ruin it with a meltdown in the van."

He nods and turns his lips upward, smiling without showing any teeth. He sighs and shrugs his shoulders. "I hoped to avoid a meltdown with everything being sensory friendly, but I understand."

"No, no, nonono, noooo." I blink my eyes quickly to balance out the bouncing. "It was all wonderful. Nobody's gone to those lengths for me. I'm just...." My brain goes blank. It's like my train of thought gave up and died. I grit my teeth and ball up my fists to try to remember. I hope against hope I don't start hitting myself.

"Too much at once?" he asks, worried.

I nod. He gets out and comes around to help me out of the van. I bolt up my driveway and to my porch. Higgins is at my heels. I slip through the slush—luckily, I don't fall—arriving at the checkpoint only to find the front door locked.

"Dammit, Kurt!" I yell. I remember why it's so dark out—daylight saving was this past week. Kurt locks the door whenever it gets dark because that's when the danger comes out or something like that. I bang on the door so hard my knuckles burn.

Maverick finds his way to me. A giant rock formulates in my throat, and I can't swallow or vomit it up. He takes both of my hands and rubs them with his slightly calloused fingers. I almost melt into a puddle at his feet again.

"I'll text you. Hopefully we can have the conversation I want to have," he says. He takes one hand and touches my headphones. "Sometimes I forget."

"F-forget?" I ask, my brows furrowing.

"That you're..."

"It's called masking," I say, correcting him. It's statistically proven that girls with autism are better at masking than boys. We put on a "social mask" to get through the day, and we fall apart at home. It's something I'm fantastic at and something I absolutely loathe.

"Oh. Sorry."

"I never forget about my autism. You shouldn't either."

Maverick looks at the ground for a moment, then back at

me. "I'm glad you and Felix are in my life." His eyes lock into mine, and the contact makes the space behind my eyes buzz. He smiles, and I think I know what's coming again.

He leans in and tries to kiss my lips softly, only to back away quickly when Kurt rattles the doorknob. We break apart and stand on opposite ends of the doorway as if that'll convince Kurt that nothing happened.

"Hey, kids," Kurt greets us, opening the door slowly. "Did you have f—"

I squeeze in under his arm and run straight to my room. I slam the door and lean against it, breathing heavily as sweat and makeup pour down my face. I pull out my phone and text Maverick.

> Me: Sorry, thanks again. Talk later.

I crumple to the floor where it breaks beneath me. I keep falling and falling until I realize I'm not falling at all—I'm still on my carpet. The room spins as if I have a migraine. Maybe I do, but I shove the thought aside and proceed to let my meat computer decompress. I allow the euphoria of every emotion I avoided in the past few hours wash over me—fear, anxiety, elation, embarrassment, and a whole slew of others I can't identify. Time to go over everything again, and again, and again. It was the most perfect first date of my life, and I barely held it together.

I hate surprises. I love routine. Somehow, Maverick made me love his surprises. Then he kissed me. He wouldn't kiss me unless he likes me, right?

What if he wants to tell me how he feels about me, and I completely cut him off? What if he was going to tell me that kissing a girl without liking her is how he rolls? How he's still a crap person underneath? How this was just a one-time thing?

Higgins scratches at the door. I hit it with my heel. "Go away, you douche nozzle!" I scream through the door. He whines again, and I hear him retreat into Nattie's room.

Why, oh why can't I enjoy a date like everyone else? Like the heroines in my books? I rub my forehead on my carpet because it feels good, as if my brain wants a massage.

My heart leaps out of my chest, my skin tingling all over as I replay the night. Crap person or not, Maverick is my safe person. He makes me hold out longer when it's time for a meltdown. He makes me feel like I can do anything. He makes me feel both lightheaded and confident on my feet.

He kissed me twice. I replay those moments, lying there, torturing myself over the fact that I ran away from him when I could've had more. He might ignore me in class. What will happen the next time we see each other?

CHAPTER 18

"GOOD MORNING, DINAH," Eliza says, entering my bedroom. "How did you sleep?

I can barely keep my eyes open as I look at her. "I didn't sleep," I bark.

"At all?" Eliza asks, a look of concern on her freckled face.

Higgins sniffs with annoyance in my ear. "I didn't sleep *at all*," I repeat from my cocoon under the blankets.

Eliza tries to coax me out of bed for a bath, but I'm not having it. My body slumps like gelatin that has sat out on the counter too long.

Sometimes my brain won't turn off, and I'm hyperactive all night. It can happen when I'm recovering from a lot of emotion or fixated on something I can't get over. In this case, it's both. I'm feeling too much. I'm fixated on everything that happened last night. My brain can't recover in order to help me shut down into a state of unconsciousness.

"I guess we're homeschooling today?" Eliza states with what could be irritation or expectancy, I can't tell which.

"Today and the rest of the week." I sigh. I can't sit next to Maverick's empty seat in English. I hope his Denver trip isn't horrible.

I most certainly can't talk to the wall at lunch. I'll spiral. I'll explode. I'm used to texting him, but not seeing him when he's become such a staple in my everyday life now would be way too much.

Eliza raises a brow.

"Thanksgiving is this week. I want to transition into the holiday mindset and schedule. I think this'll help," I lie. Homeschooling could help me, but mostly it's an excuse to lay in my bed and text Maverick all day. My overstimulated brain senses that I need to give him some space, but I want to text him. The high of interacting with him may ease my feelings even if it's too hard to see him. Exchanging words is easier and gives me time to process his responses.

"Keep this up, and you'll have to work extra hard to graduate in the spring," Eliza says with a nice voice and a hint of an ulterior motive. She's trying to persuade me to work by threatening more work. Didn't Jenny train her on this tactic and how it almost never works?

I'll pay for it later, but I flip my middle finger in the air and disappear back under my covers.

Eliza stomps out of the room to give me some space. It's one of those days where we're not going to get along. While Jenny and I love each other, we had plenty of days like this too. I snuggle back up to Higgins, my brain going a million miles an hour, every other organ in my body sagging like mush. I can close my eyes to try to rest, but Maverick's face will be there, cupped in my hands.

Ding.

> Maverick: Heading to the airport. Have fun at school. I hope you are okay

My heart's aflutter at the surprise text. But also, there's no mention of last night.

I frown as my heart skips a beat. I think for a second about gritting my teeth and going to school, but that would only amplify my attitude because of my lack of sleep. No, I'm better off in my hidey-hole, texting Maverick, with thousands of miles between us.

> Me: Don't think I'll be going, didn't sleep. ☹

The dancing dots appear quickly.

> Maverick: Is that my fault?

My heart drops further down into my stomach, squeezing through my duodenum, determined to get itself digested. I type at lightning speed, my eyes blurry with fatigue.

> Me: Last night was absolutely perfect. I just had to ruin it by freaking out at the end.

I have to reassure him somehow that I'm okay with his actions last night, even though I'm not sure of his motives.

> Me: Have fun in Denver. I'm going to miss you.

He sends back a red heart emoji. My own heart blasts

off, shooting back up my esophagus and plants itself in my brain, giving me all the serotonin.

Higgins snores in my ear—he's fallen back to sleep. The rise and fall of his chest puts pressure against my torso perfectly. His snores are steady, comforting, and the perfect sedative to allow me to finally drift off.

I grab my phone and check the time—I've been asleep for five hours. Not exactly the full amount of rest I need, but it'll do. Maverick must have touched down in Denver by now. I swipe at the screen, only to be met with a blank home screen. I don't want to be clingy, but I can't help worrying about whether he and Felix landed safely and got to their dad's. I do, however, have a new message from *my* dad.

> Dad: Hey sweetie, looking forward to Thursday?

Dad is coming for an awkward Thanksgiving like every year. While Mom and Dad don't get along well anymore, Kurt and Dad have no beef with each other, which is a huge relief. I would rather eat regular food in my room instead of being forced to sit at the dinner table with everyone and take nibbles of fancy food that tastes horrible. Why can't Thanksgiving food just involve rolls and mashed potatoes? Why does everyone think it's weird when I eat the pumpkin pie on my plate but leave the crust there, empty, like the pie shed its skin? I do like to watch the Thanksgiving Day parade on TV with Higgins, though.

Nothing can really help "prepare" me for the holiday

besides psyching myself out about it. Given my schedule has been unusually out of the loop thanks to an upheaval of change, I believe I'll handle the holidays better this year. My detail-oriented habits have been tucked away lately for whatever odd reason—somewhere between logical reasoning and hormonal rampage. I'll dig it out when I need it.

I open the WorldVid app on my phone. I've developed a little routine of watching a few videos a day when I'm doing nothing. At first, it was fantasy and sword-fighting video game techniques, but I found myself drifting to interesting topics in my "recommended" column. I've found WorldVid has helped me learn practical stuff too, like how to do my hair and finding new book series. There are people like me out there trying to learn about people stuff. I once watched a video about ten ways to interpret social cues. It was *fascinating*.

A low knock comes at the door that sounds like my mother's knuckles. I tell her to come in, but I instantly regret it. The stern look on her face means I'm in trouble.

Oh yeah. I flipped Eliza off hours ago. I try not to snigger, keeping as straight of a face as I can.

"Sorry?" I attempt. Higgins bounces off the bed and heads out the door to conduct business as usual. Going potty, scavenging for food, and looking for other people's pets, I'm sure.

Mom folds her arms and exhales loudly through her nostrils. "You have an appointment with Jason in an hour, remember?"

That's convenient timing. Maybe he can help me figure out my uneven mood swings while I unload my Maverick issues. Mom grabs a black hoodie and rainbow-striped leggings from my drawers and tosses them my way. I don't like clothes on the floor, so I try to catch them before they succumb to gravity. Mission failed. The itches begin in my feet, but they quickly go away when I lean over and pick the clothes up.

Moments later, we pile into the car and head to Jason's office. I love everything he has to play, paint, and distract me with, but I hate how I openly spill my guts to him.

"I know this is going to be a rough week, Dinah," Mom starts. I can already tell a not-lecture-but-really-a-lecture is coming. "We need to muddle through this the best we can. Hopefully you'll start being a bit nicer to Eliza?"

"She was being a turd today," I mutter under my breath, hoping Mom won't overhear. Of course, she does because I forget that we're in a small, confined, moving vehicle together.

"Dinah!" Mom says, taking her eyes off the road at a stop sign and glaring at me. Higgins playfully brings his head between our heads like he wants in on the nosy gossip, but Mom gently pushes his head to the back seat.

"She was!" I repeat, hoping my mother will be on my side. "I didn't sleep, and she was saying that I wouldn't graduate."

"You will graduate as long as you do your work," she assures me. "Remember, just as you are transitioning to a new aide, she's transitioning to *being* your aide."

Whatever. She'll never replace Jenny.

Freezing rain pitter-patters the car window by the time we pull up to Jason's office. Mom keeps an umbrella under the front seat just in case—I had a few too many meltdowns as a result of getting wet in the rain and snow for it to not become a staple in our car.

I grab Higgins' leash and open the back passenger door. He takes a few seconds too long to decide if he wants to step in the wet slush or not.

"Dude, we have an appointment. I need you," is all I say. Then he decides to strut his therapy dog stuff.

Jason never goes over the time limit with his patients, which is awesome. I hate waiting, and I love getting things over with as quickly and painlessly as possible. I'm also thankful that his office is quiet. I'm confident enough to hand my headphones to Mom for safekeeping.

Ding.

My heart stops. Is it Maverick, finally reaching out to let me know he landed okay? I swipe my phone open with hope, but soon deflate like an old party balloon.

> Dad: Did you get my earlier text?

I read it in my head with his concerned voice attached to the words on the screen.

> Me: Yes, fell asleep. Long day. Excited to see you. Going into therapy now.

I need to be better about texting Dad. I don't want him thinking I used him to get a phone and don't care to keep in touch. Even though I totally did.

"Hey, Dinah, Higgins. Come on in." Jason's tone is deep yet soothing.

"I thought we could paint today." He brings over a canvas, paints, and a brush from beyond his desk. He grabs an easel behind the couch and sets it up in front of me. I'm handed a bib like I'm a toddler about to indulge in birthday cake. The tie on the back looks scratchy, so I politely refuse. I take the brush and run my fingers over the hard wood—I haven't painted since art class in middle school. The handle is cold, the bristles still wet from being recently cleaned. I can tell they've had many therapy sessions behind them.

"Oops, you need a mixing palette too," Jason exclaims, hurrying back to his desk. "I think this'll be easier for you, Dinah. Paint what's on your mind or just mix colors while we talk. You don't even have to see my face." He hands me the palette and sits in his executive-level-of-comfort-looking chair, scooting behind the canvas so he's blocked from my view.

The itches crawl all over my skin. To let out some of the excess energy, I tap the toes of my sneakers on the wood floor, causing a steady beat throughout the office. Right on cue, Higgins trots over and slumps onto my feet, giving me warm pressure right where I need it. I exhale and decide to try to paint a starry sky. I squeeze out some violet, dip my brush into it, and dance it along the canvas.

"How have you been since our last visit, Dinah?" Jason asks from behind the easel.

I think about it for a second while scraping the last bit of violet on the top of the white canvas. "Fine, I guess. There's been a lot of change."

"Do you want to talk about the change?"

I squeeze out and dip my brush in some black, mixing it with a little blue to create the midnight blue I need.

"I've been having a few nightmares, along with trouble sleeping," I confess.

Higgins' panting and me dragging the brush along my artwork sounds louder than usual. I make little dollops that collide with the violet to make it look like the sky is changing colors.

"Okay. How do you feel about the nightmares?" Jason continues.

"I don't know. Scared, I guess." I sound like a little girl who's afraid of the dark, but I can't help but express my true feelings. Jason's superpower is sucking the truth out of everyone.

"Being scared isn't always bad. That's a valid emotion," he says, analyzing my thoughts already.

"I don't like it." I dip my brush into the red a little harder than I mean to. Little flecks splatter onto Higgins' fur, but he doesn't flinch.

"Are you ready for Thanksgiving?" Jason asks, changing the subject, for which I'm momentarily grateful.

The itches have mostly disappeared from my skin, helping me relax into the squishy couch. I recognize something like joy flowing through me. I think I'm actually enjoying putting my feelings into art.

"Sure, we all hate holidays at my house," I reply.

"Why is that?"

"Because there's no schedule. No schedules make me uneasy."

"And that affects the family?"

The joy dips a little into embarrassment and uncomfortable self-awareness. "Yeah." I swallow, admitting one of my least favorite things about my autism. I like having control of the house, but I don't. I don't like how everyone switches their schedule around for me, but I'm grateful that they do. I don't like how things can get canceled at the last minute for me, and I certainly hate any injuries or hurt feelings I've caused over the years simply because I couldn't process what was happening or what I was feeling.

"Tell me more about your safe place." Jason sounds farther away than the few feet he is.

An elegant, metallic-silver paint catches my eye. It's perfect for the stars I'll dot using the tip of the brush.

"It's a fantasy I have depending on my mood. Plus or minus some heroes."

Higgins scratches the red paint specks in his fur with his hind leg.

"That sounds delightful. Tell me about it," Jason says. I've never had anyone really be interested in my safe place. What's the catch? My lizard brain is confused—should I shout at Jason to mind his own business, run out the door toward Mom, or let him into my deepest secret?

"I know you like to play video games and read books, too. Answer me this question: Do these things help you escape?"

I fleck more silver stars in clusters. "No, running helps me escape."

Jason chuckles, to which Higgins raises an ear. He's listening intently, daring Jason to make fun of me.

"True, but imagination can be a powerful tool to escape from reality. Your brain is an amazing dream factory that will let you go anywhere you want to go. Be anyone you want to be. It can be very tempting for creative minds such as yours to get lost and avoid overstimulation."

I wash my brush off in the sink next to the couch. I guess Jason does a lot of art therapy in here, and I can see why. I'm like an open book because of it.

"If you say so," I mutter, much more interested in the masterpiece I'm constructing.

"You said something about a hero in your fantasies," Jason says.

I say nothing as I dip into more midnight blue. The sky needs more drama.

"Do they look like anyone you know? Are they the same person or someone different every time?"

I pause for a minute and think of the one standing on the peak: ocean-blue eyes. The lute playing elf: ocean-blue eyes. The boy that cupped my face in the movie theater and kissed me: ocean-blue eyes.

"Nope," I answer. Heat rises up my spine and spreads out, but I keep this reaction to myself. There will be too many emotions if I talk about Maverick.

Higgins gives a dismissive sniff.

CHAPTER 19

MAVERICK MUST BE TIRED. Probably settling in or helping Felix calm down from the plane ride. There's no need to panic. At least that's what I tell myself. This doesn't stop me from briefly checking the internet for crashed airplanes or fiery car accidents along the Denver metro.

Twenty-four hours have passed since Maverick's last text when he said he and Felix were about to fly out to Denver. I surmise this is enough time to justify a slightly worried text that hopefully sounds cool and collected. I spend about half an hour formulating the right words to say in my mind, then take my opportunity while Eliza is on a bathroom break.

Hey, you dead? No, that's too blunt.

Hi, just checking to see if you made it okay. What am I, his mom?

Ultimately, I go with:

Me: How's Denver?

I click the volume off my phone so that I don't get in

trouble in case he texts back. I quickly shove my phone back under the love seat pillow when Eliza's steps thunder down the hall.

"All right. Back to math?" she asks.

I nod and pull my worktable closer, hoping that school-work will take Maverick's radio silence off my mind. It doesn't.

Tuesday passes in a whirl. So does Wednesday. And still nothing from Maverick. By this point, I've texted him about nine times and have come to the conclusion that his phone must have died and he forgot to pack a charger. It's the only explanation that stops the buzzes in my brain. I don't want to ask Mom to text Sherri because then she'd wonder if something is up between Maverick and me. I mean, there might be, but I have no clue. More communication is needed to determine that, and given his radio silence, it doesn't look like that conversation is going to be happening anytime soon.

Dad arrives Wednesday night to avoid any Thanksgiving traffic. When he comes in the house, my therapy time is just about up. Eliza is gathering her things and saying her holiday goodbyes.

"I'll be back Monday morning, Dinah. Have a great holiday and use your tools if needed. I'll have my phone with me," she says in a high-pitched voice laced with an edge of fatigue.

I've been trying to be kind since my little stint on Monday, but freaking out about Maverick without telling anyone is taking its toll on me, and that consequence usually falls to Eliza.

My teeth hurt from the tension I'm holding in. But I can't stop worrying. Mom doesn't seem to notice as she's busy rolling out pie crust while Kurt is chatting with Nattie. Higgins is sound asleep by the fireplace.

A pair of hands slide on my shoulders.

"*Someone's in the kitchen with Di-naaah...*" my dad sings.

I turn around and give him a hug around his torso in hopes that he'll reciprocate. He does. The weight and pressure of his arms around my shoulders takes the tension away, if only for a few seconds.

His aftershave can be a comfort or a trigger. Today, it's a comfort, though the scratchiness of his clothes clues me in that they were newly purchased and unwashed, no doubt a tactical move, like a peacock strutting. Dad likes to send signals to Mom that he's doing well without her. Today, he's signaling it through stylish clothes.

And they say *I* have issues communicating.

After breaking away from the hug, Dad chitchats with me. "How're you doing?" He gazes at my face, his mouth and jaw identical to mine in a smile minus the extra crow's feet at the corners of his green eyes. I notice he cut himself shaving under his ear.

My jaw locks. I try to swallow, but my tongue is superglued to the roof of my mouth. I'm about to swallow my tongue and choke.

"Dinah?" Dad asks, lifting my chin with a concerned hand.

I swallow and curl my lips into a small smile. "Okay."

Higgins is awakened by Mom dropping an empty pan on the floor in preparation for the big meal tomorrow. The crash rings against the tile and rattles my eardrums, prompting Higgins to sprint to my side. I grab his fur and bend down to bury my face in it. I'm not supposed to wear my headphones in the house, but I'm going to try to get away with it tomorrow. Who knows what other things Mom might drop?

"Sorry, Dinah," Mom calls from the kitchen, a stressed tone to her voice.

While my headphones will help tomorrow by drowning out kitchen noise, they never suppress the smells. Some smells are good—like the buttery, creamy mashed potatoes—but overall, Thanksgiving smells are putrid. Stuffing, gross. Yams, double gross. Asparagus, triple gross. It's the same thing every year, and I'm mentally preparing myself for tomorrow.

Higgins always senses holidays are a duty for him. He hardly leaves my side.

Jenny helped my family understand autistic aversion to holidays. It took Mom a while to come around, but we have it down to tradition now. Me eating by the fireplace away from everyone equals fewer meltdowns. Growing up, Dad tried to make me eat a piece of everything on the table, grounding me when I spat it out. Many holiday hours were spent banging my feet on the wall in my room, my screams accompanying the beat.

Once the ringing in my head stops, I peer at Dad. I shake off the concern he has in his eyes with another, "I'm okay," and run off to my room, Higgins at my heels.

Escape. Escape. Escape.

I do what anybody in their right mind would do when

there's too much holiday craziness and their best friend is nonresponsive: dive into videos about how to stay calm when someone doesn't text back. I scout WorldVid for what seems like hours and hours before Nattie finds me and asks if I need anything, no doubt commanded by Mom to do so.

I catch Nattie's gaze. My heart takes charge of my bodily functions instead of my brain. It spills out in a sea of confession-vomit.

"Maverick hasn't texted me back since he got on the plane to Denver two days ago." My cheeks are about to burst from holding in the tears I need to let out.

"Since Monday?" she asks, taking a seat next to me on the bed. Her expression is either frustration or concern, and I don't have the patience for either at the moment.

I stare at the floor when a giant tear falls mercilessly from my right eye onto Higgins' golden fur. I twist the affected fur with my hand, rubbing the salty water back into my skin and feeling the furry warmth spread to calm the itches.

"Yeah." I sniffle. Higgins puts a paw on my leg.

"Why didn't you tell me?" she asks in a low whisper. It seems she's wondering why I'd keep a secret when she rarely takes an interest in what I do with my life, Maverick being the exception.

I shrug, and another tear falls onto my hoodie. "I'm worried. Either something happened to him, or... or... what if he's using this time in Denver to avoid me? To, you know... ghost me?" I gulp, in desperate need of air. The thought never entered my brain that he could've been lying and playing me for a fool all along. For what payoff, I have no idea, but the thought of it makes my skin crawl.

"No. No way." Nattie cups my cheeks in her hands and

forces me to make eye contact with her. I struggle to move my head, so I move my eyes toward my door, suddenly uncomfortable with the confrontation. I realize she's trying to tell me something important, but my lizard brain wants to fight and fly at the same time.

"No. No self-deprecation," she adds. "You are gorgeous, wonderful, and unique. I think Maverick is a genuine friend, and he's really sweet. Maybe his phone got lost?"

"I don't know." I sniffle again, still looking at the door. I blink more tears out of my eyes as my breath catches. Higgins reaches up on his hind legs to give me a calming bear hug. He's a little smelly, but I welcome the embrace all the same. Everything's starting to point to Maverick purposely avoiding me.

"If he is ghosting you, boy, does he have a problem when he gets back." Nattie forms a fist. "I'll kick his ass."

While I know she's trying to help, the idea of fifteen-year-old Nattie trying to kick bulky Maverick's ass isn't exactly a comforting thought.

I feel like an elephant has stomped on my brain, squeezing my juices and lymphatic fluid out over the floor. I take it as a sign that a migraine is knocking on my proverbial door, an all-too-familiar symptom with my emotional melt-downs. I take deep breaths through my nostrils, and Nattie follows suit.

"What do you need?" she asks quietly between breaths.

"I don't know," I whimper, my voice breaking. "I'm so worried about him. At this point, I don't even care if he likes me. He's my best friend, and we text every day."

"Yeah, he's become part of your regular routine, that's for

sure," Nattie says more to herself than to me. "When is he supposed to come back?"

I try to think back to our last conversation about his travel plans, and I can't exactly remember. "He will probably be back in time for school next week. We have an English test."

"Tell you what," Nattie begins, squeezing my hand a little harder, "we will get through the big meal tomorrow, and then we will do more pampering. Just you and me. My friends are out of town this weekend anyway."

My chest rises with a big sigh. "What about Dad? It's tradition to watch movies over the weekend and the parade."

"Dad can be pampered too if he wishes." Nattie laughs, shaking my shoulders a bit in reassurance.

My head pounds like a drum solo in a rock song. I close my eyes to see if it helps, but colored spots and bright stars dance across them. I know what needs to be done.

"I'm going to bed," I say and stand to go get a onesie pajama out of my drawer. My body feels off-kilter, like the earth decided to adjust its axis out of nowhere. I'm going to fall if I don't lie down ASAP.

Nattie goes to grab Mom while Higgins lies on my feet, making sure I don't lose my balance.

I can't stop thinking about Maverick as I change, lie down, and try to fall asleep. Pain sears behind my eyeballs, deep between my brain and spinal cord. I can't stop worrying about him. He's my best friend and genuinely cares about his autistic brother; therefore, I thought he genuinely cared about me. I got a phone just so I could communicate with him every day. He wouldn't stop after weeks of texting, would he? Was this all part of the secret he wanted to tell me before, but I wouldn't let him? Was "Denver Maverick," aka his dark side, taking over once again?

I should stop worrying about him when he probably isn't thinking about me at all.

Higgins lays his entire body on me, forcing pressure therapy on me to keep the itches from spiraling out of control. His wet nose occasionally nudges my face, assuring me he's still there, as if the eighty pounds of smelly animal on my body didn't already tell me that.

I indulge in some WorldVid on my phone. After a few minutes of mindless scrolling, I discover a girl named Leilani who guides me through an ASMR session accompanied by some new age music. *Try not to focus on all the noise. You don't have to eat the yucky food if you don't want to. Try to not take in other people's stresses and negative energy today...*

The videos do help, but then I slip into something else entirely.

My heavy ball gown tugs on my chest, threatening to expose my breasts to the entire court. I straighten my extravagant wig decorated with glittering trinkets. My breath catches in my corset, and my lower back stings, a sign I have eaten too much. Everything on the grand table appeared so delectable, I couldn't help but sneak in a few extra bites. Candied tarts with icing that melt on my tongue with a hint of raspberry tang at the back of my throat, custard that slid down my gullet happily, and smooth rice pudding ripe for taste testing.

The court is doused in firelight, the orchestra plays merrily with hundreds of patrons dancing along. I've never seen such a slew of bright colors weaving together as I do from the spectacular show of the attendees' wardrobes.

Handsome suitor after handsome suitor fills up my dance

card, though I know it's out of obligation to try to court the princess rather than interest in my looks or personality. Only one catches my attention, the one with the striking eyes.

After several dances with pleasant young men trying so hard to impress me, I'm perspiring buckets under my wig. I say a silent prayer that my heavy cologne will cover the stench by the time the blue-eyed stranger reaches his hand out for mine. His stare is mesmerizing, I dare not look away.

I am simply swept away by his gaze, his strong stature, and the music carrying me away to a fantasy that is surely just a dream.

"What is your name?" my cranberry-red lips ask him.

He says nothing as he leads me around in a ceremonial dance.

"What is your status at the court? Is your father a devoted patron?" I continue.

Silence. He stares at me hungrily, as if he wants to say something but dares not to. His eyes envelop me, wholly inviting me in toward his pools of bright blue. I see my heavily made-up reflection in them, like sea glass.

The music speeds up, the orchestra struggling hard to keep up with the overly-enthusiastic conductor. The hundreds of patrons begin laughing at God knows what, as the magnificent ballroom starts to swirl like a painting melting in a sweltering oven. The mysterious suitor spins me round and round, and I long to be done so I can vomit into a bush in the nearby gardens.

Finally, my handmaiden grasps the suitor's arm and flings it away, carrying my weight upon her side and walking me away from the festivities.

CHAPTER 20

THERE'S a message from an unknown number.

My heart leaps into my throat and pounds. Thanksgiving went about as smoothly as possible. I even got through pampering with Nattie without any meltdowns. For the first time in days, I'm calm, watching a movie with everyone. Then this happens and my nerves shoot out my fingertips and toes.

I swipe my phone open and find a lengthy message.

> Unknown: Dinah, sorry. My dad took my phone as soon as we landed. He's drunk, so I snuck into his office to get a message from his phone to my mom and you. He's trying to file for custody, an amendment to their divorce that would keep us here. He took the paperwork to court yesterday and told us we can't be out of state while it's processing. It could take months. I'm so worried for Felix

> Don't worry about me. I turn eighteen soon
> —January. I won't be in his control any
> longer then, but we need to fight the
> courts for Felix

My world has turned upside down. Everything Nattie did for me today crumbles into a heap of broken dreams. It takes a minute for me to distinguish who is screaming—me or the girl who is trapped in the world of glass.

Trish comes over in a flood of tears an hour later. Sherri went to the airport straightaway to get on the next flight she could to get to the boys. Kurt is taking my vitals and making sure I'm not about to have a syncopal episode and pass out. Higgins is flustered with everyone distressed being in one room. While Maverick is my best friend, my mom, Trish, and Sherri have all become friends too.

Mom holds Trish, letting her cry on her shoulder, her beautiful black hair soaking from the sobs. Nattie clutches a mug of eggnog in one black-painted-fingernail hand, staring into the fireplace, speechless. Dad has no idea who the Wrights are, but he soon gathers they are important to us. I'm not sure if he has figured out just how important Maverick is to me.

"I have nobody here now but you, Meredith," Trish cries. She keeps switching topics and conversations, unable to hold it together. "He's so emotionally abusive toward them. Maverick fights back. But Felix, poor Felix... and Maverick had such bad friends..."

I'm numb. I feel like I'm cold and dead on a slab in the

morgue, though Kurt has a blanket over my shoulders. Higgins makes the rounds to my lap after trying to comfort everyone else.

My brain cannot physically process this sudden change. I know there is a text, Maverick is in distress, Felix is in danger, and there is no return date for either of them.

Nattie keeps trying to catch my eye. I will not meet her gaze, though, I do feel it searing like she has laser vision. Kurt pumps up a blood pressure cuff on my left arm every ten minutes, which I think is overkill, but whatever. I can't feel the tightness of it, nor the sweet release of the pressure. I can barely register the blanket on my shoulders. All I really feel is a black hole formulating in my stomach as my heart drops inside.

Dad removes himself from the conversation and gestures for Nattie and me to do the same. Dad saunters toward the guest bedroom, but Nattie and I stroll into the hallway, both of our brains on the same wavelength.

It's time to eavesdrop. I stay by the corner and listen in.

"I don't know how he got this case filed with several CPS files open on him." Trish sniffs. "If Felix is without his therapy schedule, he'll cry all day. And Maverick has a record. He had to do ten days in juvenile detention before Sherri left that bastard. I'm so worried his old friends will come around again."

"Oh no," Mom replies, fatigue heavy in her voice.

"Yes. Drugs, alcohol, girls, and parties at such a young age," Trish mumbles.

My chest is struck by a battering ram.

If Mom knew how close Maverick and I have become, that we might have become more than friends, she'd freak out. If she ever found out Maverick was a troubled boy who moved away from his problems to find a second chance at some success in his life, there would be no way she would ever allow me to ride his motorcycle, let alone date him. She might not even let me see him.

I peer at Nattie, who's unfazed and probably texting her friends this gossip. I may not be able to completely comprehend empathy, but that sure isn't it.

I turn around and walk to my room, shoving my sister out of my way. Higgins is still busy comforting Trish.

Closing my door and locking it tight, I slump on the other side of the door. I can't help but slide to the floor and wrap myself in my blanket.

I'm immature, inexperienced, and foolish to think Maverick was going to care enough to want to be with me. He is a bad boy with a motorcycle, plenty of sexual experience, and has partied enough to get drunk without throwing up. I can feel it. He tried to tell me in the van after our date, but I ran away.

I shrug off my blanket and begin to rock back and forth on my tailbone, trying to shake the terrible thoughts out of my head. He's kissed other girls with the lips I kissed. I try not to think of Maverick kissing someone else, let alone being naked with another girl. Touching each other, taking each other in, warming each other with their tangled bodies. My stomach writhes at the thought. I dry heave several times.

Meltdowns usually entail crying and screaming.

There's no screaming present this time, besides internally. Tears flow down my face.

My lizard brain wants to run. It wants to run barefoot through the icy slush onto the black ice that bombards the streets of Milwaukee. It wants to carry my feet through downtown, over the barriers, and to the beaches of Lake Michigan where the icy depths would be a welcome friend to accompany my numbness. I want to sink to subzero temperatures so I'm frozen from feeling anything.

I knew having close friends would only bring me heartache. For once, someone wasn't making fun of me, keeping their distance from me, or bullying me. He was caring, funny, interested in what I had to say, and *wanted* to know me.

Now he's over a thousand miles away for the foreseeable future. Maverick's old friends will probably be happy to see him, maybe even some girls he left behind too. I want to file away the thought of Maverick in the back of my brain like I do with other things, but that part of my brain seems to be out at lunch.

I collapse on the floor, my hair falling out of my onesie sloth pajamas, and stare at the ceiling dotted with soft lights. I think about that starry winter night when Maverick kissed me twice, the electricity that jolted through me, the out-of-body experience, the softness of his lips on mine. My chest contracts as my brain locks my heart behind a steel vault door, topped with a barbed wire. Maverick is far away and may never come back. The space behind my eyes fizzles and pops into complete emptiness, leaving my skull feeling hollow. My heels scoot back and forth on my carpet, causing some static hairs to float in front of my face. Then I touch my phone again. Shock.

I repeat this behavior for I don't know how many hours. For whatever reason, it keeps me breathing. It fuels my desire for stimulation and prolongs a meltdown about

Maverick, school, or basically anything else. Back and forth, back and forth, back and forth, shock. Itches. Buzzes. Speed up heart rate. Back and forth, back and forth, back and forth, shock. Bite my tongue. Hold my breath. Back and forth, back and forth, back and forth, shock.

Eventually, Higgins snores so loud he wakes himself up, like the golden retriever nut that he is. He notices I'm not in the bed with him, so his head pops up with concern, his eyes combing the room for me. I soon feel his teeth tug at the sleeve of my pajamas, begging me to come to bed. I can't move from this spot. This is where I'll live until I'm dragged off to school. This is my space. Nobody can make me move.

Eventually, Higgins gives up and goes wandering out my door that's slightly ajar. I throw a pillow at it to shut it, and fall into a fantasy.

As I pull my cloak around me tighter to protect my fair skin from the biting wind, dried-up dead roses crunch beneath my heels. I follow the hollow path of crackling petals my dead lover left for me eons ago. Mist hints at filling the air, bringing an eerie feeling down the path.

I lift my lantern and blow into it, my magic filling it with light to part the mists. Looking ahead, the rose petals seem to go on forever. My legs pick up speed as I sweat with sudden urgency. I hear his moans of pain, his cries for help never heard by another. His shrill, ghostly voice echoes off thick tree trunks enclosing me into the hollow.

"Dinaaah..." his voice whispers on the wind. The brisk cold slaps at my face and hair as I struggle to lift my lantern to head level. The air is so thick, it feels as though anvils are resting on my chest and limbs. It's getting difficult to breathe, each gasp for life threatening to be my last. My muscles

scream, *fighting against their very fibers. My bones seem to bend, warning that should I take another step, I could shatter into a thousand pieces.*

Tears fall freely from my eyes, freezing onto my cheeks. I know I'll never make it—I'll never be able to lift the curse I laid on him. Redemption is not in my stars. Our love story was not meant to be—a galaxy-crossed fate that would never end happily.

Hundreds of years ago, it seemed kinder to cast a curse that would enable him to forget me entirely than to try to pursue our love. The residual magic created this frozen hollow, trapping me in it and forcing me to live the rest of my days with him, but not with *him.*

It isn't long before someone comes to check in on me, but I'm surprised to see that it's my dad, who has Higgins in tow. I scoot my butt forward until the door can open to fit a grown man through.

"Long day, huh? You ready to get some sleep?" Dad asks.

I sigh through my nostrils as Higgins plops next to me, ready to snuggle.

"I brought your dog. The drama's over for now."

"Thanks, Dad."

He flips off the light, and the twinkly lights illuminate us. He's about to leave the room when I call for him. "Dad?"

"Yeah, honey?"

"I've been through a lot lately."

He nods like he's not sure what to say, but then agrees, "You sure have. I'm proud of you for how well you've handled everything."

"Really?" I sit up a little straighter.

"Oh, absolutely. I'm incredibly proud of your growth. I just wish I could be here to witness it all the time."

There's a short silence before I ask, "Do you?"

Dad kneels beside me, and I can hear his bones crackle. I can see his furrowed brow from my twinkly lights. "What do you mean by that?"

"Why'd you leave?" I ask. Blunt. Right to the point. I thrust the dagger in, hoping to catch the kill. "I'm old enough now, Dad. I have a right to know."

He swallows a lump of courage to get him through the next sentence. Higgins is already breathing heavily, exhausted from the work he's done today.

"Was it me?" I whisper. I already experienced so much heartache in today—another difficult truth won't be that hard to take. I'll just add it to the accumulating pile of numbness.

Dad grabs my hand with both of his, the calluses on his hard-working hands are soothing to my skin. "Absolutely not, Dinah, it's a hundred percent not your fault."

"But did my diagnosis contribute?" I persevere. Every second between answers is like a mark on a dungeon wall I make with a shiv—long, drawn out, and heavy with intense effort. The tension is as thick as peanut butter, and normally I'd be escaping by now, but my eyes are fixated on my father's identical green ones.

"One thing you have to understand about being a grown-up, Dinah," he begins what sounds like a lecture, but I know the subject matter is deeper, like a layered dip, "is that there are constant stresses and responsibilities. Eight-hour work-days, bills to keep the lights on, medical insurance, and what-not. Maintaining a marriage and parenting while keeping everything at bay takes work. When you were diagnosed, we weren't sure how our lives were going to be from then on. We didn't know what to expect. Would you live to old age? Would you be able to be independent and live on your own? Would you still succeed even if all the intervention and therapy failed?"

I'm trying to uncover the unspoken rules about telling the truth. Figuring out how to socialize when everyone only tells half-truths or thirty percent of the truth is almost as hard as deciphering emotions. I stay silent but keep eye contact with Dad, who understands it's a big deal.

He continues, "While we were so worried about getting the right treatment for you, your mom and I drifted apart. With the added stress of your health, we forgot to take care of ourselves. We were short with each other after using up our patience each day."

So, it *was* my fault.

"I'm sorry," I whimper, another tear creeping into my duct when I thought I had cried it dry.

Dad wraps his strong arms around me, rocking me back and forth on his lap. The rhythm is soothing, but I still stain the front of his black shirt with my tears.

"This is what I'm getting at, Dinah. Yes, your diagnosis was hard. Your mom and I decided to put your health over our own marriage. That was my fault. I should've stepped up and took her out more, allowed her to pamper herself more while figuring out your meltdowns and routines. I should've handled the insurance claims, pet therapy bills, and everything so she could process everything healthily. In the end, her life was easier without me being around all the time. It absolutely is not your fault. I want you to understand this, honey. I love you more than anything in this world. You are unique, and there's nobody like you." Now Dad's tears contribute to the stains on his shirt.

I swallow hard, wondering if opening up to someone else in my family is a good idea. The numbness begins to fade, replaced with a temporary warmth. Dad's love for me seeps through the unfeeling to try to make me feel again.

Drained from emotional exhaustion, I can't remember when I fell asleep, but I know I did in my dad's arms. I'll deal with Maverick tomorrow, even if I have to convince myself to let him go.

This is the end of our friendship, or whatever it was. I can't handle thinking about him, no matter how badly I want to talk to him. The only cure is to cut off all contact. Even if I want to worry, it's not how I'll get over him.

CHAPTER 21

DESPITE SHERRI LANDING SAFELY in Denver, lawyering up, and staying with a friend—Maverick continues to be radio silent over the weeks ahead, straight into the last week of school before Christmas. It's apparent his dad still has complete control over his phone, and he either got caught or didn't dare try to reach out again. Trish keeps Mom in the loop—allegedly Maverick's dad had a few friends on the inside of the courts, including a lawyer buddy who is trying to help find loopholes and cut corners to gain control over the kids. He's slapping Sherri with mediation and other paperwork to keep her under duress. From what Mom understands, he claims that their divorce settlement included fifty-fifty custody, and moving to Wisconsin violated that order.

To keep me from hyper-focusing on the situation, Eliza and Jason both insisted I return to school as often as possible.

"Good morning, Dinah." Eliza sits on my bed. "Time to get ready."

I'm struck by a pang of annoyance that jolts down the front of my heart and fuels my adrenaline. "Fine, fine, fine, finefinefinefi-nah," I retort as I freefall backward onto my blankets.

"Well, if you're going to be a booger about it, maybe I won't give you this surprise," she teases, irritating my nerve endings. I hate surprises—mostly the frustration of my brain unable to figure out a mystery. My family has learned that you *do not* tease me about something I'm going to receive. Just gimme the damn thing.

I hate that I'm intrigued. Her last surprise made my Halloween costume a fantastic hit, and her execution was spectacular. No teasing whatsoever.

I ball my hands into fists and dig my fingernails into my palms in anticipation.

Eliza digs into her bag, her curls dancing across her face. She reemerges with a purple ball, which Higgins sniffs to make sure Eliza isn't handing me a keyless grenade.

I'm underwhelmed until she motions me to take it from her. I expect a rough texture, but it's soft and squishy. It takes the shape of my hand when I squeeze it and takes time to expand back to its original shape.

"It's a stress ball. For when you're feeling frustrated." Eliza smiles.

The steel wall I had put between Eliza and me seems to crumble, decimating quickly down to a pillar of ash, which almost fills the Jenny-shaped hole in my heart.

Molasses-thick emotional tension fills the air, as if super magnets are pulling me toward Eliza, and my body is no longer under my jurisdiction. My arms outstretch automatically, and I clasp my hands around her neck, finding her skin smooth and chilly. Her arms reciprocate the hug and hold me at the perfect pressure, not suffocation tight, not carelessly cautious. It's the way Jenny hugs.

A silent tear streams down my face. "I'm scared," I whisper.

I'm always on edge. The meds make me jumpy. I'm hormonal and emotionally unstable.

But I don't want to be.

I think I catch Eliza off guard with the first hug I've ever offered her because she says nothing for a beat before finally replying, "You can do anything, Dinah."

A few moments later, we break apart and she gives me space to get out of bed. My room is still bathed in soft twinkly lights, like a fairy hollow. I get out of bed and retreat to my love seat, my brain whirring too fast. I open the Eliza folder in my brain, flip through all the negative things about her, and surprisingly, add a positive.

I stride into the bathroom, ready to try to shower. I can do this, or at least try to.

Andrew was so excited that I was back to play *Thelena's Wrath* with him, he nearly peed himself. Higgins got loads of extra good-boy pets for being absent. He was lapping up the attention like spilled milk on the kitchen floor. He tried to behave himself, but I found myself tugging on his leash a lot more than usual to remind him to do his duty.

It's a new week, so I hope I can be a new me.

English, my absolute favorite class, quickly becomes unbearable. To see Maverick's empty seat next to mine, on a daily basis, kills me inside. I try not to look at it to the point where Higgins has to keep pressure on my lap the whole time to maintain the "green zone."

These past few weeks, Eliza taught me a new system to help me cope with lizard brain. It's called "the zones of regulation," and its color coordinated to my mood. Being in the green zone means I'm feeling great, no itches or buzzes. The yellow zone means I'm beginning to feel uncomfortable—emotions are rising, and I'm not sure if I'm going to be able to control a meltdown that's on the horizon. The yellow zone is my in-between, where I watch WorldVid videos, read a book, squeeze my stress ball, or get close to Higgins. Then there's the dreaded red zone—I've lost control, my senses have lost all reason, and I'm unable to calm down without help. I really like the zones of regulation because something as simple as color coding is easier to understand where I'm at and if I need to ask for help.

The anxiety medications are well and good, and so are my aides, but I can't help but feel angry that I'm not able to express how I feel.

What if I feel out of control? Just let me thrash and cry.

A best friend came into my life and then went, like a match burnt too bright. Far too quickly.

I think that deserves some grief.

I can't help that I'm wired the way I am or that my brain is constantly going *what if, what if, what if.*

I'm angry. I'm sad. I'm devastated. I'm confused. I'm treated like a baby. I'm unable to act my age.

Higgins begins to brush his paw against my skin, his cold toe beans begging me to stay calm. His soothing, rhythmic motions allow me to forgive and forget and to give no heed to my thoughts.

A faint buzz sounds from my phone again and again. I ignore them.

Until lunchtime that is.

Swiping my phone open, I exhale bittersweet disappointment upon seeing Jenny's text message.

> Jenny: I'm thinking of you Dinah! I miss you!

I send a red heart emoji back in response.

A heart emoji. The last genuine thing Maverick sent to me before his dad took his phone away. Next to the Jenny-shaped hole in my heart that is under construction is a massive, Maverick-shaped one. It's hard to forget him. I never thought I'd have so many emotions for one dumb boy.

I haven't written to Maverick for weeks now. The shocks assume control of my limbs and I open our text message chain.

> Me: I'm getting on my own nerves without you, lol

It doesn't feel like enough. My feelings are set off like a rocket breaking through the stratosphere, the momentum impossible to extinguish.

> Me: You once said that our friendship wasn't for brownie points in heaven. How do I know the legitimacy of your kiss, when your lips were on plenty of other girls' lips according to your stepmom? I want to talk. I want to write notes in class and figure this out. I can't wrap my head around you, in fear that my mind will explode. I hope you'll be back soon.

I think about ending my message here, but to end it on a lighthearted note, I text:

> If you don't hear from me after tomorrow, I've run away to the forest.

I hit send, a shock shooting through my index finger as I lay my phone back down.

Am I the redemption arc in Maverick's fantasy story of his life, or is he mine? I certainly don't need saving. I'm my own person, albeit one who has autism. Do I need some help figuring out the unspoken rules of society? Absolutely. A knight in shining armor? No way.

I just want my best friend back.

My safe place becomes more morbid by the end of the school day. Here's to hoping the next day gets better.

It doesn't.

My back is a hot mess of crackles and pops when I wake up on the floor.

Not a good way to start the day.

A louder-than-usual knock sounds at my door.

"Mom wants me to remind you to get in the shower and get ready, or something like that," Nattie's annoyed voice calls through the woodwork.

"Nooo!" I yell back more grumpily than I should.

"She doesn't feel good and has an article due today so hurry up, you turd!"

Today is cursed. I slept horribly, my back is broken, my hormones are everywhere, and the schedule is already off.

I respond by throwing the stuffed Higgins Jenny gave me at the door, resulting in a loud bang followed by Nattie's yelling, "Mooomm! Dinah is being a brat."

Our holiday sisterly love didn't last long. Maybe it'll make another appearance at Christmas.

I roll over with full intention to climb back into bed and pretend this day is already over. When I climb to my knees, a blinking light catches my eye.

My phone has several new messages. I lunge for it, swiping it open to see I have over nine texts. They're all from Maverick.

Something comes swimming back to me—stimming, anxiety attack, the texts I sent.

Oh no.

Swallowing a gallon of saliva into my dry throat, I tap open the texts and begin to read furiously.

> Maverick: I couldn't sleep, so I wandered the house in search of my phone's new hiding place. At first, I was glad I found it, but now I wish it would've stayed hidden. My heart hurts knowing you feel this way

> I'm sorry I'm not there for you. It's beyond my control, which I know you understand. If I could, I would teleport there to help you through this scary time

There's about an hour's difference between the first two messages and the next ones. I wonder if Maverick went back to bed because he heard his dad waking up, or spent the next hour trying to figure out what else he wanted to say to me.

> Maverick: In case you haven't figured it out, Mom coming out to us was not easy. Dad took it extremely hard and hit the alcoholic button faster than a fighter jet. He always was a hothead, but hitting Felix was the last straw. We moved out, Mom met Trish, and I channeled my teenage angst into terrible decisions

> I tried to tell you what I used to be. When we finally got away from my dad, I was determined to have a second chance at life, start over, and redeem myself. It's freeing, moving somewhere where nobody knows who you are or what's in your past. I promised myself I'd be a better person for Felix

I freeze in shock. My heart is a giant pincushion, a thousand sharp points sticking into it, each puncture wound inflicts a different emotion. With each pump of blood, the pins float with it, sending the prickly sensation throughout my body.

Maverick's dad hit Felix. Maverick acted out against all the change in his life. If I didn't know any better, I would say that he acted exactly like me when things don't go as I plan them to. Only instead of partying, drinking, and going out with all sorts of people, I simply explode with emotions and throw things.

I wonder if that's a huge difference between atypical and

neurotypical people. I can be impulsive, but it rarely involves other people. Being invited to a party would require the social skills that are agreeable and engaging to those around me. Maverick is charming, I bet he can talk his way out of, or into, almost anything.

> Maverick: Dinah, you drew me in like a magnet. Not because you were a damsel in distress that needed saving or as a chance for me to prove myself as a better man. It was your focus, your love of reading, your imaginary places, and the love you have for your dog. I wanted all of that

> I think about you every damn day, about how us not coming back is affecting your schedule, how I can't give you a Christmas present in person, how you're going through meltdowns and I'm not there. It's killing me

My feet tap nervously under my blankets. Higgins notices the strange movement of the cloth and perks his ears up, watching me intently. He lays a fluffy paw on my chest, prepared for anything. It isn't long before my feet are sweaty.

> Maverick: I'm sorry if I hurt you. You didn't know me back then. Hell, I didn't know me. I lost my best friend Jake over a stupid argument while I was drunk and high on coke. I'm sure Trish told you about juvie too. It was no cakewalk

My mind races back to the Halloween fundraiser cakewalk and how I didn't participate in it before my freak-out. I don't understand the comparison, so I shrug it off as a figure of speech and move on.

> Maverick: My kiss was legitimate. Just thinking about seeing Kingdom Delivered with you makes me smile

My chest awakens, butterflies bursting through the steel door surrounding my insides. They aren't just fluttering; they're soaring atop the slipstream, not planning on coming down to earth anytime soon.

> Maverick: I haven't heard from you, so I guess you did run away. Awesome

The prickly blood rushes to my head as I sit up quickly, almost throwing up. I type frantically, not caring for once about proper spelling or grammar.

> Me: Maverick, I'm glad you're all right. I'm alive. Didn't run away. Thank you for ezplaininh everythinh. I don't mean to be paranoid, I'm kust worried about you and Felix. I hope you can come home soon. I feel the same way abrt Kingdom Deliveref.

I hit send before proofreading.

Wow.

I hope he can decipher everything.

I wait for ten minutes just to see if his phone is still in his possession, but no dancing dots appear at the bottom of the screen.

I hope I hear from him soon, so I know he's okay. His dad's house sounds like a nightmare—a hothead that hits his autistic son and is keeping his kids hostage for Christmas. I hope Sherri can get the courts figured out quickly.

The butterflies and prickles mix to form flying prickles in my chest. My heart beats against my rib cage like a fist that wants to punch through a wall. I know what I have to do to avoid a meltdown. I bury my face into Higgins' fur and travel to my safe place as fast as possible.

CHAPTER 22

CHRISTMAS COMES and goes without so much as a word back from Maverick. My brain is now used to the idea that until he is back in Wisconsin, his texts will be information dumps with many days in between to play it safe with his dad.

I'm glad my family does most of the traditional holiday things but incorporates me so they aren't as overstimulating. Presents are opened in the morning by the firelight, one at a time with breaks in between so I'm not too overwhelmed. Kurt stayed home one night so my mom and Nattie could go out and see a movie on opening weekend—for which I was grateful. I wasn't up to big, last-minute schedule changes just yet, or probably ever.

The best Christmas present ever was a week to relax. Eliza went home to Green Bay to visit family, Mom submitted most of her articles ahead of time, and Kurt was on call for holiday emergencies, but the break from both school and therapy was nice.

The Friday before classes start up again, I have an

appointment scheduled with Jason. Mom has been careful to schedule the appointments around my ever-changing routine, and she figured I would need one after Christmas and before school began. Jason's visits have started to coincide with the awful "T" word—transitions.

"Are you transitioning well after the holidays?" Jason asks from behind the canvas. We found that painting is the best way to get things out of me and keep me calm during our sessions.

"To what?" I ask dully, dotting some cotton-candy pink in the fluffy cloud scene I'm concocting.

Higgins sneezes on Jason's shoes, and he recoils. I stifle a laugh from behind my painting.

"Well," his deep voice rumbles, "regular home life, I guess? How's life at home?" He shifts in his seat, composing himself after the nasty dog sneeze.

"Eliza's back after the holidays. We put a puzzle together, took turns picking WorldVid videos to watch, and played a game about interpreting emotions yesterday," I answer. I'm always drawn to the beautiful, metallic silver paint. I think Jason orders it for me, especially, to make sure it's always in stock.

"That's good. Is Eliza prepping you for your return to school?"

"Yeah." I can tell he wants more detailed answers. Maybe if I give him details, then I won't have to keep coming here so often.

"Okay. Are you having any more nightmares?"

This particular question gives me pause. I'm having more unpleasant dreams about places that aren't as safe as I would like them to be.

I spread a happy yellow at the tips of the pink clouds. "More like... invasions of my safe place, making them seem wrong." I struggle to find the correct words for what I want to tell him.

"Would you like to tell me about them, Dinah?" Jason prods. Higgins glances up at me nervously when the itches begin. It's like my dog can sense when I don't want to press subjects further. My toes bounce in my shoes. I try to control my knees so they don't bump my canvas, but the buzzes are spinning out of control. I need to rock back and forth to make the air not so thick. It helps me think. The leather couch squeaks as I rock on my tailbone, and the easel makes a threatening jerk that prompts Jason to jump up and save it, gently putting it to the side.

Jason faces me, but I avoid his gaze. I don't want to see my reflection in his glasses or the concerned furrow in his dark brow.

"I can see you're heading into the yellow zone, Dinah," Jason says calmly. Eliza must've filled him in on the zones of regulation. Yellow and red zone are where my lizard brain fights, flights, or freezes.

I really don't want to fight or freeze, so I try to plot an escape out of Jason's office. Just then, Higgins sits on my feet and lays his paws on my thighs, inviting me to grab his fur. I oblige with my left hand.

Jason lets me rock and smell Higgins' freshly washed, lavender-scented coat of fluff. After a few deep breaths, the rocking stops, but my toes are still bouncing. I try to steady my shaking right hand that is holding my brush—sending a few silver paint drops falling like heavy snow onto the carpet.

"Take your time and breathe, Dinah. If you need to talk, breathe deeply first." Jason talks me through my escalating emotions.

I breathe as slowly as I can in my hyperventilation state. Blood pounds in my ears as the backup singers to my hammering heart. Somehow, I'm able to get some oxygen in my nostrils and down to my lungs, which results in a heap of backed-up word vomit.

"Maverick is trapped in Colorado and turns eighteen this month. I don't know if he'll come back here or if his dad will keep Felix and him hostage. But since he's been gone, he's been showing up as the villain in my safe places, and it makes me insane to think that he's kissed someone else before he met me and has had a stint in juvie. It's all too much."

Wheeew.

Higgins buries his face into my lap, shifting his weight, while Jason stares at me. I've involuntarily given more information to him than ever before in previous sessions.

Crap.

"Please don't tell my mom about this," I whisper, tears welling up in my eyes. Getting the words out helps the pounding in my ears, but my heart feels like I just sprinted a mile.

"About which part, Dinah? That was a lot to take in. I can understand why you're so anxious if you're holding feelings inside of you," Jason says coolly. I appreciate his bedside manner, but I want to make it perfectly clear that the doctor-patient confidentiality is respected in his office.

"Can this stay just between us?" I inquire cautiously, peering around the canvas to see his expression. Emotionless. Robotic. Poker face. Chocolate eyes baring into my soul.

"As long as there's no information that's bringing you direct harm, such as abuse or the like," he replies.

I take another deep breath through my nose, slowing my heart to a somewhat normal rhythm.

"The part where Maverick was in juvie," I whisper.

"And who is Maverick? The hero in your safe place?" he digs deeper, scooting to the edge of his seat to hear me properly.

I nod, adding, "Now he's the villain." My eyes dart to the small window on the far wall, encrusted in a beautiful frost on the outside. My left fingers are still rubbing golden retriever fur. My toes are still bouncing in my shoes. My right hand has found a place to set the brush down and has joined my other hand in the ritual of clutching onto Higgins' fur.

Jason leans back and crosses one leg over the other, exposing his hipster-like moccasins that are totally impractical for the winter weather outside. I guess since he's an independent adult, he could wear a thin bathrobe and bunny slippers in the snow, and no one would say boo.

"To be honest, Dinah, it's not the worst teenage drama I've ever heard." He grins, his extra white teeth shining across the room. "While your feelings are completely valid, I'm proud of you for accepting some social emotional normality and expressing your emotions in a healthy way."

My brain takes a minute to catch up to what Jason's trying to say. It doesn't help that Higgins' bushy tail is pummeling the floor in a rhythmic beat.

"You're... glad I got my heart broken?" I conclude, blinking in disbelief.

"No, not glad. I'm proud, that's different. Your feelings are a victory of the emotional range you're expressing. It's normal. Concerns like these are things almost every teenager goes through." Jason nods as he clasps his fingers together.

The teeth in the back of my mouth grind together. Jenny's lessons of etiquette are clashing with her lessons of authenticity, and I can only choose one to focus on. I struggle for a few seconds, then pick one and roll with it. Authenticity it is.

"I feel deeper than almost any other person," I start, my hands balling into fists full of dog hair. "I hear things louder than other people. Life exhausts me. Change crumbles me. So, don't presume my feelings are normal or act like I'm turning into a normal teenager," I scold him, determined to put the so-called professional in his place. He may put a canvas in front of me to act as a confessional, but I'll be damned before this hippie-wannabe therapist tries to understand the whirlwind that is me.

"Dinah, I said your feelings are valid—" he tries to interject.

"Which is a fancy way of saying, 'Hey! You're normal! You're neurotypical! You don't need Medicaid. You don't need your service dog. Since you're normal, why can't you follow everyone's conversations quickly? Why do you need someone to tell you multiple times how to do a simple task? You should understand your school assignments perfectly!'"

I stand so quickly, Higgins falls off my lap and crashes into the easel, sending my poor excuse for a painting flying to the ground. I grab my dog's leash and stride to the door.

My ears ring with a high-pitched sound, as if I've blown a circuit in my head's computer. There is nothing in my brain besides the van and getting into it. All of life's other details are blurry while I hyperfocus on my escape, determined to get away from Jason's ableism.

I head straight for safety, passing Mom in the hallway. Luckily she left the van unlocked, so I sit and wait for her inevitable face of disappointment to join me. I invite Higgins to sit on my lap and provide therapeutic pressure, but he hesitates. I look around to see what I'm possibly forgetting before realizing he's waiting for me to put my seat belt on. Mr. Furry Smartypants.

It isn't long before Mom walks out of the building toward the van. I chuckle while the Lake Michigan wind blows her hair straight into her face. She doesn't look embarrassed or upset; instead, she looks calm, which throws me for a loop. She enters the driver's seat and looks back at me with a smile on her face.

"Therapy went great, I see?" she says. I can't quite read her mood. Either she is about to break down and cry, or she's holding back laughter.

I squint at her as if that will help me interpret her facial expression better. Higgins' tail beats against the passenger seat in the few seconds of awkward silence.

Then Mom bursts out laughing.

At first it scares me enough to make me jump. If Higgins hadn't been on me, I might've flown through the roof of the van. Mom, still snickering, passes me back my headphones. I left in such a hurry that I forgot I didn't have them on me.

Mom lets out a dramatic sigh as she turns the key and puts the van in reverse. She's still smiling as she shakes her head and says, "Looks like we need to have a talk with this psychotherapist!"

I stare down at my boots. This situation feels like the time I was six and I got kicked out of ballet classes. Well, I wasn't really kicked out. The teacher asked Mom to "find another activity" for me. My ballet teacher couldn't handle my emotional outbursts when I didn't get a move quite right —apparently, I was disrupting the class too often.

I tug on Higgins' fur in anticipation.

"I yelled at him. It sounds like he's got a lot of work to do on himself. And if he ends up not being what you need, we will look for another therapist for you, no problem." Mom says all this as cool as a cucumber.

My anxiety melts away instantly, my heart filling with a warm appreciation for my mother. Sometimes she gets frustrated with me, I have no doubt about that. After all we've been through, it feels so good to know I have someone in my corner.

CHAPTER 23

ELIZA IS surprised on Monday morning when I'm ready and willing to go to school. I'm not feeling depressed for the first time in weeks, and I've convinced myself that trying to embrace change will be worthwhile. Getting my feelings out, even though it was rough in Jason's office, and having Mom fight for me made this morning different.

My nerves are on edge, so I keep a tight hold of Higgins to help me through it. Mr. Peterson is pleasantly surprised when I play *Thelena's Wrath* fairly, resulting in Andrew's triumph for the first time this school year.

I grab my headphones just as he realizes he won. He cheers at the top of his lungs and runs a victory lap around the classroom.

Andrew yells a slew of triumphant profanity. A contagious smile grows on his face. The rest of the room gasps— one aide is particularly red in the face. Mr. Peterson jumps up and holds Andrew's shoulders to help him calm down and explains that nobody should use that sort of language in the classroom, no matter how many months they have been trying to win. He says this sternly, but I could tell he was trying his hardest not to laugh.

When I'm not in the classroom, I visit the library to keep my mind off of Maverick and Felix. On one particular trip with Eliza, I see a poster at the front desk that says they are looking for volunteers. While checking out the books, I give myself the itches by talking to a stranger—the librarian.

I glance around and then ask, "What do volunteers do?"

"Oh." The librarian jumps a little at someone suddenly speaking but then smiles. "Hello. We just need some help putting returned books back on the shelves, organizing new displays, those sorts of things." Her black curls bounce as she nods.

That sounds like fun. It's routine, and I get to spend time with tons of books. I might try it. Eliza nods nonstop, seeing me move out of my comfort zone. She's so eager, she practically signs up herself to be a volunteer on one Saturday a month next to my name.

As a sidebar to my tumultuous love life, seniors at school have been talking about graduation. I don't see what the big deal is, other than I've completed twelve long years of homework, singing, and games in the disability classroom—plus or minus some regular classes sprinkled throughout. I'll be glad to not have anything to do all day, but thinking about not having an eight-hour schedule every day does give me the itches.

Eliza and my parents have been discussing what to do once I turn eighteen next month.

Do I want to go to college? I don't think so. Too many people. Too much noise. Too much independence. I'm not ready. Now if the people were books, that'd be a different story.

Do I want to work toward living independently? I mean, sure. I can't rely on Mom, Kurt, and Dad for the rest of my life. What will I do when they die? I can't play video games every second of every day.

I don't want to hyperfocus on those thoughts. I'll cry myself into a meltdown.

I want to be up for improving myself, but it's getting past the itches and the subsequent panic attacks that are the looming dragons in the corner of the cave.

The day flies by with thoughts on top of thoughts.

As I stim in bed at night, I watch one of my favorite creators, Leilani, talk about her WorldVid career and why it's the perfect one for her.

Maybe *I* could do that? It's basically staring at a recording device in the comfort of my own room.

The only hard question is what I would even talk about. What talents do I even possess?

I inhale deeply and imagine what it would be like to have lots of people listening and learning from *me*.

The thought overtakes me overnight and into the next morning.

I look at myself in the mirror, smiling as if it's a camera. I start with a "hello" and "welcome to my universe." Then I giggle because it sounds silly talking to a bunch of strangers.

I've had a lot of good days in a row, and I think it's because I'm growing comfortable with different types of stimuli. I want to try this—something a little different than my usual habit of escape. Maybe it has something to do with the relief of having Christmas vacation over with? Perhaps it's that I go to sleep to cello music instead of white noise? Whatever it is, something is different, and I like it.

The rest of the week, I write different scripts for my introduction video. I have to figure out the number of words, the appropriate tone, pitch, facial expressions, and duration.

Meltdowns are nonexistent throughout February, and I don't worry about whether Maverick is coming back anytime soon. My focus has shifted to imaginings of me as a queen on top of a video throne.

In between my career-planning thoughts, I had sky-high hopes I would hear from Maverick at some point, but we heard from Sherri instead. She and her lawyer are fighting the court order, citing obstruction of justice and neglect, which sounds serious to me. I think about Maverick and how free he must be feeling knowing he is no longer under his dad's jurisdiction. I imagine him on his motorcycle, smiling and riding away into the sunset. He probably hasn't been smiling much lately. I frown as I think about Felix and how worried Maverick and his moms are about him. That morbid thought leads me down a path where I think about what a douche nozzle Maverick and Felix's dad is. I really wish I had a solid confirmation that everything is okay with everyone.

Nattie and I have a good talk one chilly Saturday in March about it all.

"I can't worry about things that are out of my control, I guess. What can I do about them, anyways?" I ask her.

She paints her nails neon green with sparkles. The unpleasant fumes sting my nose. She blows on her nails to help dry the polish faster. "Probably a lot healthier than complaining about it every day."

I don't know what to make of her comment or whether it was helpful at all.

I sit on my love seat with Higgins in my lap, running my fingers through his soft coat. Petting him helps me think.

I try to slowly piece together exactly what I'm feeling.

Is it relief? It's more like a heaping bowl of confusion mixed with a dash of relief, a pinch of fear, and a sprinkle of bittersweet.

Or is it hope? Now that Maverick is eighteen and no longer has the burden of his record as a minor, will he return? Will we pick up right where we left off, or have both of our lives changed too much?

No. He'd never leave Felix.

As for my sudden awareness of my more-than-friendly feelings for Maverick, I sigh. I allowed myself to dive too deep and prevented my heart from locking down. It flew out of my chest and gave itself to Maverick freely, all without me realizing it. I'm not even sure when I gave my heart to him, but it was probably around the time when he became the villain in my safe places. It was a defense mechanism that was trying to protect me.

Well, that plan backfired spectacularly.

A knock sounds at my door, and before I can say, "Come in," Mom pokes her head into my room. I hate it when she does that. The itches are about to tingle my spinal cord, but I tell them to back off through my brainwaves.

"Is there a pampering party going on in here?" she asks, inviting herself into my room.

Higgins bounds off of the love seat and out the door without hesitation. Apparently, he has important business to attend to that cannot wait.

"Not really, what's up?" Nattie answers for me. It's my room, feel free to use it as a communal area or whatever. No need to respect my privacy.

"It's Kurt's birthday, and I thought someone could help me make the cake?"

Nattie says no because she's doing her nails, but I don't mind. I actually like leveling the flour to the precise tip of the measuring cup, ensuring the recipe is followed to a T.

Someone's in the kitchen with Di-nah.

Someone's in the kitchen I know.

Someone's in the kitchen with Di-nah.

Strummin' that old banjo.

Mom is careful to let me measure and dump the dry ingredients in when they're needed; then she does the messy stuff like crack the eggs and roll the fondant. She's a talented baker—it's one of her many hobbies, like writing. Kurt's cake is going to be a red heart with a pulse line in white icing.

In the middle of kneading the fondant, Mom's phone rings.

She nods her head at me. "Dinah, could you?"

I don't know if she wants me to answer it for her or put it on speakerphone. It's Sherri and I want to hear every update there is to hear. I tap the answer button, put it on speaker, and set it down on the counter, bouncing on my feet.

Please tell us there's good news.

"Hello?" Mom flusters, flyaway hairs falling onto her face while she continues kneading.

"Meredith, it's Sherri," a frantic voice pipes through the phone. She sounds like she's being trampled in a mosh pit at a concert. The sound is so disturbing I run to grab my headphones off the hook, nearly tripping over Higgins who is lying on the tile floor, sprawled out lazily on his back.

Mom bends closer to the phone on the counter. "Sherri? What's going on? Are you okay?"

Sherri's voice blends in with the background noise. It's giving me a headache behind my eyes, even though I'm smushing my headphones on my ears extra tightly. I can only make out a few words of her response.

"At the airport... home... charges... Maverick... for Felix..."

"Sherri, hun, I can barely hear you." Mom picks the phone up with a greasy hand.

I overhear Felix screaming. My anxiety spikes for the first time in weeks. Then I pick up a voice that makes my heart leap into my throat.

"We'll call you when we land!" Maverick's voice comes through loudly and clearly, as if the phone is so close to his mouth that he could eat it.

"Have a safe flight," Mom choruses, unable to contain her excitement.

When the call ends, Mom and I beam at each other.

"They're coming home?" I ask. An unfamiliar feeling rises in my chest. I identify it immediately as optimism. My heart leaps through the ceiling and dances among the clouds.

"It sure sounds like it. They were definitely at the airport. I think Sherri said something about the case charges, maybe they've been dropped?" Mom guesses, returning to knead the fondant. "Do you think they'd come over for Kurt's birthday tonight and have cake with us? I'll text Trish while the fondant chills."

Tonight?

After months of not seeing him, or hearing him, and barely texting him, I'll see Maverick tonight? I'm not ready one bit. How does one prepare for the return of their best friend in a few short hours?

I spent these past months getting so used to change, I didn't anticipate any old change revisiting for a second round. The soles of my feet have magically changed to wheels as I escape the kitchen as fast as I can. I swear I jump a ten-yard leap that would get me a medal in track from my door to my bed. I twist my blankets between my toes, trying to get a stim going. Lizard brain definitely wins over this situation, but I must figure out how to get rid of it before the Wrights make their way over for cake tonight.

While Mom finishes the cake and tidies up in the kitchen, I group text Jenny and Eliza for advice. I quickly summarize a text encompassing my feelings.

> Me: MAVERICK IS COMING BACK AFTER MONTHS AWAY AND I DON'T KNOW HOW TO DEAL WITH MYSELF I LOOK LIKE A MESS WHAT DO I DOOOOOOO

Completely out of character, Eliza answers while Jenny is MIA. One calm response text later.

> Eliza: With all you've accomplished this year, I have complete faith in you!!

I decide to get up and take a shower. I steal one of my sister's special, soft conditioning masks for my hair so that it's silky smooth. In a heat of panic, I wash up faster than I can process and before I know it, I'm drying myself off.

I cover up an unsightly pimple on my left cheek and recruit Nattie's help for some fierce, dramatic eyeliner.

I get more than I bargained for when she goes into full makeover mode.

"I don't know why you're making such a fuss if he's just a friend," Nattie mutters.

I remain silent, unable to interpret Nattie's whirlwind of attitude.

"Did he kiss you or something?" she persists.

My lips are sealed, but blood rushes to my face.

"Shut the hell up," my little sister scolds while applying blush to my cheeks. "No way! He likes you. This is so cute and so disgusting."

"He might like me, but I want to be careful. I'm still having a hard time trusting him after..." I can't finish that sentence.

Nattie swarms my head in a cloud of heat protector spray. Higgins sneezes about fourteen times beneath my vanity chair.

I look in the mirror and barely recognize myself, but at least I'm presentable for visitors. I'm not just getting dolled up for Maverick. It is Kurt's birthday after all.

That is what I keep telling myself, anyways.

I pick out my sparkly leggings that my mom got me from an internet website designed specifically for people with sensory issues. They're one of my favorite pairs because they're so soft on the inside. While the weather has slowly warmed, living in Wisconsin my entire life has prepared me for a freak snowstorm or two before spring is officially here.

I can't be too careful.

I pick out a lavender hoodie with bright yellow tie-strings.

I'm so wound up that Nattie volunteers to go on a walk with me. This is suspiciously out of character for her. I narrow my eyes when she grabs Higgins' harness and leash while I tie up my shoes.

I snatch a granola bar to combat my low blood sugar and high anxiety combo. After I finish the verse of my must-sing-in-the-kitchen song, we're out the door.

Nattie holds the leash. I skip down the sidewalk, admiring the melting snow and springing flowers—tulips and daffodils that bloom too soon every year. Their petals sparkle with hope, but their evolutionary need to be first is always their downfall. There's almost always a late-spring snow-storm that takes them out in Wisconsin.

I try to take deep, steadying breaths while walking toward the park, but my heart is pounding against my rib cage, trying to break out. Nattie slides her free hand into mine, which is a huge deal since she's always clutching her phone. This simple gesture fills my chest with love, like a depleted battery filling up on juice.

"You charge my batteries," I say to Nattie before I can stop myself.

She giggles and shakes her head. "You're such a weirdo."

"Higgins does it too, but in a different way," I add. I can tell I'm overstimulated by the way I'm talking. Sometimes when I get too excited about something, Jenny says, I speak in a more childlike way. Simple and to the point, but not as mature. I can't help it though.

I'm so ready to see my best friend for the first time in months.

Time moves like a sloth. Even our fifteen minutes on the swings in the park go by painstakingly slow. With my headphones still on, I think about how my swinging back and forth is a lot like my life, there's no smooth sailing in the middle. After the thrill of the height from going up, I think I'm on my way back down to stabilizing, but instead I find myself swinging almost as far backward. The whirl of the wind through my eardrums is suddenly too much to handle.

If I could fly in silence, that would be *perfect*. I could take off from the velocity of the swing and keep going high enough until I decide where I want to go. Lots of books explain the sound of silence once you reach a certain height. I'd like to experience that one day if I can handle the flight up.

After a fierce twenty minutes, we gather Higgins' leash to head home. My phone dings, and I'm about to have a heart attack. Could it be Maverick?

It's Mom, telling us to come home. The Wrights are on their way over.

Higgins and I sprint down the street.

"You'll mess up your hair!" Nattie calls after me.

I don't care. I need to get back home before the Wrights arrive.

CHAPTER 24

TEN MINUTES and a restyling of my hair later, the doorbell rings. Higgins sits by the door without moving, having learned not to bark at the doorbell when he was a pup in service dog school.

Mom rushes forward, after also styling her hair to keep up the appearance that she isn't a hardworking mother of two with a job. She opens the door and gasps.

"Hello," she whispers, a hand up in front of her face. "Come on in, please. What an ordeal you must've been through." I can barely hear her through Felix's crying. I'm glad I have my headphones handy.

The Wrights walk through our front door, all four of them looking equally exhausted, Sherri most of all. She and Trish are holding hands so tightly, it's like they're handcuffed together. Trish, in her medical assistant scrubs, has her other arm around Felix, who's wearing his own pair of bright blue headphones. Maverick brings up the rear and looks straight at me. His hair is long enough to tuck behind his ears. The strands fall in his eyes.

Maverick sports two black eyes, scrapes along his fore-head, and a split lip with stitches. His right shoulder must be either recently broken or dislocated as it's in a sling, and he's visibly limping. I glance from Felix to Maverick several times, comparing notes. Felix doesn't have one scratch on him.

I assume the worst. My heart sinks like an anchor and crashes into the basement.

I don't rush forward and hug him like I thought I would; he seems too fragile for that. I focus on Maverick, and the world blurs around me.

Nearly losing my balance, I take a few steps back and fall on the couch. Higgins arrives in a split second to rescue me, of course. I clutch his fur in anticipation of what horror I'm about to hear in the coming minutes.

Mom gives Sherri a long hug. Maverick escorts Felix to the living room and helps him sit in the recliner. Felix's wet face soon lights up as he crosses his legs and rocks back and forth—a freedom he surely didn't have on the airplane.

Maverick and I avoid eye contact. When he catches me looking at him, I pretend to be interested in Felix's stimming. When I catch him looking at me, he quickly snaps his head around in a different direction.

My eyes start to itch from my lack of blinking. I don't want to miss a second in case seeing Maverick again isn't actually real. In case this is just another one of my daydreams.

"What happened?" Mom asks, still in shock.

Trish wanders over and sits by Felix while Sherri holds on to Mom's arms. I can't tell if it's for emotional or physical support. She looks absolutely drained, and I'm astonished she's able to get her neurons to synapse, let alone form words.

"The case was dropped. Shane was arrested. Domestic abuse." Sherri groans, her frame shaking. Tears trail down her face as she glances over towards Maverick.

"I'm fine," he mutters, stealing a quick glance at me and then averting his eyes to the floor.

"The six hours you spent in the emergency room says otherwise!" Sherri snaps.

"You've all been through hell. Sit down, take a load off. I'll make some tea while we wait for Kurt to get home." Mom leads Sherri to the love seat by the fireplace and strokes her hands. That method usually works on me, but I guess it works for distressed neurotypical people as well. Trish digs a manga book out of her purse for Felix.

"Do you want to sit down, Maverick?" Mom points to the empty seat next to me.

I gulp as quietly as possible. He shakes his head and keeps a hand on Felix's shoulder, letting him know he's there, even though his little brother is fully immersed in a book. I can't imagine what they have been through in the past few months, let alone the past twenty-four hours. I long to know, but at the same time, I fear the truth.

After abandoning me for a few minutes, my brain returns home to my skull. The familiar buzzes are there, accompanied by loud ringing in my ears. A sheet of water covers my eyes. I finally lower my eyelids, accompanied by searing pain. Never again will I starve my eyeballs of their natural essence.

Keeping my eyes closed, I realize I'm not going to bear being a part of this conversation. So I escape.

I run from the oasis and into the cold desert night. The dunes rise like mountains from another world, terrifyingly high waves on an untamed sea. Twilight glistens on the other end of the sky with every star that ever existed in sight. It would've been gorgeous if it wasn't freezing cold. My brain can't decide if the waves are water or sand. I try to get away as the waves crash together, sending millions of grains to and from into the air and falling to the earth like feathers.

I conclude that my safe place is not only unsafe, but it's on a planet and in a setting I have never experienced before.

A large ripple of sand bobs up and down beneath my feet, and for a split second, I think I'm going to sink beneath the surface and drown in the sand.

My white, sheer gown is of no help while the sun is away. I crave warmth as a rush of iciness coats my skin. The only option available to me is to return to the oasis, but my feet are filled with lead.

I have no desire to go there. I don't want to face the truth. How will we ever repair our friendship? It isn't how it used to be at all. There are far more serious conversations to be had.

I want to go back to laughing about video games, talking about books, and watching a movie.

But we can't. We have to break through the barrier of tough discussions first.

It suddenly feels like we aren't two teenagers anymore.

I open my eyes, meeting a pair of ocean-blue ones surrounded by bruises looking at me. Maverick sat next to me while I was away in my mind, but the goosebumps from the cold desert are still here. I can hear Kurt's voice and many other conversations going on in the kitchen. Everyone must be catching up before serving birthday cake.

I jump up and escape from a possible awkward conversation and join everyone in the kitchen.

"Dinah—" I hear Maverick begin, with his footsteps following close behind me.

"I want to place the candles," I volunteer, swerving around the counter. Mom truly outdid herself with Kurt's EMT-themed cake.

Out of the corner of my eye, I see Maverick sit at the table, giving up his pursuit of talking to me.

As I place the candles on the cake, Mom says in a stern voice, "Dinah, honey, we need to talk to you."

We? That can be a whole lot of possibilities. Maverick and Mom. Nattie and Mom. Kurt and Maverick and Mom. There are dozens and dozens of possibilities. I tell myself there's no need for itches.

"Why?" I mumble, my anxiety jumping through the ceiling.

I dart my stare towards Maverick talking to Nattie at the table.

Higgins' big eyes fix on Trish next to us, relieved that he isn't the one in trouble as she scratches his ears.

Mom doesn't answer, she just motions for me to join her and Trish in the living room.

I scratch Higgins' fur for comfort, and he takes the hint to follow me. Every nerve in my body shoots out like electricity. There are so many thoughts racing through my brain that I swear it vibrates against my skull. Is this Maverick's way of telling me we're just friends? Are they moving again?

Trish and Mom sit on the couch. I brace myself and hold

Higgins like a teddy bear, plopping myself down. His hot breath on my cheek lets me know he's here for me.

Mom takes a deep breath and gets on with it. "Dinah, we want to talk to you about Maverick."

At the mention of his name, my heart nearly leaps out of my chest. I keep myself from looking at him through the open arch to the kitchen.

"What about? Is he okay?" I ask.

I sneak a glance. He looks okay. He still looks handsome despite his injuries.

Trish and Mom give each other a knowing look before Trish answers quietly, "As far as I know, he's fine. No need to worry, we're all here and safe."

I loosen my tight grip on Higgins and clutch my chest. I'm panting like I just ran across the state of Wisconsin. I narrowly avoid a meltdown right here and now. I collect myself and do my breathing exercises before Mom continues.

Trish and Mom glance at each other. They exhale at the same time, which makes my skin crawl. I stare at the wall behind them. Trying to make eye contact with either of them is too difficult in my current state of mind.

"I'm concerned about you and Maverick," Mom says like she's defusing a bomb on a classified mission.

A sharp pain shoots down my spine and limbs. My nervous system is organizing a mutiny.

How could they know about him showing up in my dreams and fantasies?

My feelings melt into liquid and drip off the couch to the ground. This confrontation has smushed me into a puddle of goo on the floor that Higgins would probably love to lap up.

I don't feel human.

This isn't real.

This is totally a break-up on his behalf. If not that, then it has to be the kissing thing. Although that was months ago, so I don't know why anyone would want to bring it up now.

Then again, maybe Jason broke his promise and told Mom every one of my feelings about Maverick. That is the last straw; this calls for me to fire Jason for good.

"He told me that was just between us," I whisper.

"Who told you what was between who?" Trish asks.

"My therapist. I told him that I've been having night-mares. About how Maverick has been showing up in them, and all the worries and thoughts I have about Maverick, and he went and *told* you, violating doctor-patient confidentiality!"

Mom raises her brows. "Jason didn't tell me anything."

Whoops. "He didn't?"

Mom shakes her head.

"Then... what is it?" My gaze fixes on Trish, like she is a glitch in a perfectly coded system. The intruder. An invader.

Maverick must have spilled his guts.

"Dinah, we're worried for you—" is all I hear.

We're. Mom called Trish, and they discussed it together.

So much for being in my corner.

The humiliation bubbles up in me like some sinister acid. I'm ready to evaporate into the air from embarrassment and become a translucent thought, haunting my disgracers for life.

"Dinah, it's totally fine to have a crush, okay? I'm just worried you're getting in too deep, and that you'll get your heart broken," Mom's voice echoes to my ghostly self.

I'm a deadly mist, floating down to my unsuspecting victims. My ears heat at the thought that Maverick can hear this conversation.

"I think honesty is the best way for you to find out, dearie," Trish adds, using her best bedside manner to boot. "Maverick had a different girl on his arm every week in Colorado. It really came as no surprise to anyone when he was booked into juv—"

"People can change!" I bellow, my threatening, bodiless voice filling the room. "He changed."

I am sure he heard *that*, because he twists his head to meet my gaze.

"Okay, Dinah. No interrupting," Mom whispers. "Do I need to get out the timer?"

Curse the damn timer. My poisonous smoke will soon fill their lungs, and it will be all over. Their falsifying lips will tell no more tales.

"No timer," I command.

Trish plows ahead, crossing her scrub-clad legs with ugly shoes that are probably super-comfy for standing on her feet all day. "I want to make sure Maverick hadn't behaved badly around you. Your mom told me you went on a date with him before he and Felix left."

Is nothing sacred? Is none of my business private? My blood would have boiled if I still had a body. Alas, it has melted and evaporated, and soon, Trish will quit spewing these hateful words.

Mom nods. "Yes, and they texted often as well. *Maybe* he considers you more like a friend, Dinah. I wanted to see how you feel—"

"It's not like that!" I blurt out, unable to contain my

anger any longer. The mist disappears, and my body reformulates in seconds. Higgins is nearly in my lap, and I rub his ears frantically while I anxiously bounce my knees.

Mom purses her lips and slaps her hands on her knees. I know what that means.

She runs down the hall and is back within seconds with the dreadful sand timer. Inside it is a minute's worth of purple sand. It's used for taking turns talking. It's condescending. I'm not in kindergarten.

My cheeks are on fire as this happens in front of Maverick. Not *in* front of him per se, but he can see us from the kitchen. He and Nattie seem to be talking about video games. Felix is showing Kurt his manga, and Sherri is cleaning the dishes.

Mom upturns the tiny timer and holds it between her thumb and index finger.

"Go ahead, Dinah. You have one minute. Then it's our turn," Mom says, her tone settled. It's so calm, it throws my nerves for a loop.

My blood nearly boils over, and I'm prepared to call my mom out hard for ableist behavior. Usually, she does a great job defending me and supporting me with others, but she still needs educating about some things.

"I can't believe you think autistic people can't foster a genuine romantic relationship with someone. Why would you think that I can't achieve love?" I ask, holding my lower lip to keep myself from whimpering.

They'll never believe me. I must show them proof—give up mine and Maverick's only privacy. Nothing will be a secret anymore. I bite my bottom lip so hard that I can taste blood.

It has to be done.

I stand up with a force that sends wind into their hair. My brain lurches like it's about to launch into space. I guess all the blood rushed to my head along with the feelings I'm holding inside. I stride to the other side of the couch. Higgins tags along as I dig my phone out of my hoodie pocket and hand it over to Mom.

"I don't need a minute. Help yourselves," I snarl. I plop back down on the couch hard and try to make myself as small as possible. Tears well up and flow down like a burst dam. I can't believe that my private life, the one thing I have going for me after Jenny left, is like a buffet being eaten up by adults that have no idea what I'm feeling. They may think they understand me, but they sure as hell don't. If they had to endure what I do from the moment I wake up to the moment sleep greets me, this conversation would be going quite differently.

Higgins puts his snout up against my face. I pull his golden coat into a hug. The fur absorbs my tears, his heart beating rapidly against my arm.

Through my watery vision, I watch Mom and Trish scroll through my phone. All they need to know is in his last information dump. How dare Trish accuse Maverick of not being genuine to me? Sure, I was concerned about that at first too, but the movie date that we had? The lengths he went to give me comfort? The kisses we shared? I wasn't sure about it when I spilled my guts to Jason, but I know right here and right now that I don't just like Maverick. I'm deep in like with him.

No ten-day stint in juvie is going to change that.

Soon the women on the other end of the couch glance up from the phone with uninterpretable expressions.

"What?" I ask with a sniff, wiping my wet cheek.

"I'm sorry, Dinah," Mom whispers.

Trish nods beside her. "I'm sorry too. I should have given both you and Maverick the benefit of the doubt. How wonderful the move here made him want to be better. That was one of our hopes."

Did my brain just short-circuit? Did I actually win an argument? My heart soars across the room and carries me with it. Before I know it, I hug my mother tight around her neck. My fingers are tangled in her hot-rolled curls, but I don't care. She *was* in my corner.

"He's my best friend, Mom. I've been so worried," I say between sniffs. I try to contain my emotions in case Maverick jogs over to ask me what's wrong. That will definitely have me running away and never talking to anyone.

"Seems like he's your best *kissing* friend," Mom corrects, and the two women laugh. I hate being teased, but this time I'll allow it.

"I'm proud of Maverick. I can't deny that I'm relieved. I hope his friends learn a lesson though," Trish admits. I have no idea what she's talking about, but Mom lets go of my embrace and nods.

"I bet you're really proud at how far he's come," Mom whispers.

"I need some water," I say and get up, nearly stumbling over Higgins. I'd rather be in the kitchen than the living room, despite how warm my cheeks feel.

CHAPTER 25

I PEER AROUND MAVERICK—FELIX is still engrossed in his manga. Maverick and I play the don't-look-at-each-other game until it's just us three.

"He's okay," Maverick mutters, nodding his head toward Felix. "How are you? I saw you talking to our moms. Is everything okay?"

I can't believe Maverick is worried about how I am at a time like this. He's the one that needs the worry.

"What... Maverick... what happened?" My breath catches on each syllable.

Just like months before, he captivates my gaze, even though I hate eye contact.

He bites his bottom lip ever so slightly. The left of the upper lip is stitched up, and I imagine it hurts. I think of a scenario where I can empathize like Jenny had taught me, but nothing comes up.

"Dad got impatient with Felix. I intervened. I boiled over and let out everything that bothered me about him. He threw the first punch. It didn't help that he was on his twelfth or thirteenth beer." Maverick's face softens as he looks over at Felix.

Though I frustrated my parents greatly throughout the years, neither of them have ever laid any of their hands on me.

"Luckily," he continues, eyes on me again, "Mom's lawyer was delivering papers to the house and heard the commotion. He called the police, then Mom, and here we are."

My brain fuzzes over with all the information I just received, knowing that I'm likely going to have to endure more.

"What else? Did you get to see your friends? Did you have anyone there for you?" I'm amazed I can piece some questions together.

Maverick looks pale, like he swallowed a fast-acting poison.

"No. That whole situation was awkward as hell. Because I turned them into the police. It's partially why my dad wanted us back in the first place, for me to accept responsibility, but ultimately it was to be a dick and get back at my mom," he explains.

"But you served time in juvie. What other responsibilities did he want?" I whisper, dreading any answer.

"That's the thing. He knew I took the beatdown for my friends. He wanted me to do the right thing and turn them in, all while he's sitting around being a negligent parent." Maverick sighs.

"But... you did turn them in."

"I know."

Both of us are silent.

What do I do? What do I say? Do we talk about his past? Do I forgive him? Is there anything to forgive? Hasn't he been through enough? Haven't I been through enough, worrying about him? Is he worth worrying over?

"Dinah...." Maverick pauses.

Oh crap. Here it comes. Nope. Nope. Nope. Nope, nope, nope, nope, nooope. I gulp, which signals Higgins to put his paws on my knees. Maverick is going to make me spit out what his mom told me.

"I don't want this to be weird between us." He stretches out each word.

But it is. I'm not worried about his past. I'm worried about the time we've spent apart.

I've got new routines now.

Ringing in my ears. Buzzes in my head. Nope, nope, nope.

"Like I texted before, I didn't know you back then, but my actions were despicable. I haven't found anyone besides Felix who trusts me fully. Even my mom," he plows on, piercing the silence around us with his rumbling voice that's full of regret. No Maverick smile, no warmth from his face. The sounds of chairs scraping against the tile is a sign that the gathering is waiting for us.

We walk over to the cake to sing "Happy Birthday" to Kurt.

"You can trust me," Maverick whispers to me. "I've learned my lesson. I'll never touch drugs again."

And there it is.

Drugs?

A bomb goes off in my chest. All emotions that I've been holding back, all the stimulation I've suppressed, and all the frustrating changes have reached the surface of Mount Dinah. My bones shake, sloshing my organs around in their designated pockets of my meat computer.

Our families are singing "Happy Birthday" to Kurt. I stare at my knees, thinking a million thoughts.

I take one big breath to answer him before I make my escape. "I can't," I tell Maverick.

I fly down the hallway to my room where I slam and lock the door. I don't want anyone to hear my meltdown. I grab the nearest blanket and screech into it. Scorching-hot magma bubbles up from beneath, pouring from my cavity with ferocity over the floor, the vanity, the carpet.

Oh.

That's not lava.

That's puke.

Scratches and whimpering come from the other side of my door. I want Higgins to snuggle me, but at the same time, I question if I really want his presence. Dogs are gross with vomit and the like. Luckily, I have my phone. I send one text to my mom before I fall into the flowing lava.

> Me: Help.

Knowing he did drugs, got beat up, and made poor decisions sends me into a panic. Most people would probably talk to him and ask what help he needs. But I'm drowning in all the changes and news of the Maverick I once knew being someone I don't even recognize.

I don't blame him for anything, but the Maverick files in my brain just blew up into a mess I don't know how to clean up. It's too much. Maybe Trish and Mom were right to be concerned about me not being able to be in a relationship with him.

Because I cannot do this.

But I don't want him gone forever.

Maverick only abruptly entered my life, made it wonderful, suddenly left it, made it horrific, and unexpectedly came back, resulting in one bumpy roller coaster. Trusting him is going to take time.

Then there's the awkward fact that we like each other, but that situation is extremely sensitive. I feel like I'm walking on broken glass around him. I want to get that safe space back. I miss the warm feeling I used to get by simply standing in his presence.

It's been almost an hour since I ran away to my room. It's quiet enough to tell me the Wrights are gone. I tell myself there's more to this story.

We will get close again once more. I hope. But it'll be as if we're getting to know each other all over again.

We start with a text. After a few sentences, I get a headache and have to go to sleep.

Over the next few days, we don't really pass notes in English class anymore. If we do, I'm unable to focus.

CHAPTER 26

SEEING Maverick walk toward the disability classroom a week later to eat lunch with Felix gives me a lump in my throat. One day, I'll be able to put the awkwardness aside and fly into his arms, kissing him with all my strength, as the world fades around us. At the moment, though, I'm in a whirlwind—pictures of him and some drunk girl tangled together flash in front of my eyes.

I understand I truly should get over it. Denver Maverick was a different person. I'm just having a hard time distinguishing Denver Maverick from Milwaukee Maverick.

When I get home from school, Eliza asks me each day if I'm doing okay. I'm numb but trying to find my footing. It's hard to read a situation when everything feels awkward.

I've erected steel walls around my heart. High security. Only Mom has a secret entrance, or at least that's what it feels like. She's been trying to cancel plans to spend mother-daughter time with me, even rushing deadlines, but I've been insistent upon not disrupting her life any further. Nattie and Kurt too.

This is what true transition is about.

Life-altering event.

Panic.

Isolation.

Learning to adapt.

Short euphoria.

Repeat.

My coping mechanisms are fighting the reactions to the transition. Things like Higgins, stimming, reading, hiding in my cave, and looking at videos help to get my mind off of Maverick.

Yet I'm somehow expected to live a life and be normal like everyone else. I was watching WorldVid interviews about how people cope with anxiety and depression when I discovered furries. There are fursuits and giant animal heads where people escape into to take on a furry persona, or *fursona*. I like the idea of escape, but the rest of the lifestyle is pretty extreme for me—though I do love the term they use for "normal" people: normies.

I have come to terms with the fact that I will never be a normie.

Eliza doesn't appreciate me calling her one though, so I made it her new nickname. To cope with anxiety attacks, we've formed our own little book club. We both read a book each week and discuss it on Friday like a couple of nerds. Sometimes she films us, and we talk about posting it on WorldVid. It's an amazing therapy tactic and has taken a lot off my back. Coming home from school isn't so heavy anymore when part of therapy is diving into a fabulous fictional free-for-all. Eliza is ecstatic at my progress.

She has no idea that I have my own idea at the back of my mind about starting a WorldVid channel.

I don't know why I text Maverick about it. Maybe to gauge his reaction and definitely not to have any deep conversations about feelings.

The shutters rustle noisily against the house. I don't see myself getting to sleep anytime soon.

> **Maverick:** In my opinion, you're a perfect candidate for an autism awareness WorldVid channel

> **Me:** I wouldn't know where to start if I were to talk just about me. Maybe I should be a book reviewer instead?

The dots dance one by one. I have a feeling he's thought about this conversation beforehand, much like I've thought about having a WorldVid career. My toes scratch the edge of my bed where my blanket ends, the sensation strange but oddly calming.

Higgins snores in my ear, his hot breath raising the temperature so high that I have to flip down my blankets to free myself from the wrath of dog breath.

> **Maverick:** It could be you and Higgins! You could explain day-to-day life, talk about what it's like to be you, and answer people's questions. Talk about why the Autism Around the World walk is important to you

A natural smile plays casually on my lips for the first time in a long time. I forgot what an advocate for autism awareness Maverick is. I forgot that he genuinely has my best interest at heart. My chest warms, and my brain tingles in my skull. The steel walls in my chest come down around my heart just a bit.

Then I remember how I've forgotten about helping Felix get a service dog. Maybe we can work together to make some kind of video to introduce ourselves. Especially considering that the Autism Around the World walk is next month.

> Me: Maybe you should come over tomorrow, and we can browse ideas?

The dots barely dance before Maverick replies.

> Maverick: I'm 100% there!

He accompanies his text with a winking emoji. Progress. This is progress. I am confident we can be best friends again.

School the next day consists of our usual avoiding each other, funnily enough. During lunch, I text Maverick to tell him that he can walk with me and Higgins home after school, if he wants.

Usually, he rides the bus with Felix or takes his motorcycle. I think he's so happy I'm finally letting down my walls that he doesn't care how he gets to talk to me.

We meet outside the boys' gym after the last bell which is next to Maverick's last class of the day.

My blood pumps in my chest speedily when he emerges from the building. Sporting wet hair, he pulls on his leather jacket and backpack while keeping direct eye contact with me. Ocean-blue eyes. *Hero* blue. The scent of his fresh deodorant and light cologne hits me, combining into a surprisingly pleasant aroma.

Like a prepared nerd, I've written down topics of discussion on a piece of paper during science and memorized them. I'm finally ready to get my best friend back, flaws and all.

Topic of discussion number one: the Autism Around the World walk.

"Hey there, Dinah," Maverick says. Higgins stands on all fours in eager anticipation for pets. "And fuzzy companion." He bends down on one knee to give Higgins neck scratches, ear scratches, and even gratuitous belly scratches before looking at me and smiling the old Maverick smile. The one I haven't seen in weeks.

"Ready to go?" I ask, tugging on Higgins' leash to make him behave himself.

He nods, and we head toward the sidewalk. The air is slightly crisp, so I want to get moving. The wind tangles my hair around my headphones while it's merely drying Maverick's.

I look down at the ground to make sure I don't run into anything. "So, does your mom have the donation booth set up for the walk?"

"Almost," he replies before asking hopefully, "Are you guys coming?"

"Of course, we never miss it."

He nods, and we keep walking, eyes on Higgins' fluffy tail leading us along. I bet we look like a cute couple to the cars passing by.

Dinah. Stop it. He's just your friend.

For now.

Dammit.

My brain wants to be at war with my heart, so I strike up topic of discussion number two: Maverick's dad.

"Is your dad still in jail?" I ask.

Maverick pins his lips to one side of his face in a puzzling expression. I can't tell if he's uncomfortable talking about the subject or if it's just the face he pulls when he talks about his dad.

"No. His buddy paid his bail, but he's on probation. He can't leave the state. The courts gave sole custody of Felix to Mom and Trish," he says.

"Well, that's good then," I reply, making a mental note to never bring up Maverick's dad again. However, he plows on with the subject before I can change it.

"I do have good memories of my dad," Maverick begins. "They're sprinkled with moments of me walking around on eggshells, not knowing if he was in a good mood or bad mood. On rare occasions we'd play shooter video games together. He taught me how to ride the motorcycle, but a short temper combined with frequent alcohol use finally drove Mom away."

I take in the information, trying to put myself in Maverick's shoes. Dad, Mom, and Kurt have been impatient with me at times, sure, but they have shown me and Nattie nothing but kindness. I can't imagine being constantly on edge, not knowing if today was going to be a good-temper day or a bad-temper day.

"Living there was a nightmare. No communication to the outside world, him attempting to homeschool us while drunk off his ass. I'm glad that part of my life is over." Maverick shrugs.

"Yeah..." is all I sputter when we stop at a crosswalk.

"Dinah." He looks directly at me.

I freeze, the sound of my name bubbling up inside me like a geyser about to go off. I stare across the street before making a break for it as the cars stop. Higgins gets the hint and sprints alongside me. We book it to the crosswalk.

Maverick wants to talk seriously.

I don't.

I want my friend back and to discuss the fun WorldVid channel.

"Dinah!" he calls after me as I turn off the sidewalk, cutting through the field behind my house.

Higgins and I trample through the mud and flaccid hay. My left shoe gets stuck in a patch of extra-sticky mud. I immediately regret this decision. I'm helpless. Maverick catches up in no time while Higgins proceeds to freak out, trying to figure out what he should do next.

"I'm stuck!" I cry, the geyser nearing eruption.

Maverick circles around until he faces me, breathing hard but smiling. "Now you and I can have this conversation we've been avoiding face-to-face."

Crap on a cracker.

Escape, escape, escape, escaaaape...

"Listen. I know I was a terrible person before I met you. I told you I wanted all of that to change as soon as I moved. I just happened to have met the most wonderful person in you. On my first day at school." He smirks, his eyes glued to mine.

I can't help but listen intently while continuing to attempt to free my left foot from the mud. I have to run. I have to escape. I can't handle this conversation.

"Please believe me when I say I never intended to hurt anyone. The past few months without you were torture. Please don't torture me anymore," Maverick pleads as he inches closer.

Higgins doesn't know what to do but whine, so he plants his rear in the mud and waits for further instruction.

I need someone to give me instructions too. I'm frozen in place. Figuratively and literally. The gray sky parts, rays of sunshine playing peculiar shadow patterns on Maverick's face. He holds out his right hand.

Higgins, once again, is not trained professionally for a situation such as this. He stands at the ready next to us. It no doubt looks like two dogs playing together to him.

This whole time of separation, I thought *I* was the tortured one. Torn from my comfortable routine around my friend and crush that I barely functioned. Hearing he experienced the same hurt tugs at the switch of my rib cage—my heart is ready to open the gates wide and free.

I take his hand, using the leverage to free myself from the mud.

Then I run.

CHAPTER 27

IT'D BE great if I knew where I was running to because the oak trees and brick houses don't look familiar. There's a park nearby, and I go there to rest. Texting Eliza my location according to my phone's GPS, I tell her I got lost and I'm taking a moment to rest on a bench.

What do I do about the feelings that we have for each other? Maverick scares me and excites me. I want him to look at me but also not at all. I miss him and need to escape him. It's overwhelming my breathing to the point of panic.

Eyes closed, I take in three breaths and glance back to make sure he didn't follow me.

When Eliza says she's on her way, I slump onto the ground. Higgins rolls in the grass, and I do the same. Even if home is a block away, I don't have the strength to push on at the moment.

Eliza's laugh drowns out the chirping birds in the background. "Looks like you had fun."

Not exactly, but I'm too exhausted to explain anything.

She lets Higgins off his leash as I sit up. I allow him to

trot around the playground so I can take my time getting back up and sip on the water Eliza has brought me.

"You've progressed so much this year, Dinah. I'm very proud of you. Even if it includes rolling around, this is a nice change for you." Eliza's words echo off a crystal palace in my mind. She feels far away even though she's next to me. In a strange sort of way, after all the crap these past months have unloaded on me, I'm proud of me too, considering the state I am in at the moment.

"I was running away from Maverick," I admit.

"Why were you running away from Maverick?" she asks.

I sigh, hating to answer the question. "He was trying to apologize. He was talking about feelings, and it was really awkward. I had to run."

"I feel like I'm missing an important piece of information," Eliza presses. "Did you forget about therapy?" She puts her hands on her hips.

I pick my words carefully. "Uh..." is all I can say.

"Dinah, I'm teasing you," Eliza says, chuckling and shaking her mane of red hair.

Relief sweeps over me. I'll never grasp the concept of sarcasm. If I had a magic lamp, I think my first wish would be to be able to tell when people are being sarcastic or not.

"You're making plans and walking home with friends. Neither of those are on your usual schedules. That's fantastic." She claps her hands. "Tell you what. I only usually stick around for two hours on Fridays anyway. If you want to do something by yourself when you get home and showered, I'll just be off. Okay?"

"Sure. Sorry for not texting you about that first," I say.

Thinking back, it would have been the sensible thing to do. Social awkwardness wins again.

Higgins whines his "there's a bee!" whine and hurries back to us before sitting by us, his tail wagging with anxiety. Any bee dumb enough to be out before the spring snowstorm deserves what it gets. I'm just glad he didn't chomp it like he did the first summer we had him—his snout was swollen for days. I chuckle at the memory.

I glance at my smartwatch and am pleased to see my heart rate is returning to normal. I sigh, wishing I could roll in the grass again, but I need to push on. I can only imagine what Mom's reaction to my dirty clothes and shoes will be.

Before Eliza can say it's time to go, I grab Higgins' leash and secure it to his harness once again. I glance at Eliza for reassurance before she nods. I tug on the leash to go to the left side of the street instead of the right.

"This isn't our normal route, but a new way can be a good change," Eliza says.

Higgins looks confused but obeys the leash as we stroll on.

The houses are similar, the street nearby is still rather busy—so far so good. We stride along the curve of the side-walk, which takes us to the next cul-de-sac over. The first house has no fence, with rowdy kids playing on a swing set in their yard. My anxiety spikes, but I calm myself with deep breathes. Eliza helps me with overexaggerated inhales and exhales, reminding me to do the same. Higgins leads on, his tail giving away his excitement of a new neighborhood to look at with plenty of new sights and smells.

An unfamiliar bark roars. It's so loud, it rings in my ears even through my headphones. Our eyes dart to a lawn across the street where a massive, unleashed dog is baring its teeth. He's a short-haired breed, which allows him to exhibit his strong, muscled body. The jowls are huge, and I gather the dog must be some sort of mastiff. I love dogs, but this one was not bred to be friendly but rather one to scare off intruders.

I freeze in place, and my lizard brain begins ordering me around.

Fight? Hell no, I'll get my guts ripped out.

Flight? Definitely, but what if it's faster than me?

Freeze? What good would that do?

Higgins growls back in full protection mode. Eliza grabs his leash and tugs on it to run back in the direction from which we came, back to the safe, known route where we turn right instead of left, like in a video game when you've made a wrong decision and have to shut it off before it saves. This way you can fix your mistake before suffering any of the consequences.

Horrifically enough, there's no rewind button in reality. This isn't my safe place or a video game. This is all happening, albeit in slow motion.

The two dogs bark at each other, no moves yet made. The owner comes out of his house and stands on the porch, ordering his dog to stop, but he doesn't. Instead, the massive beast leaps forward toward us, roaring barks and drool in its wake.

Eliza snatches my elbows and jerks me sideways, yelling at me to run. The world spins into a blur. The colors and sounds crash together like a violent painting in process. Lizard brain adrenaline kicks in. I run to the end of the street, my shoes pounding the pavement with as much force as a two-ton elephant. I can't stop. I won't stop until I'm home. My motivation of remaining unharmed is playing across my mind like a marquee until I notice that I don't have Higgins' leash.

I snap back into focus, glancing around at Eliza gasping beside me.

I grab her hands.

His leash isn't in her grasp either.

"HIGGINS!" I scream in an unearthly, high-pitched noise.

Echoes ring in my ears as I hear chunks of fur being torn from flesh. Red puddles start to form in the street as Eliza calls Kurt on her phone. Vicious growling meets howls of pain in the most unpleasant melody to ever invade my senses.

My knees buckle, and I fall to them on the cement, most likely bruising them. I'm seeing stars. The owner of the overly large dog has gotten in between the two canines and pulled his dog away, giving me the opportunity to jump up and run toward Higgins.

My knees ache with every pounding step, but the adrenaline coursing through me helps me to ignore the pain. I hear Eliza calling my name, and I know she's running after me. I collapse next to the bloodied ball of fur, his whimpering and heavy breathing breaking my heart.

The world is a blur of streaked colors through my tear-flooded eyes. A car attempting to drive through the neighborhood stops. The kind person gets out of their vehicle to offer help while Eliza recounts the horror to them. I don't want to cause any other pain to my poor Higgins, so I gently rub his ears as Mom's car pulls up next to us.

"I'm so... sorry, Higgins. I... left you. I... feel like... a traitor," I say between sobs.

Warm arms swoop around me, and I instantly thrash against them. I want to comfort my dog. Kurt has his EMT kit and begins applying pressure to his wounds and wrapping them.

"Dinah." Eliza's shaking voice tries to remain calm in my ear.

"No! Don't try to calm me down!" I yell toward the sky. I refuse to let go of Higgins' fur. I need to be near him, to comfort him. He's been there for me every step of the way, and I'm here for him.

"Dinah," Kurt's voice is loud but steady above my dog's painful whimpers. "We're going to load him into the car and get him to the emergency vet right this second."

My breathing is still heavy, my chest just might collapse on itself at any moment. With every exhale, I'm wailing. With every second that ticks by, my dog's life could hang in the balance. I want Higgins to be well again, right now. I want to stop time and rewind to ten minutes ago. Even a half hour ago.

None of this would've happened if I hadn't run away from Maverick.

"You're hyperventilating," Eliza says, attempting to take my arms away from his fur again.

My face burns hot and tears boil down my face. I blame me. I blame Eliza. I blame Maverick. I blame the owner of the beast. I look up as Eliza manages to help me step away from the scene and let Kurt do his work. Mom unleashes her mama bear on the owner, her face as red as a beet and his face reflecting remorse.

In what seems like an instant, Mom and Kurt load the crumpled fur-lump of Higgins into the backseat of their car. I run and fling the back door open, fully intending on being with him every second of this process.

"Dinah, should we go home and talk this through? We can get through this together." Eliza's meek voice comes from my side.

I stare right into her tawny eyes, her freckled face wrinkled with worry. Her hair is a stressed-out mess, and the only thing I want to say to her is rude, emotional, and totally out of line.

"I can't talk to you," I say through gritted teeth.

Time can't go any faster as we drive to the vet. I'm as still as Higgins in the car, even when Mom and Kurt take him inside. They have to come get me because I don't know how to leave the space his blood and fur left behind.

Everything is too much. No amount of time seems enough to shake me out of this state. Even the next morning at the breakfast table.

CHAPTER 28

THE MILLIONS of pieces of me are scattered on the floor, each one is sharp enough to draw blood. Whatever I was, what life that may have existed outside of my room before the attack is gone. I am a mere speck of dust, floating aimlessly in a vast, endless universe that has no objective.

Am I human? I'm not sure. I lost all feeling two days ago. Every breath, every blink, every swallow goes by without my notice. I awoke this morning clutching my blankets instead of a warm ball of fur, without Higgins' heart beating against my skin. I must be a malfunctioning machine.

I'm sinking into a pool of bottomless mud, which reminds me of Maverick. I think of our awkward rendezvous in the field that seems like centuries ago, not days. Not even that memory can bring any reaction to the surface. He's texted, he's called, but everything has gone unanswered.

I can only take so much.

My mind thinks it can take more. Everything in my meat computer has completely shut down except for my essential organs, but my brain is going a million miles a minute. It keeps making me experience phantom fur on my arm. Invisible weight on the other side of my bed. Transient snores in the middle of the night.

The first twenty-four hours in the pet hospital were nerve-racking. Higgins had to have three separate surgeries and is currently heavily sedated. When Kurt asked the vet over the phone if he would be able to continue his service dog duties, the vet seemed positive, so I have high hopes. That doesn't stop the endless itches, though.

I keep replaying the attack in my mind. The sounds that ensued, the screams, the moments afterwards. Rushing to the emergency vet. Leaving him there overnight in critical condition.

Higgins is more than a dog, even more than a partner to me. He is a magical sidekick. He's the other half of my body. My external calming system. My meltdown detector.

I want to see him, but Mom and Kurt say I shouldn't see him in this condition. It'd hurt me too much emotionally. I eavesdropped a little earlier on the conversation between Kurt and the vet—the illicit activity revealed Higgins' wounds are costing over four thousand dollars, to which he subsequently repeated the conversation to my mom in the kitchen.

Higgins' jaw is broken. He needs stitches in eleven places. His back left leg has significant tendon damage that requires major surgery. His spleen was punctured, but the vet saved him. That bastard beast will pay for his medical bills.

I assume Kurt is speaking of the aggressive dog's owner.

Knowing my best furry friend was close to the brink of death unhinges me. Thinking about the pain medication he's on, the healing he'll have to go through, and not knowing when I'll hear his heartbeat cuddled next to mine in my bed next...

I need a heartbeat tonight.

Grabbing my phone from the nightstand, I remove the charger and scroll through Maverick's twenty messages, each pleading for me to answer, for him to come over.

It buzzes in my hand, announcing Maverick is coming in thirty minutes.

I tiptoe to my door and lock it, then quietly go to my window to punch out the screen. Kurt still hasn't replaced it since I left it open from a particularly rough windstorm a few years ago, and it's still loose.

Little raindrops tap on the roof. I hate the rain, but part of me wants to run out and scream at the wetness.

My mom knocks at my door again. "I have news."

Is Higgins okay? Is this good news or bad news?

"Come in."

Mom opens the door wearing her wrinkled flannel pajamas with her hair up in its nighttime bun. My heart pounds at the thought of the consequences that could come should Mom discover that a boy is on his way over here. Let alone the fact that I had punched out my window screen specifically for him to climb into.

"It's not about Higgins, though he is doing good. He was awake for a little bit today." Mom smiles.

My heartbeat slows down a tiny amount. The thought of Higgins already fighting to be on the mend sends warm fuzzies through me.

"So, it's *not* news about Higgins, but it *is* news about Higgins?" I ask, the impatience grows within me.

Mom looks tired as she closes her eyes with a sigh. "Jenny's coming to visit in the morning."

I long for Jenny. A large part of me resents Eliza for letting go of Higgins' leash when he was attacked, even though I know she was in a state of panic and was trying to keep me safe. In my mind, I tell myself that Jenny will whip out her superhero cape and save everyone.

"I can't wait to see her," I say, stifling a fake yawn so Mom would get the hint and go to bed. It's almost midnight, anyway.

"Goodnight, honey," Mom says and closes the door without making a sound.

I clutch my blanket to my chest and count down the seconds until I hear the buzz of my phone announcing Maverick's arrival. I tell him the window's open.

Grunts sound from the ground, and I suspect he's about to climb in. A part of me oozes with excitement to see him. The other part wants to escape. Everything has been a mess, but the joy of being next to him wins over and the corners of my mouth curl up.

He climbs through the window with one pull-up like he's an expert at sneaking into girls' bedrooms. I wipe that thought away as soon as his shoes touch the carpet. His black T-shirt and pineapple pajama bottoms sway with his movements. His messy light-brown hair is a little askew from wearing his helmet. Who gave him permission to look this attractive tonight? I've never found him sexier.

Maverick takes me in his arms and secures my body in a warm embrace, giving me the comfort I've needed these past two days in Higgins' absence.

I exhale into him. For a millisecond, I worry how he feels

about his friend being in flamingo pajamas meant for kids, but to hell with that. I decide I don't care.

"I'm here, it's okay," he whispers against my cheek. "I'm really sorry about Higgins."

And then, I do something impulsive.

I cup my palm onto his jaw and bring his face down to mine and kiss him, my vulnerability at an all-time high. I need to feel something. I need his warmth. I need his hands on my skin.

Maverick breaks apart and says, "Hold on just one second."

His words make my heart stop. All I want is a warm body to comfort me, and in the moment, I forgot about my anxieties and apprehensions I had about Maverick a couple of days ago.

"Sorry," I say, quiet as a mouse.

"No, no, it's okay. I just want to clarify something." He clears his throat, his sparkling eyes looking into mine. "Does this mean we're friends again?"

I gulp, embarrassed at how I threw myself at him. The social norms of conversations throw me for a loop on a normal day, so functioning under extreme stress and trauma seems to have left me desolate when it comes to etiquette.

Maverick is my best friend.

I have feelings for my best friend.

"We're friends," I reply, and rub my palm in his several-day-old stubble, which sends electric shocks up my arm.

Maverick sighs. "Well." He places his hands on my waist and pulls me toward him in a flash. My heart jumps into my throat, sending endorphins all over my body. "I'd say we're more than friends."

Then he kisses me with one quick swipe.

My human safe place has returned.

His heavy breathing between passionate kisses is doing something to me I've never encountered anywhere else. I have read about these urges and situations in books all the time but had never planned on experiencing them anytime soon. My teenage hormones make an appearance out of nowhere, and my mind is racing with rather playful thoughts. The things coming to mind can only be found on that one fan fiction website I sometimes wander to while browsing aimlessly.

My fingers ruffle through Maverick's hair while his heartbeat thumps next to mine. Our bodies are practically plastered against each other. His stubble tickles my face in a frenzy. I'm pretty sure I've discovered a new form of stimulation to calm the itches.

Maverick's lips part from mine once we're both out of breath. He raises his face to look at me. I notice his pupils are dilated like a black hole vortex in the middle of the sea. His smile is back on his lips, though something is different about it. It isn't forced.

It's honest.

I can't stop myself. He sucks on my bottom lip and grazes it gently with his teeth. He's never done that before. He kisses the nape of my neck and explores my shoulder when we fall, both weak for each other, onto my bed.

Every kiss electrifies me down to my toes. Maverick's fingertips on my face and neck send shivers over my body.

"No, wait, we'll wake—" I begin to say, but then remember. *Higgins.* He isn't here, but I'm so used to having his body on my bed. The way his ears perk up at any sound in the night, the way he splays his furry legs and snores.

Maverick stares at me, the concerned look back on his face. He's still breathing heavily, but I can tell he senses our moment of passion has ended.

He sighs, stroking his fingers through my hair. "I'm sorry, Dinah. It sucks, but I know he'll recover. He will."

"I just... I just..." I whimper.

Maverick presses his hand on the back of my head and brings it to his chest.

"I'm here for you," he says. His shirt smells freshly laundered with a hint of lilac and citrus.

"I like your moms' laundry soap," I say.

Maverick laughs as quietly as he can. He brings my face away from his chest and up to his with both hands and kisses me gently, not with ferocity like the previous kiss, but with tenderness. I'm unprepared for what he says next.

"Dinah, you make me feel like I've never felt before."

Every pore on my body roars alive with an unknown sensation. I'm supposed to be fretting, not celebrating. I guess I'm experiencing a deep and meaningful friendship turned infatuation, something I never imagined would happen to me. It's an invigorating connection, one that could last eons. I can see it in his eyes.

Often, I say things without thinking. Maverick makes me ponder my words before they come out. I don't know if it's because I'm scared of messing up what we have, but I usually count to three and rehearse what I'm about to say. I take a deep breath and think of something to say that would suit this moment.

"Me too."

As Maverick holds me, he provides the heat, heartbeat, and breath that I miss from my hospitalized dog. Our teenage hormones go unquenched throughout the night.

When morning comes, I awake at a knock at the door. That's not good.

"Crap," I whisper.

I look up at Maverick's darling face, open-mouthed and dead asleep. I poke him hard in the chest and he yelps, "Ow!" a little louder than he should have.

"Dinah?" Mom's voice wafts through the other side of the door.

"Be right there, getting dressed," I reply, hoping there's little to no panic traces in my voice.

Maverick jumps up and tiptoes over to the open window, making me realize how cold my room has become with us forgetting to close it. He slips his shoes on and slides himself noiselessly out the window, which I then close as quietly as possible, but it's no use. I know Mom is listening to make sure I'm okay.

I'm a dead woman walking.

CHAPTER 29

I PRAY to the fairy gods, magic gods, and anyone who is listening that nobody in my house notices Maverick running like hell away from the side of our house to his motorcycle. I can't help but laugh, but then I remember how much trouble I'm about to be in, even though nothing happened but cuddling.

I unlock and open my door with haste to greet my mother, who eyes me up and down.

I forgot I said I was getting dressed. Yet here I am, still in last night's flamingo jammies.

"I... thought you said you were getting dressed?" Mom asks with a raised eyebrow. She's dressed early today, though her hair and makeup aren't quite done.

"Yeah. I... slept in my underwear," I lie. So unsmooth. Mom knows I like to be encompassed by soft, fluffy things, plus my room being as cold as the arctic is a dead giveaway.

"Oh my gosh, Dinah. Please tell me you at least used protection," she says, her voice rising.

Nattie opens her door and peeks her head out, unable to

resist the early morning show that's playing out in the hallway.

I wish I had superpowers to vaporize myself on the spot. I bury my face in my hands. My vertebrae meld together in a squeamish sensation in my back like I'm about to crumple into a heap. The heat in my body rushes to my face as I admit, muffled into my hand, "Nothing happened, Mom." I want to die from embarrassment.

Between my fingers, I spy Nattie waggling her eyebrows at me.

"Lord have mercy. What am I going to do with you?" Mom groans, then raises her arms and drops them like dead weight.

I don't know what to say. I just stand there, my head hanging in shame. Nattie giggles at the same time Mom invites herself into my room and gently lays her hands on my shoulders, an invitation to look into her eyes.

"Just tell me, did anything happen?" Mom asks, her eyes glazed with genuine concern, not anger.

My heartbeat slows when I realize I'm not about to be scolded.

"We kissed a little, then I had a breakdown over Higgins not being in my bed. So, Maverick became my Higgins weight. That's all," I confess.

Mom breathes in through her nose, a nerve twitching in her cheek. When she breathes out, I can tell it's in relief.

"Thank you for being honest," Mom says, a smile playing around the corners of her mouth.

Just then, the doorbell rings. For a millisecond, I think it's Maverick coming back, but then I remember that Jenny is coming to visit today. Nattie's bounding steps down the hallway confirm that she is running to get the door.

"It's me," a voice sounds from beyond my door. A voice I haven't heard in months.

A mushroom cloud of adrenaline awakens in my chest, along with a rush of serotonin that overcomes my entire body at the thought. I jump behind Mom and fling my door open, almost accidentally hitting her in the head.

"Jenny!" I wail and race ahead.

There she is—puffy eyed, high blonde ponytail and all. She practically flies to gather me in her arms like a mother hen.

Her goodness spreads over my skin and pierces through my tough exterior to awaken my grief at her long-missing presence.

We cry in each other's arms for who knows how long. The happiness of seeing her mixes with my cloud-nine feelings about the boy I spent the night with and dead-inside feelings about what happened with Higgins, setting off an atom bomb of emotion in me.

"He was... attacked..." I whisper.

"I know, honey. I know, shhhh," Jenny says, practically rocking me like a baby. She caresses her nails on the skin of my arms like she used to. They send calming vibes from my outer layers to my inner ones.

"Eliza... she let him... she let him go," I pepper into Jenny's shoulder.

"She didn't mean to, Dinah-Doo. Absolutely not," Jenny assures, wiping a tear from her face. "You've got to know it was an accident. She's positively sick over it."

"She made us go left. You never made me go left. We

always went right!" I cry, begging Jenny to take my side. I knew Eliza was a bad idea the moment she first walked into my home. My fear mixed with hatred becomes a truly malicious concoction boiling in my blood, just waiting for an excuse to boil over. And yet... while thinking these things about Eliza, I know the opposite is true. She is a good aide. But I have to channel my grief *somewhere*.

"She was trying to get you used to change."

"Well, this is one way to freaking change my life. Higgins almost died!" I yell, not at Jenny, not particularly at anyone but at the universe, cursing it for hurting my precious golden retriever.

Jenny cups her hands on my cheeks in her loving way, in the way that I missed so terribly.

"Let's talk. Like we used to," Jenny says with a forced smile, one that shoves the tears back in her eyes and helps her be strong for me. "I'm sorry I stayed away so long. With the wedding, the honeymoon, and training for my new job, then the bad winter driving—they're lame excuses, really."

Moments later, we're on my bed when Mom delivers scrambled eggs and toast to us. Nattie sheepishly invites herself in. When I ask why she's not at school, she looks at me like I'm clueless. I know why I haven't been in school the last few days, but I've never seen her not be in school.

Apparently, it's Saturday. I've lost all track of time since Higgins' incident.

"It's time to celebrate instead of worry. Get every feeling out," Jenny says, hugging Nattie fiercely before they both sit on the end of my bed.

I exhale. "I miss him so much."

"Me too," Nattie echoes.

I want to know how Jenny has been, to keep my mind off of Higgins.

Jenny tells us about her life. She tells me about her fancy new apartment, her job, and even some of the new kids she's working with. For a change, she's working with a lot of toddlers and preschoolers instead of teenagers, and she misses the attitudes versus the tantrums.

She asks me about my life, and I spell it out from October to April. My fainting spell, Eliza, Halloween, Maverick's drama, how we're kind of together now, my anxiety over graduation, and my worries about Higgins' future. What if he can't be my service dog anymore?

We talk for hours and hours, but it seems like only minutes have gone by.

"As much as I don't want to, I have to leave," Jenny admits, her bottom lip quivering a little.

I thought I was dehydrated from crying so many tears, but I'm wrong. More well up in my burning eyes.

"I love you so much," I say, giving her the most ferocious hug my strength can muster.

"I will always love you and your family. I love Higgins with all my heart. Don't worry, Dinah-Doo. He'll heal fast," Jenny says and sighs.

She briefly leaves my bedroom, and before I can fret about her leaving without a true goodbye, she returns with a package. Jenny consistently gives gifts for sad or happy occasions. The last one being my Higgins stuffed animal, which on the day of his accident I threw out my door, unable to look at it. My mom, undoubtedly, put it somewhere safe for me until I'm ready.

In slow motion, Jenny pulls a large, bulky present out with a squished pink bow.

She hands me the package. "I know you hate pink, but it's what I had. Forgive me."

I unwrap the shiny paper one corner at a time, prolonging her visit for as long as possible. When I finally tear it open, I gasp because it is both smooth and bumpy at the same time.

"A weighted blanket. To help you sleep and calm down, especially while Higgins is away," Jenny says. Her thoughtfulness knows no bounds.

"I don't know if I can do the Autism Around the World walk without Higgins," I say. It has hit me now that it's only days away and he'll be in the hospital for at least another week.

Jenny rubs my hands. "Be with the people who can support you. You've come so far, and I believe in you. You may have had difficult moments in the past, but it doesn't mean you should stop. Nattie told me she's going to help you in school. How do you think that'll go?"

"Fine." I try not to think about going to school without Higgins, but I will survive. I try to think positively, accepting that it might actually be nice to spend the day with my sister.

Looks like I have to do the most important event of the year without Higgins no matter how much I don't want to.

A few days later, I ask Maverick to come over. I'm ready to have a serious conversation with him. Plus, get my first WorldVid video planned out. Not having Higgins reminds me how important service dogs are. Like Felix, who has coincidentally sent me pictures of his favorite dog breeds via Maverick's phone.

"Good morning, Dinah." He steps into my room. "Dines," he says with a smirk.

"Morning," I say.

We settle on the love seat, a notebook and pen in my hands to jot down ideas. We can share the video with people at the walk so they can donate after the event as well.

"Okay, where do we start?" I ask, not making eye contact. I'm in my concentration zone until Maverick puts his arm around me. The warmth in my chest spreads to my shoulder and the nape of my neck.

"How about we start with us?" he asks, an annoying cheeriness in his voice. "I liked kissing you."

"Friends who kiss," I reply, trying not to make a big deal out of it. We came here to talk about a WorldVid career, and I intend to stay focused.

"And maybe more?" He squeezes my right shoulder, bringing me closer to him.

I forget that an eighteen-year-old boy in a girl's bedroom can't focus that much.

I don't know how to react, so I stare down at my paper and start writing basic ideas. My lizard brain is not fighting, flighting, or freezing this time. I'm in charge of my brain, and I'm going to do what I came here to do.

"Eventually I will probably need a ring light for my phone. And a computer to edit the videos with," I say and scribble in my neatest handwriting. "Or a laptop with a really good camera."

"Your birthday is coming up, right?" Maverick asks in my ear.

Shivers run down my spine, but they aren't bad shivers. I've never felt anything like them before. I like it a lot, but there is no way in hell I'm letting Maverick know that.

A thought flashes through my mind. The bad boy with the motorcycle, seducing others with his charm and silky voice.

"Don't make me get my headphones," I threaten with a smile on my face.

He chuckles and backs away an inch. "All right, all right."

I'm turning eighteen, and I've always wanted a laptop. I usually do my homework on the family desktop or in the library but having my own would be so much better. I remember the hassle I put up with to get a phone out of Dad. If I want to convince Mom I'm responsible enough for a laptop, I have to give one hundred percent to this cause.

I place the end of the pen in my mouth to chew off some of my anxiety. Meanwhile, my knees bounce to accompany the chewing. My body feels like an underground tank in a mad scientist's lab undergoing all sorts of experiments—hormones, anxiety, impulsive changes to my schedule, pulling down the red flags that usually set me off. I'm delighted in my progress, but I'm also wary of being over-stimulated. I don't want to be a ticking time bomb going off at some random triggers.

Maverick picks up on my anxiety and doesn't push his body language any further for the rest of the afternoon. We brainstorm, jot ideas down, and do a recording test of an outlined episode on his phone. Whenever I become hesitant about the whole thing, he shows me other people on WorldVid who have spread awareness about their disabilities: dissociative identity disorder, agoraphobia, type one diabetes, and even furries who take off their masks and explain their social anxiety. They give me the courage I need to go on.

It's difficult not to relive our romantic moments repeatedly, especially right in his presence. I focus on our friendship and our ideas about the channel, but it's too much. His broad shoulders, his sturdy back, his too-long brown curls against his neck. I watch his thin lips as he talks, reminding myself to never take them for granted again. That genuine smile that is always reserved for me—oh, how I missed it.

I've never had a comfort person besides my family members and aides. A comfort person is like a security blanket that calms the lizard brain. Maverick is one normie I'm keeping around for as long as I can.

When Sherri calls Maverick to tell him to come home and help with dinner, the awkwardness returns. A pang of worry hits my chest because we don't quite understand what our relationship or friendship has turned into. And without discussion, I'm worried that it will fall to the earth like a big heap of dirty laundry. I try not to worry as Maverick leaves, the hours after that, and as I get ready for bed.

Before going to bed, I do a solo yoga session. Even though I'm not on my period, I find solace in doing the stretches Eliza taught me. Near the end of the session, my phone buzzes across the room. I nearly fly to swipe it open.

Maverick: Felix wants to say hi

A video message is attached, which Maverick has never sent before. My curiosity piques as I download it with a tap of my index finger.

Maverick and Felix are at their house, presumably in one of their rooms. They're both wearing sunglasses and backward baseball caps atop their heads. Their arms are crossed like they're "cool." I laugh before either of them makes a sound, a warm sensation heating the back of my neck.

Maverick attempts beatboxing, badly. Felix sings, or rather, is humming, his own rap tune interrupted with giggles. At the end of the short song, Felix holds up a piece of paper he has drawn on. I can make out the shapes of two people standing in a field, under which are words neatly printed in Maverick's handwriting:

Dinah + Maverick forever

When I hyperfocus on Maverick, I imagine the possibilities of our future, the alabaster clouds of fortune that may shine upon us. Who's to say we can't conquer anything together? I used to say the sky is the limit, but who knows? We could be astronauts if we wanted. The universe is our limit.

I text back a smiley face, and we keep texting until I fall asleep and wake up in the morning to my alarm clock going off.

While we no longer sit together during English, we do at lunch. It took me days to go to school without Higgins, but Nattie helped me the last several days as she promised. She gets permission from the principal to leave her classes early and walk with me to my own classes, just so that I'm not alone. It may seem silly, but it has helped me out a lot. When Maverick's not helping Felix, he helps me. I don't know what I did to deserve such wonderful humans in my life, but I'm beyond grateful.

I even learned how Nattie doesn't always like her friends because they don't let her pick which video games to play.

When I talk about how Nattie and Maverick are helping me at school, Kurt and Mom are hesitant about mine and Maverick's relationship. Dad is all for it, funnily enough. It's another normal thing I didn't know I could have in my life. I grew up scared that love would be unobtainable for me. I believed most people found me strange and unrelatable. I had even pictured me and Higgins alone together forever and accepted my fate.

CHAPTER 30

THE AUTISM Around the World walk in downtown Milwaukee is here, and I'm in better spirits. I have a boyfriend, even though we haven't officially called each other that or been on another date, but our texting and kissing game have been consistent. Plus, Higgins is recovering faster than expected.

The morning is bright, and I can barely contain my excitement. I throw on random clothes in such a hurry that Mom has to remind me to wear the hoodie I got at last year's walk. It's in the Autism Around the World yellow color that reads: "Make no mistake, I'm just as human as you."

I bounce along in the van the whole way to the park while everyone else is groggy from the early morning.

"I hope lots of people will help Felix today," I say, unable to think of anything else but meeting the Wrights at the walk. The nonprofit allowed the Wrights to set up a booth to raise money for Felix's service dog, and his moms have been working hard by passing out flyers.

My mom sips her coffee behind the wheel. "Ahum. I'm glad you are helping them, honey."

Arriving at the walk is a breath of fresh air. My headphones block out any unwanted noise, but I can focus on birds singing and happy laughter. Blossoms and buds cover the park trees. I can't think of a more wonderful place to be at this very moment.

Sherri and Trish sit at one of the several booths near the entrance to the 5K walk. It's covered in a green tablecloth with a poster of Felix's face off to the side on an easel. The booth reads: "Felix needs a service dog!"

There are dozens of hearts around the big bold words. Trish is clutching a receipt book and a large money wallet while Sherri is scattering green rubber bracelets printed with Felix's name and big yellow stars adorned with the words: "Accept All of Us!"

Every autism diagnosis is different. Anyone who knows more than one person with autism can probably see that. Society needs voices to bring awareness and acceptance. This walk represents the awareness, but the acceptance part is a whole other issue that needs extreme work.

I really wish I would have started my WorldVid channel before the walk, but my excitement got the better of me. I did write down a different video idea we could do that captures the walk. I fish for my phone in my pants pocket, ready to record some good moments.

A pleasant sensation of a calloused hand slipping into mine warms every cell in my body. The perfect amount of weight is balanced against the rest of my arm up to my shoulder. I know Maverick is holding my hand, standing inches away. His arm hair touching mine is the only thing that could potentially give me the itches, but my hoodie provides a barrier.

I glimpse at his face. It's a little red from shaving this morning but still bright with his full smile and eyes that hold pools of endless ocean blue. His lip stitches have healed into a scar that gives him a rough, bad-boy look which conveniently makes him a bit sexier.

"Hi," he says in my ear. Felix stands next to him. They both have green shirts on emblazoned with the same message displayed on their moms' booth poster: "Felix needs a service dog."

The warm sensation in my chest grows. I'm unable to contain my large range of happy emotions.

"I have something for you," I say, digging into my front pocket. I pull out a neatly folded piece of notebook paper where I brainstormed topics for WorldVid videos last night in bed.

Maverick eyes the paper and takes it from me. His pupils go side to side as he reads. I impatiently wait for his response.

> How I got my service dog
> How I was diagnosed with autism
> The difference between sensory seeking and sensory avoiding
> A day in my life
> Why disabled kids need advocacy

The corners of his lips curl upward. "Dinah, these are perfect."

I bounce on my toes. My chest screams with excitement as I hug him with as much pressure as I can. The three of us spout off ideas for my first video, the channel's name, silly gimmicks I could do, and so on. I capture a few shots on my phone of Felix motioning his ideas to Maverick.

We proceed to enter the raffle, get some swag at other booths, and eat complimentary bagels and schmear for breakfast before lining up at the starting ribbon. Though not having my usual yogurt is a little unsettling, I tell myself to ignore any triggers. I want today to be perfect, and so far, it is. The tulips and daffodils are in full bloom, unknowingly preparing to frost over when my inevitable birthday freak storm hits.

Mom has disappeared into the booth to sit with Trish while Sherri takes Felix. Kurt walks with Nattie and some of her friends. I spot Eliza with her group of behavior aides from the company she works for, each one holding a yellow balloon. We've talked since Higgins' attack, but it's not the same yet. I need a little more time to accept her with open arms again. She helps me as before, but I don't share everything with her the way I did in the past. She gives me a big wave but goes back to holding hands with a tall handsome bulky guy.

A gulp catches in my throat, and my heart almost stops. Is Eliza going to get married and move away too? I've gotten used to her therapy methods. A wave of melancholy envelops me like a swarm of wasps, threatening my perfect day with an incoming meltdown.

Heart rate rising.

Body temperature dropping.

I'm somehow still able to put one foot in front of the

other in the crowd of people, probably because I'm clutching Maverick's hand to death.

A voice, warped and distant, sounds in the distance as if I'm a fish trapped inside a tank, hearing the outside world for the first time.

I shake my head to try to jolt myself out of it and bring myself back to reality.

"Dinah? Did you hear me?" Maverick's concerned voice comes from my left side. "You're squeezing my hand. Does that mean you don't like the idea?"

Apparently, I missed a whole conversation during my dissociation.

"Um... tell me what it is again?" I ask, hopefully in a convincing voice. People's various noises creep through the protection of my headphones.

Eliza whispers something to the guy she's with before walking over, strutting an aerobic walk in her gym clothes.

I let go of Maverick's hand and narrow in on Eliza, my eyes filling with tears. My chest rises and falls.

"Dinah? What's wrong?" Maverick whispers.

"Great turnout, huh?" Eliza asks in a chirpy voice.

I slip far away into my safe place.

I terraform the earth, making mountains and rivers out of thin air. I hunt with lightning and tremors. Wherever I step, craters and valleys result. With a brush of my hand against the ground, fields of gold and green plumage rise up at my command. I stretch my hands forth and conjure up millions of cherry trees, eternally blooming, never fading. Pink leaves on trees are a necessity in my world. Gray clouds that cover up the sun are forbidden, and the temperature never rises above seventy-five degrees Fahrenheit.

The goddess of all creation is rudely interrupted by a sudden whoosh sound that rips the ceiling and walls of her cave from around her, bringing blinding light in.

"Enjoying the sunshine?" Eliza asks.

The battle has begun.

"Rude, you just ruined a million-year terraforming process in my world," I say.

"I know you must be upset Higgins isn't here, but you are out here, and that is progress," Eliza says calmly, though I can tell she's determined to get me moving forward.

"How dare you disrupt my universe...."

"Your *neurodiverse* universe?"

I roll my eyes. Sometimes, Eliza will play word games with me like rhyming to get me to focus on positivity instead of negativity.

"My... immerse universe," I say.

Eliza frowns.

"That doesn't make sense. Wouldn't it be an immersive universe?"

"Hey, just be happy it isn't a *perverse* universe."

"How about we take a seat and talk? I brought your stress ball." Eliza keeps the calm determination in her voice, handing me the ball. Two can play at that game, even though I take the ball and squeeze it.

Immediately following, I realize I need to be up front with Eliza.

Maverick leans closer, his warmth radiating into me. He inches closer, the weight of him comforts me.

"Who's that guy you're with?" I ask, staring directly at her freckled face for an answer.

She crosses her arms and stares right back.

My eyes begin to itch, the need to break eye contact prevalent in their dehydration, but I stubbornly stare harder.

"Derek, my boyfriend. We've been together about three months now," she replies, her tone softer.

I shut my eyes and rub them with my index fingers. Little pink dots flashing under my eyelids remind me that my cherry-blossom-filled world was ripped away from me.

"If you want, I won't answer any more questions until you're in a comfortable place like your room instead of an unfamiliar place in public," Eliza says, taking the first step toward a bench.

I huff in prime teenager fashion, displaying my annoyance with every move. Having autism means I wear my emotions on my sleeve, and it's impossible to hide what I'm feeling.

"Or we can just walk to get our juices flowing and chat later," Eliza compromises.

"Juices flo—gross," I groan, my stomach churning a little.

"It means to get your metabolism going, your blood pumping faster, your intestines digesting," Eliza clarifies through soft laughter.

To get my thoughts away from bodily fluids, lizard brain jumps in and makes my mouth drop a bomb on her.

"Are you going to get married and move away like Jenny?" I ask.

Eliza whips her head around at me, a serious expression on her face. "Is this what your anxiety is about?" She holds out her hands and grabs my shoulders, halting me on the sidewalk. Without warning, she wraps her arms around me and puts a hand in my hair.

Unwelcome hugs envelope me like I'm in a straitjacket.

"Dinah," she whispers near my headphones, "I will be here for you as long as you'll have me."

I'm filled with a confusing emotion that clashes against my determined annoyance. I thought my heart was stronger than this, but it's apparently as fragile as glass, and it shatters at this. I break through the straitjacket to hug her back. Sobs of frustration escape me into her soft jersey jacket.

"I hate change," is all I can say between the whimpers.

People at the walk know what's going on, of course. There are no gasps, no awkward tension. People walk around us knowing that I'm having an autistic meltdown.

People understand me here.

"I know, and a lot is coming. We'll discuss your birthday, graduation, and the like later, okay?" Eliza says as we break apart. She wipes my face with her jacket sleeve and nods with reassurance. "For now, let's practice little changes. Let's enjoy today. Okay?"

"Okay, like what?" I ask, sniffling. Moments like these are why I wish Higgins was by me. I squeeze my hand as if his leash is in it, waiting for his fur to rub against my leg.

Shivers snake down my spine, the bad kind.

"I don't know. This is hard." My teeth grind with anxiety, but also with willpower. I want to be able to face changes like an armored maiden with an enchanted sword. With no fear.

"Trust me, everything will be fine," Maverick says.

He embraces me into a hug, and the tension is a little lighter. At least he's here by my side.

I release a deep breath, believing his every word. And not just because Eliza repeats it as well.

CHAPTER 31

IT'S CHALLENGING NOT to get frustrated when I keep working toward a goal and it never seems obtainable. The fundraiser walk and the Halloween event brought in a bit over a thousand dollars combined. I sigh a few times just thinking about how long they could be waiting. How are Maverick and Felix's moms going to get the money they need to get a service dog?

I spend the rest of the weekend playing with my phone angle to film something. I do a "hello" video. After sending it to Maverick, he responds with him and Felix sending me their own versions of "hellos" that are adorable.

Moments later, Mom knocks on my door, telling me that the Wright boys are here to help bring Higgins home. Maverick is my emotional support human, and Felix really wants to make sure Higgins is all right.

Upon finding me taking a selfie, Mom asks what I'm doing.

"I'm practicing making a video. Higgins and I are going to start a WorldVid channel," I reply.

She raises an eyebrow. "Well, just know that Higgins might not be up to becoming a social media star until he's fully healed."

I don't say anything more because I jog through the house and into the driveway, where my boyfriend waits for me. His hands slide deep into his pockets all attractive-like. It's so early that everyone is still yawning. We climb into the van with anxious excitement, ready to bring Higgins home.

As I look at my own reflection in the glass, I smile and whisper, "Good morning, Dinah."

We're on our way to the vet emergency hospital.

When we arrive, Maverick holds my hand tight when a veterinary nurse with big muscles carries out eighty pounds of my golden retriever.

I weep at the sight of him. Higgins has a large cone around his head I know he must hate. His back leg is bandaged up like a mummy, while one side of his fur is completely shaved with a nasty-looking, stitched-up incision. Worst of all, his snout and mouth are closed shut with a medical muzzle.

An involuntary whimper escapes my lips. Maverick puts his arm tight around me. The itches return, and so do the memories of Higgins' attack.

The sheer panic. The realization. The screams emitting out of my own mouth. The owner of the aggressive dog yelling, all echo in my ears.

Higgins' eyes sparkle when he sees me but with tired and helpless pleas behind them. I won't be hugging him anytime soon. Or taking him to school. Or sleeping with him.

"How is... how is he going to eat?" I squeak to the nurse.

I may be barely functioning and shaking, but the love I have for Higgins overpowers the itches.

"You'll have to give him food through a syringe until his jaw heals. Instructions and equipment are in the bag right here." The nurse hands my mom a large folder and a plastic bag. He proceeds to carry Higgins to our car and lifts him into the back seat.

I rush to sit by him before Maverick can object. He sighs and begrudgingly sits in the passenger seat on the way home, leaving Higgins between me and Felix.

I long to bury my face in Higgins' fur, but he seems too fragile. I lean close and whisper how much I love him. He whines as if he yearns to lick my hand.

Felix follows suit and brings his face close into the cone. I smile, seeing Higgins stick his tongue out in an attempt to lick Felix's face.

My gaze centers on Felix and Higgins, the former rocking while still saying "Awww" and petting my dog softly.

"When is Felix getting his own dog?" I ask Maverick.

"The fundraisers and my moms' savings amassed about two-thousand dollars, it's just enough for a deposit to be put on the waitlist," he answers.

"There's a waitlist!" I exclaim, nearly hopping out of my seatbelt. I got Higgins when I was a kid, and no one said anything about a waitlist.

"Yep, for about four years unless we can pay for a service dog right away. Unfortunately, the time that it takes to get and train an autism service dog is demanding. We have to wait that long for Felix to get his perfect friend. Finding the funding is tough." Maverick sighs.

Four years!

Felix will be my age by then. I sink into the ground, watching Higgins exude his calming powers over Felix. The thought burns into my brain. I can't focus on anything else while we drive.

I believe what I'm feeling is... empathy.

In that moment, I realize I need to make a fundraiser video for Felix's service dog. And there's no time to waste.

When we park, everyone jumps out and attends to Higgins. We set up a comfy pillow and bed for him in the living room. His tail wags with excitement.

Mom prepares snacks for us while we bathe Higgins in the bathroom. Not bathe exactly, but pat him in the places we can reach. Felix laughs every time Higgins huffs, and I tell Felix the best way to wash him. This may be Kurt's job, but I want to try and figure out how to wash Higgins too.

Maverick keeps reassuring me that I'm doing great.

"Thank you," I say, feeling confident.

Maverick wipes a soap splatter from my face. "I wanted to tell you something at the walk the other day."

I freeze, remembering how I had a meltdown. "Sorry I ruined the walk for you."

"No, you didn't. We were there for autism awareness. That includes everything that's part of that."

I bounce on my soapy knees, not making eye contact with him. "I'm ready to listen."

"I'm thinking about getting a job," Maverick says, looking ahead to honor my discomfort in frequent eye contact. "I applied at a few places, but I really want to work at the county resource center. I want to be able to take Felix on summer field trips around the city, and other people who have disabilities as well."

"Sure, that sounds great," I mutter, only half-understanding what he really means.

"I want to major in psychology," he continues. "I think taking a year to work and volunteer will look good on a college application."

He wants to talk about more upcoming changes like college. Now? On this day? The bright hope of the day crumbles into ash. I don't want to question, but I have to.

"Where do you want to go to college?" I ask.

"I want to help out my family as much as possible. It only makes sense for me to stay in Milwaukee and go to UW," he replies.

A wave of relief sweeps over me, but once I get going on the anxiety track, it's a one-way freight train going a hundred miles an hour, zooming toward a bottomless crevasse.

I grab an oversized towel Mom keeps specifically for Higgins' baths and open it wide for him.

Graduation, jobs, Higgins, Eliza, Maverick... it hits me at once—the realization that change is inevitable. I can't get used to happiness; it'll always go away. I can't get used to boring; life itself brings too many unwanted surprises. One day Nattie will grow up and graduate, and will she move away too? Get married or get a job and leave me in a lurch?

I clutch Higgins' damp body in a bear hug. His sweet lavender smell mixed with dog stench encompasses my senses, bringing my brain back into focus. Tears fall like rain into his fur as Maverick bends down to hug us both tightly.

"We will tackle change together. I'm adamant to make

you part of my routine." His arm around my waist gives me shivers. When Maverick plays with a random strand of my hair, my body shudders and practically melts.

I spin around and kiss him, throwing my arms up around his neck.

Maverick tips my chin up so I can see his sapphire eyes, trusting and overly patient.

"Okay?" he asks, quietly.

My fingertips run along his stubbly jaw. "Yeah... thinking about change," I say.

"Awww! Oh... *awww*," Felix says to Higgins. He gently pats his head. Higgins looks hesitant at first, flashing his cautious eyes at me. I can't help but giggle and feel that tingly feeling blooming in my chest once more.

I'm thinking about what changes I can bring about to help Felix get his own therapy dog. If I've learned anything from this past tumultuous year, it's that not all change is negative.

"He can't wait four years for a service dog." I tell Maverick about my video plan. "I want to use my WorldVid channel and make it a fundraiser with the videos. I can start with talking about myself and Higgins, then about why Felix needs an autism service dog, too," I say. "He needs his own Higgins. I'll start a donation campaign to raise the money for him."

Maverick slips his hand into mine. "My family and I will support you however you need."

Maverick and I look to Felix, still petting Higgins' back like he's grooming a horse.

"How about it, Felix? Wanna make fun videos with Dinah?" Maverick asks his brother.

Felix bounces on his butt, clapping with exuberance and laughing. My boyfriend hugs his brother fiercely, which he returns. I've never seen Felix willingly give a hug to anyone else.

It's then I realize what's not so different between Felix and me. Not being able to speak isn't the same as not having anything to say.

I whip my phone out and ask Felix if he wants to be in the shots. He poses with a signature Wright-brothers smile next to Higgins ten times.

CHAPTER 32

I TITLED THE VIDEO: *A Friend for Felix and My Hope for the Future of Autism.* It's barely five minutes, but there have been nearly nine hundred views since last night. I rewatch it again on my phone. The quality isn't that great, but I'll learn how to make the next video better. There was no time to waste, and I couldn't wait to add the clips of Higgins with Felix from yesterday.

It's a bit weird telling people how I was diagnosed at nine years old and how I want to bring awareness to autism and the importance of service dogs. A comment from a viewer mentions how they can relate to being on the spectrum and how they also have difficulty with communication, social interactions, obsessive interests, and repetitive behaviors.

I enjoy talking about my daily life of hearing things much louder than most people, feeling emotions deeper, having stronger taste sensations, and more anxiety about uncertainties.

I watch the last-minute, wondering if I shared too much:

"I love to go to the movies, but outside of Washington, North Carolina, and Wisconsin, I'm unaware of any effort to provide sensory-friendly viewings.

"I love sports, but they're often loud and full of sensory overload. Precautions like stretching or yoga as a team beforehand would go a long way in ensuring autistic children could participate in sports with their friends.

"Autistic people aren't like the token autistic or eccentric characters you see on TV or in the movies. We're real people, and we're on a spectrum of diversity.

"This is my boyfriend's little brother, Felix. He also has autism and needs a service dog of his own to love and help him through life. Can you believe that the demand for autistic service dogs is so huge that the waitlist is over four years long? My hope is by sharing this video, people can help secure a friend for Felix. Please consider donating at the link below. Every little bit helps. Felix can't wait to keep everyone updated, and I can't wait to share what I plan to do for my birthday and graduation. Once I figure those things out, of course..."

It's a start, I guess. Hitting two hundred dollars with a goal of ten thousand only pushes us closer to our goal. While I want to focus everything on this fundraiser, I remind myself about Higgins.

At first, I protest to Higgins sleeping in Mom and Kurt's room, but they insist that his care will be too overwhelming for me. Kurt brought home a large fluffy dog bed for Higgins, which assures me that he'll be comfortable.

As for me, I learn to sleep with my weighted blanket.

The next morning, I try something new.

I go to school without Higgins and without Nattie. I

wear my headphones the whole time. I only last two hours, but holy crap. Look at me go. I didn't think I'd last five minutes.

The next day, I last three. Then four. Then I muster through an entire week.

As long as I can wear my headphones, leave a few minutes early before the bell, and win at board games with Andrew, I survive.

Granted, both Maverick and Felix help me, but I walk the hallways on my own. I won't be perfect at it all the time, and I can't wait to have Higgins by my side again, but it's exciting to know I can do it on my own. Something I never thought I could do.

I am making my own change and independence.

My nightmares cease, replaced with either dreamless sleeps or frequent travels to my safe place. Valleys filled with rainbows, stormed castles, far-off fantasies—all of them have been calming and wonderful.

When the sunrays warm my cheek, I open my eyes and get up before anyone comes to get me.

Maybe it's because it's May, and it's my birthday. Maybe it's because my video raised a thousand dollars for Felix. Maybe it's because I handed out flyers about the video to strangers at my school without any itches.

Whatever it is, I shout, "Good morning, Dinah!" to myself.

As I dance down into the kitchen, I sing, *"Someone's in the kitchen with Di-nah..."*

Moments later, everyone sings me an early "Happy Birthday" in a lower tone than the usual blaring volume. I appreciate it after seventeen birthdays of overstimulation. I prepare myself for about five more birthday songs throughout the day.

Maverick hugs me around my waist after I blow out the candles on the *Kingdom Delivered* cake my mom decorated for me. His present is not only a bouquet of sweet-smelling lilies but also a leatherbound collection of the *Kingdom Delivered* series. I immediately declare that they'll go in my dream library, a Beauty-and-the-Beast-worthy library I will hopefully have one day.

Kurt hands me a present while my dad beams in the corner, a little further away from the excitement. Their faces set my nerves on edge. Are they excited or scared?

"What's going on?" I ask, unable to contain myself anymore.

"Well, this present is kind of big, so it's from all of us," Kurt says.

It doesn't feel big. It doesn't look big. It looks like an average-sized box, rectangle in shape. Like a holiday box that's holding a sweater vest from the mall.

Their stares cut into me like white-hot knives. The anticipation is too much. Higgins hobbles over and sits down next to me, his cone bumping my face. I hand the package over to Maverick.

"You open it."

"Dinah, it's your birthday."

"I'm aware. Don't be a douche nozzle."

Mom *tsks* while everyone else laughs.

Maverick shrugs and carefully unwraps the box. He

turns the top of it to me and smiles his signature Wright-boy smile.

It's a white, very expensive-looking laptop. My phone can do so much, but this will help me to be better at creating everything WorldVid related.

Confused, I turn to Mom, Dad, and Kurt.

Mom sighs. "Your dad and stepdad talked me into it, since you want to get into video making and editing," she says, holding her hands up in a shrug. "Consider it part of your graduation present."

"Thank you," I say, my lips turning up into a huge smile to express my gratitude.

"Knock, knock," Eliza says, her wild red hair aflame in the summer rising sun. A bouquet of colorful daisies rests in her arms as she approaches me one soft step at a time.

Mom and Eliza exchange some muted words before Eliza smiles at me, spying Higgins with some lingering guilt visible in her eyes. I don't know if she'll ever forgive herself for what happened. I'm unable to move from my present spot, though I swear I can hear the beating of my fantasy wings ready to take off.

"I wanted to say happy birthday, but also, to look at this good boy recovering so well."

Higgins' present to me is walking again and having his post-surgery muzzle removed. He still has to wear a big ugly cone, but Felix and I decorated it nicely for my low-key party. Felix drew lots of stars in permanent marker on it, and I covered it in an assortment of multicolored stickers. I was worried that sharing some Higgins-time with Felix would bring on the itches, but I'm pleasantly surprised that the time goes smoothly and happily. I enjoy spending time with him, listening to his stimming-induced humming.

Felix keeps saying a sound very close to "Awww" as he pats Higgins' fur.

Before the morning ends, we make an impromptu video and post it.

The day has just begun, and I'm confident I will get through it on my own at school. I might even say hi to a stranger in the hall. For once, I'm actually excited to remember the last few weeks of senior year.

CHAPTER 33

I'VE HANDLED the graduation commotion without a single meltdown.

After the valedictorian's speech, Andrew and I are the first to get our names called so that we don't have to wait in the long alphabetical line. The dean asks the parents in the audience to please be a little quieter for us, but Andrew's family can't help themselves. They whoop and holler in support, their pride riding the waves of the stadium of graduation, but I survive. I have my headphones on under my cap as a precaution.

Andrew pumps his fist like a champion, clutching his diploma.

I try to wait patiently to watch Maverick walk, but his name is one of the last called in the Ws. Mom nudges my elbow when my boyfriend walks across the stage. My heart swells with pride for both of our accomplishments.

I insist that my parents not take a million pictures of us or at least turn off the flash. My dad can't stop hugging me. I have to push him off the fourth time, telling him he's violating my safe space. He says he can't help it, he's so proud. Mom does her side-eye, but I don't think anyone can be annoyed right now. What I've accomplished today is something I never thought I would be able to do.

We have a small celebration in our backyard underneath the trellis. Kurt grills hot dogs and hamburgers. Nattie and a few of her friends are on the trampoline, avoiding us while giggling and tapping on their phones. The Wrights are with us, of course, and Higgins has to be reminded to not run around to everyone begging for pets. Kurt keeps telling him he'll pop his stitches, though they're mostly healed. Maverick teases that we should give him a futuristic haircut to match his undergrown side, but he'll receive a summer haircut soon enough.

Higgins snuggles up to Felix, causing a huge smile to curl up on his face and squeals of glee.

When I check my videos, the fundraiser goal has been surpassed. I have to do a double take because this is it. My hands flap as I bounce on my feet.

Maverick and Mom rush over asking if something is wrong.

When I tell them the news, it's the best graduation gift ever.

A month later, Maverick and I sit on Trish and Sherri's couch, waiting with bated breath. This is the moment we've been waiting for. Higgins sits as still as he possibly can, but he can't contain his tail beating against the wood floor in a steady beat.

Thump. Thump. Thump.

Felix bounces up and down on the loveseat on the opposite side of the room, making happy noises. His aide, Daniel, is playing a game on the tablet with him.

Maverick squeezes my hand a little tighter, and his skin rubs against mine to create electricity. I'm excited for what's about to happen, but I can't resist thinking about the night we spent together just a mere twelve hours ago. I dislike many textures, but his lips upon my skin isn't one of them. I'm finding the more days that pass, the more I see Maverick as a permanent part of my life. And if he's not? I've grown more through the changes I've faced this year to find a pathway through that change.

But I like the idea of him being permanent so much better.

Higgins' ears perk up when he hears the slam of a car door in the driveway. Sherri and Trish are home with Felix's surprise.

With the extra money from the video fundraisers, Sherri was able to purchase Rosie outright as a fully trained autism service dog from someone who moved away. For weeks, Felix has been bonding with her, unknowing that she would become his service dog specifically tailored for him.

Sherri walks her in on a leash, a crisp new harness strapped around her torso states: "AUTISM SERVICE DOG DO NOT SEPARATE FROM HANDLER." She's a gorgeous cocker spaniel with a brilliant white-and-red coat, a bright pink bow on her collar. She trots over the threshold, panting. When she sees Higgins, she immediately sits and remembers she is on-duty. Higgins whines, wanting to sniff her in a greeting, but I nudge on his collar to remind him that he's on-duty, too.

Daniel finishes his game with Felix because pulling away midgame is a surefire way to upset his routine. After about two minutes, Daniel gives Felix a high-five and states that tablet time is over. Sherri gently brings the cocker spaniel closer to the love seat.

"Felix, Rosie is now officially your service dog," she says.

Felix's eyes widen. Daniel takes Felix's trembling hand and runs it along Rosie's fur in a swift, petting motion, her tail wagging wildly. Felix smiles and makes a rare moment of eye contact with his mom, flapping his hands everywhere. Trish and Daniel are wiping their eyes. Maybe they are allergic to her fur?

Maverick pets Higgins and looks away. I don't really understand why, so I lean over and ask him why.

"Nothing," he whispers, still looking away from me.

I grab his chin full of stubble and turn his face toward mine, finding his blue eyes watering and losing their battle to contain his tears with the bottom of his eyelids.

"I'm just really happy," he says.

I'm happy to see his little brother get the help that he deserves, too. At this thought, emotions burst through my chest and flow through me like a dam that has broken from the pressure at the core of my body. The feeling is almost too much. I must bury my face in Higgins' fur. The soft bristles meet my cheeks, providing the serotonin I need.

Higgins continues to whine, wanting to meet Rosie so badly. Just like me, he's experiencing that patience is something that needs to be learned. Maybe Rosie can be a good example to Higgins and help him relearn what behaviors has creeped out of him during the past few months.

"Awww!" Felix laughs, his squeals reaching an abnormally high key. He nearly slaps Daniel in the face with his excited hand-flapping. As if on instinct, Rosie stands on her hindquarters to give him a calming hug, and Felix reciprocates.

"Well, we better get going," Maverick says. "I promised Dinah we'd go to the store to get her a better microphone for her channel."

"Speaking of!" Sherri gasps, kneeling to pet Rosie with Felix. "Felix, honey, Dinah's WorldVid channel is what helped you get your dog. Can you tell her thank you?"

I'm totally unprepared for the ferocity of Felix's hug. It knocks the wind out of me, but the emotions that come with the embrace is a moment I'll never forget. My heart almost beats out of my chest as I smile widely, rivaling Maverick's own signature grin.

Felix getting his autism service dog is not a part of my typical morning routine, but it doesn't give me the itches. I can't stop smiling. Sometimes change is good, even when it feels scary at first. I know that not every day will go my way, and that's okay. I still need Higgins, and I still run away, but I also stay and do things on my own.

Maverick nudges me, smirking as he sees how happy I am hugging Felix. "Are you having a good morning, Dinah?"

I nod, my smile not leaving my face. "It's truly a good morning."

Tomorrow seems close enough, yet far away. Next week and next month are miles away. I wish I knew what my future holds, but I'm still trying to figure out who I am and what I want to do. For now, I'm going to take one morning at a time, one change at a time. I don't need a grand plan for the summer because I'm enjoying the little moments of reading my books on the trampoline. I don't need a grand dream for my career because I like trying different things at my own pace. I don't need to have a good morning every day because without a bad morning I wouldn't be able to experience a full life.

ACKNOWLEDGMENTS

The idea for this book came to my mind one day when I was walking our puppy, Bowser. I didn't anticipate a much bigger dog around the corner scaring him to pieces! We lucked out and nothing happened like it did in this book. Unfortunately, we had to rehome Bowser to another family when my baby daughter began having frequent seizures that sent him into his own panic attacks. The beautiful family he went to still sends me pictures of his cute, golden retriever face.

A huge thank you to the amazing Includas team. Thank you, Luda Gogolushko, for always reassuring me when imposter syndrome hit hard. Thanks to Madison Parrotta for her wonderful edits that enhanced Maverick and Felix's brotherly love, and to Catherine Valdez for always being upbeat on our virtual calls even when I was discouraged.

Thank you to Anita Mumm who loved the manuscript and brought a much-needed second set of eyes to the pages. To all the beta readers and sensitivity readers that read this manuscript, thank you for lending your voices and taking your time to ensure that the neurodiverse community would be represented faithfully.

To Amelia Shifflett, my beta reader, my best friend, and my runner-by of new ideas. Your crush on Maverick makes me smile. Thanks for enduring my strangely titled emails often inspired by TikToks that kept us entertained while reading the same chapter for the umpteenth time. To Rachel Wozniak, who inspired Jenny's character. You changed our lives, and us moving away from you was one of the hardest things I've ever had to do. Jeanette Ogara, who recognized this book's magic and pumped me full of confidence juice to keep going. To Ariel Shapiro, who dragged me kicking and screaming into my first NaNoWriMo. You created a monster. Your morbid texts kept me sane. Adriana Villanueva, for always dropping everything when I need you, and getting cheese fries at 2:00 am in Vegas. My brother Deven, thanks for recommending books to me and telling me I had talent. Thanks to Mandy and Brianna for being my cheerleaders and sending me endless texts asking when this book was going to finally come out.

Brant, my best friend, my partner in raising our two amazing girls. I couldn't do it without you. I still don't know how I queried and revised this book while you were in training, during Covid, with our two girls out of school. Also, to rub salt in the wound, you were deployed during the bulk of the editing process. Basically, this book is nothing short of a miracle. Thank you for believing in me so fiercely.

Thank you, Mom, for reading my rough first draft and instilling confidence in me, for being willing to be open-minded and learn about the neurodiversity in our family. To my siblings on the spectrum: Jordan, Lydia, and Mallorie. To my neurodiverse nephews: Seth, Braden, Carter, Benjamin, and Peter, I hope you see yourselves in this story. To my grandparents on the other side: Look! I did a thing! To Dad, who isn't here to see this day, thanks for lending your childhood dog's name to Higgins.

And to Boo-Binks, my noise-avoider (and my muse for Dinah) and Stinkerbelle, my adrenaline seeker. I can't imagine life without you. I hope we are all patient with each other, autistics raising autistics. It's my wish that more neuro-diverse protagonists find their way into the written world, so you may see more of yourselves in books and media.

ABOUT THE AUTHOR

 Emily is a neurodivergent author, mom, gamer, and military wife. Originally hailing from Logan, Utah, she's since followed her husband around the country for the U.S. Air Force. She has a bachelor's degree in Professional and Creative writing from Central Washington University. She's a member of the International Women's Writer's Guild and The Poetry Society of America. Her ultimate goal is to become a library-haunting ghost so she can finally read every book in her to-be-read pile.

twitter.com/emholyoakauthor

instagram.com/emholyoakauthor

tiktok.com/@emholyoakauthor

amazon.com/author/emholyoakauthor